I0819654

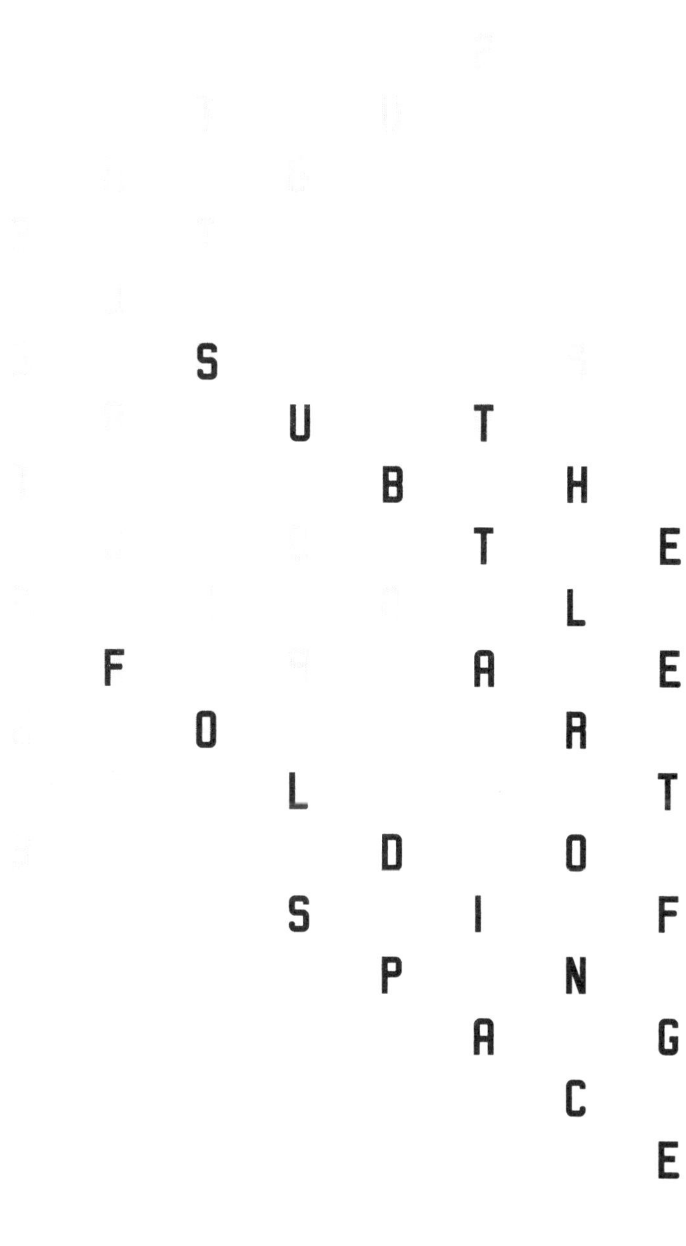
THE SUBTLE ART OF FOLDING SPACE

The Subtle Art of Folding Space

JOHN CHU

The Subtle Art of Folding Space

JOHN CHU

TOR PUBLISHING GROUP
NEW YORK

This is a work of fiction. All of the names, characters, organizations, places, and events portrayed in this work are either products of the author's imagination or used fictitiously.

THE SUBTLE ART OF FOLDING SPACE

A Tor Book
Published by Tom Doherty Associates / Tor Publishing Group
120 Broadway
New York, NY 10271

www.torpublishinggroup.com

Tor® is a registered trademark of Macmillan Publishing Group, LLC.

EU Representative: Macmillan Publishers Ireland Ltd, 1st Floor, The Liffey Trust Centre, 117–126 Sheriff Street Upper, Dublin 1, D01 YC43

The Library of Congress Cataloging-in-Publication Data is available upon request.

ISBN 978-1-250-42540-9 (hardcover)
ISBN 978-1-250-38208-5 (ebook)

First Edition: 2026

Printed in the United States of America

10 9 8 7 6 5 4 3 2 1

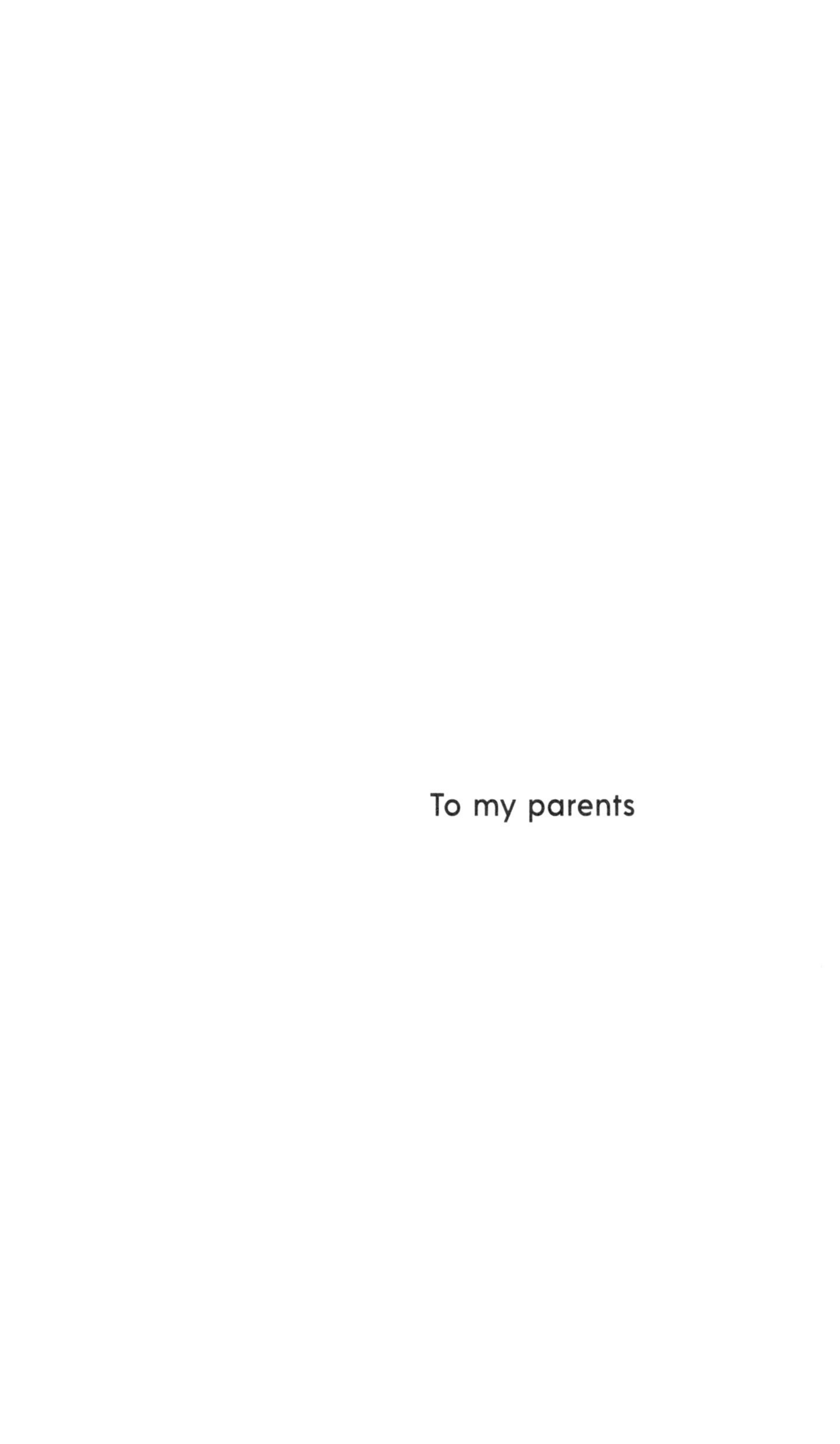

To my parents

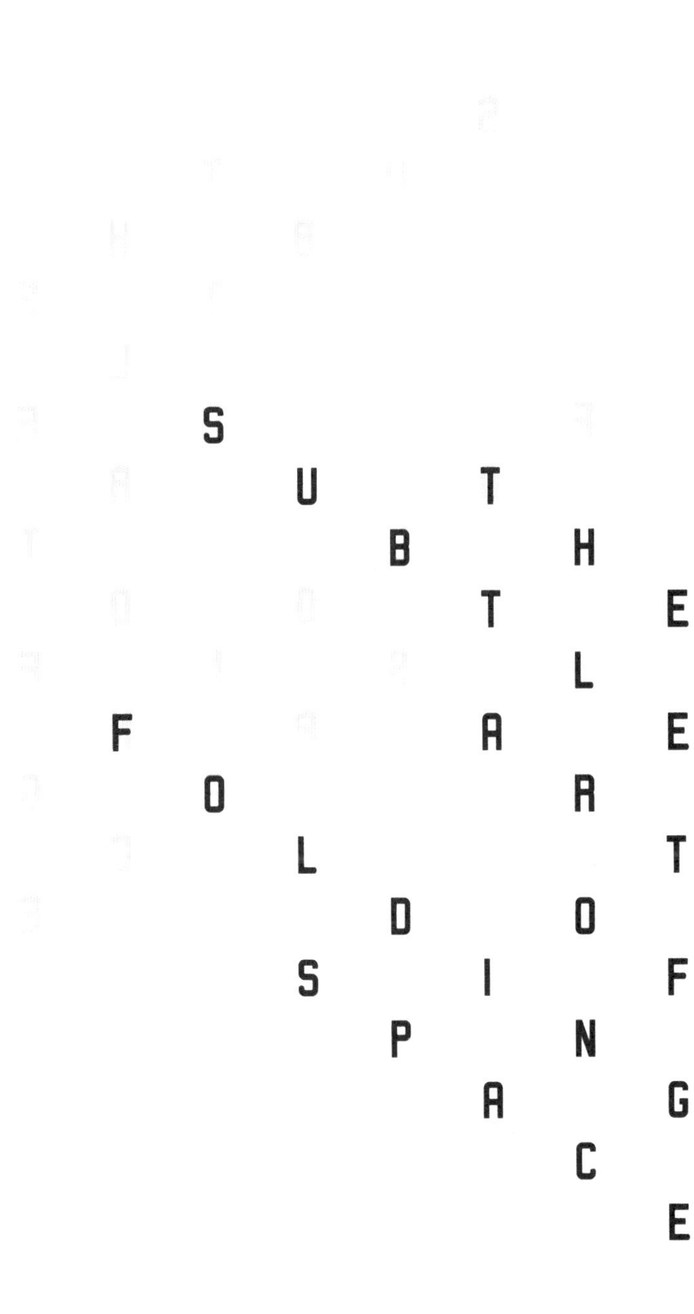
THE
SUBTLE
ART
OF
FOLDING
SPACE

CHAPTER 1

"Attention passengers: The next Red Line train to Alewife is now approaching" echoes off the walls. Not only has the next Red Line train to Alewife arrived but its passengers have already flooded the station, a torrent rushing up the escalators, through the turnstiles, then down the concourse to spill out the doors to Cambridge. The deluge arriving as the PA system squawks catches Ellie off guard. It's rush hour. When a train arrives on one side of the platform, the one on the other side leaves seconds later. She sprints, a beleaguered salmon racing against the current of bodies. Her pack sloshes between her shoulder blades, a sloppy fin batting the waves of people surrounding her.

No one has tried to kill her today—yet. Her sister, Chris, arranges something at random intervals. It's to keep Ellie sharp, Chris claims, because, occasionally, skunkworks isolationists try. Not that Ellie believes Chris has her best interests at heart. Well, not anymore, but she doesn't know how to stop the attempts on her life, and they do keep her sharp.

Maybe the mistimed announcement is part of today's attempt. She'll be caught in the rip current of bodies, a wave will overwhelm her, and a shark hiding in the swell will tear her to pieces. Compared to the attempt with the Mylar balloons, the jar of Marmite, and the US men's Greco-Roman wrestling team, an ill-timed flood of people at Alewife Station is downright practical and likely.

None of that happens, though. The crowd flows around her as she plunges down the stairs toward the platform.

The car doors shut just as she reaches them. While the PA system blasts "Attention passengers: The next Red Line train to Alewife is now arriving," the train clatters away. The train supposedly now arriving sits already emptied on the opposite side of the platform. It beeps as its doors slide shut.

As the crowd streams up the stairs and escalators, the platform quickly clears, leaving a couple of people who must have, like Ellie, just missed the train. Some guy wearing shorts that stretch across his thighs, no shirt, and more self-possession than Ellie thought possible hovers in front of one of the train doors. Someone else sits on a bench, staring at her e-reader. A thin woman reaches for Ellie like a drowning person reaching for a buoy. Her luggage crashes to the floor. She asks in rapid Mandarin whether Ellie knows how to get to the Best Western. Her oboe-like voice skips through her words.

Ellie blinks. Strangers start conversations in Mandarin with her all the time at school. Not so much outside of school. The Best Western is only a short walk away. With luggage, though, the woman will want a taxi, but there's almost always one dropping someone off outside the station. All the woman needs to do is go up the escalator and cross the concourse. She tells the woman all of this in Mandarin. Ellie's response doesn't draw laughs, her irrational fear whenever she talks to a stranger in any language that's not English. In fact, the woman thanks her. Ellie decides she is not today's assassin.

The woman doesn't turn to the escalator. Instead, she freezes for a moment, then glares at Ellie.

People randomly start sounding like her sister way more often than Ellie would like. Some people text. Her sister commandeers convenient strangers. It's never less than creepy, and it always catches Ellie off guard until the glare.

"If you'd quit school after Mom's diagnosis like I'd told you to, you'd have moved back to DC," the woman says in fluent English, her voice now husky and incongruously casual. "You wouldn't need to worry about missing the Amtrak now."

It's not Chris's voice, but it absolutely is. A childhood in Taipei clashed with an adolescence in Buffalo to give Chris an accent that's all non-rhotic and flat nasal vowels. She's always sounded like a panhandler in 1930s New York, albeit one who made unreasonable demands on your life rather than begged for a nickel. After Mom was diagnosed with glioblastoma, Chris became a 1930s New York panhandler who's always promising to send Ellie to sleep with the fishes.

Chris has always treated Ellie like this. Ellie was mostly through her undergrad when she had even an inkling that anything was different. None of her university friends have older siblings who talk to them like this. Granted, their older siblings are only a couple of years older, not practically a decade. Still, the idea that Ellie became a full-grown adult before realizing this is too embarrassing to think about, so she usually doesn't.

"Even if I miss this Amtrak, it's not like there won't be another one tonight. What do you have to tell me that's so urgent that it can't wait until, at worst, tomorrow afternoon?" Ellie folds her arms across her chest. "You did not waylay some random stranger so that you can taunt me about missing the train."

As Ellie says this, it strikes her that maybe Chris did. The obvious opening to needle Ellie is right there. Whenever Chris does it, she is, of course, always "just joking."

The woman only comes up to Ellie's neck. She glares down at Ellie anyway.

"Of course not. Who do you think I am?" The woman folds her arms across her chest. "If I have to stay at home to watch Mom, you have to go to the skunkworks and repair the physics of this universe. Mom brought you with her so many times that you have to be dense if you can't make a straightforward repair by yourself."

Ellie ignores the jab. When Chris doesn't have to play the good, dutiful sister around witnesses, Ellie has to ignore a lot of jabs to get through a conversation.

"What's the problem?"

"Everyone's wrong about why the International Prototype of the Kilogram is losing mass relative to its official copies. We'd see divergences between them even if the kilogram were defined by something more fundamental than a cylinder of platinum alloy. The notion of the kilogram, itself—"

"Has become unstable." Ellie frowns. "Fundamental physical constants are changing—"

"Yes. Now the good news—"

"There's good news?"

"—is we've found some hold-time violations in the skunkworks. Probably caused by some leaking valves. They must be why the kilogram's unstable. Fix them and I promise I won't judge you when you don't get here until tomorrow afternoon. First time for everything."

By "first time," Ellie isn't sure whether Chris is talking about repairing the skunkworks by herself or not judging her for being late. Probably the former. The skunkworks that generates a universe lives within the surrounding universe. She's only ever assisted Mom, albeit more times than she can count by now. There are an infinite number of skunkworks and universes. Nothing in the matryoshka doll that is the set of nested universes can prevent Chris from judging Ellie. She would ask, but Chris has already gone.

The woman turns around as though she hasn't said a thing. She goes to the escalator, trundling her luggage behind her.

At least someone gets to go where she wants to. Ellie doesn't. Chris won't let anyone else stay by Mom's side. Mom lies comatose, the end stage of glioblastoma, on a bed in Chris's den. She needs constant attention from Chris the way dolphins need tax advice. However, taking care of your parents is a filial obligation and no one is more Taiwanese than someone who no longer lives in the motherland. All of the relatives see Chris as the good daughter, the dutiful daughter. Even though Chris wants Ellie in the same house as Mom, she never lets Ellie do anything.

Ellie visits every weekend anyway. She does because she's more like Chris than she likes to admit, just as stubborn and also someone who no longer lives in the motherland. Also, once in a while, Mom shifts in bed. She yawns. Her eyes open a crack and, for a moment, she stares right at Ellie, as though she's about to wake from her long nap. Then her eyes close again, and she slumps back into oblivion. This seems like much more than random firing of neurons in a brain about to die. Ellie, even though she knows better, can't help thinking that the next time might be the time she wakes for real.

The train beeps. Its doors slide open. Passengers stream onto the train. Ellie shakes her head clear, then joins them. Everyone else is headed toward Davis Square. Ellie, on the other hand, is headed to the universe that surrounds this one. She blends into the crowd, so no one notices when she disappears.

CHAPTER 2

The air in the skunkworks feels spackled onto her skin. It burns into her lungs like hot fudge, slow and slick, its aftertaste at once sickly sweet, bitter, and sour. It takes effort to force back out.

The skunkworks looks like the masterpiece of some mad plumber who failed perspectives class in art school. The labyrinth of pipes surrounding her make her dizzy at first. Standing on one of the broad swaths of transparent mesh stretched between pipes, she bobbles until she gets her bearings.

Fat pipes pass overhead. They form a de facto canopy hiding the rest of the skunkworks, which stretches for miles above her. In actuality, it stretches for miles in all directions. Fixes have piled on top of so-called improvements have piled on top of emergency repairs forever. Rust covers the gates and reservoirs at the intersection of pipes. Most pipes block each other's way and have to zigzag around each other. No pipes are unscarred from dead welds of stubs where pipes used to join together.

Data pulses through the pipes in all directions. The pipes ripple, but stabilize in time for the clacking of valves and the burbling of reservoirs. Probably because she already knows which ones they are, the pipes that violate the hold-time requirement look out of sync even to the naked eye. Pipes are supposed to be stable from a little before reservoir valves clack shut until a little after. The pipes that violate the hold-time requirement start to ripple again too soon, corrupting the reservoirs they feed.

Someone stands on a mesh below her. Daniel. He's a verifier, not an isolationist. None of the latter have found her yet. Ellie lets go of the breath she didn't realize she was holding.

Even though Mom always pulled Ellie into the skunkworks with her, she never admitted, at least not to Ellie, to the existence of isolationists. She had to learn who they are from Chris. They believe whatever universe a skunkworks generates is by definition correct, even as a skunkworks inevitably decays. Any change introduces error instead of removing it. They're what Chris used to scare Ellie into doing what Chris wanted when Ellie was a kid. *Be good or the isolationists will get you.*

Mom only ever talked about maintainers. They fall into three rough groups, with some overlaps. Architects design the configuration of gates and pipes that generate the next universe in. Builders, like Ellie and Chris, install those gates and pipes, translating the architects' designs into reality. Verifiers, like Daniel, check whether architects have designed the right thing and whether they have designed the thing right. They understand the skunkworks better than anyone, to the extent that anyone really understands the workings of any universe. The first one to show up when the skunkworks has gone wrong is almost always a verifier. Or a generalist, who's skilled at all three jobs.

Even looking down from above, no one can mistake Daniel. His long legs are proportionately too short for his torso, and his shoulders are too wide. He manages to be both lithe and stocky at the same time, as though he were the runt of a family of impossibly elegant giants. He was voluntold to play football in high school and, even now, he does not look like someone you want to tackle you. A black T-shirt is draped over his left shoulder.

The pipes beyond his gaze blur as though a giant thumb has smeared a broad swath of petroleum jelly on the air. He holds his hand out. The blurred air twists and swirls into a ball on his palm. It coalesces into an egg tart. Bright yellow custard sits inside a pale, blond serrated crust. The perfume of eggs and sugar hangs in the thick air.

Every verifier Ellie has met except Daniel generates equivalence reports as sheafs of something crystalline. Daniel's, for reasons best known to Daniel, are always edible.

He studies the egg tart from every angle. His neck cranes and his hand twists. Crumbs fall when he lifts the tart to look at the crust's bottom. He brings it to his nose to sniff. The custard jiggles slightly when he shakes the tart. He frowns.

Ellie bounces from mesh to mesh, swinging around pipes and ducking under reservoirs, landing next to Daniel. This mesh, already taut from his weight, barely registers her.

"Cousin! Your first time solo." Daniel's voice, despite being practically subsonic, is never the thunder she expects from an elegant giant. He speaks with the rustle of leaves and the rush of water as it smooths rock. "Congrats."

"Chris mentioned hold-time violations, probably valves gone faulty. Should be an easy fix. Otherwise, she wouldn't have sent me instead of coming herself." Ellie's arms wave in slow-motion semaphore as she steadies herself. "Your egg tart shows a mismatch between how the skunkworks that was built functions and how the skunkworks that was designed functions, right?"

"Yeah, no point calling in an architect. The design itself is fine. The problem is in the implementation. It's all yours."

She sets her backpack down, then walks around Daniel to a knot of intertwined pipes. Reservoir valves clack, and the pipes they feed ripple too soon. Data races through those pipes, corrupting the reservoir they feed in turn. All of the valves, however, are fine. Their actuators swing smoothly. Their seals fit perfectly against the pipes and reservoirs. Nothing leaks.

She could add some delays to satisfy the hold-time requirement, to make the data take longer to reach the reservoir they feed. That's almost as simple as the leaky-valve repair Chris expected. That, however, would merely get rid of the symptom. Mom taught her better than that. She has to find the cause of the hold-time violation first.

The skunkworks predate humanity and, if she's guessed the age of the hardware right, no human has ever made any changes to this section. Any mismatch in construction should have been found eons ago. She checks anyway, working through the checklist her mom taught her, hoping that's what the problem is. If the design is fine and the hardware is correctly constructed, the remaining alternatives are all unthinkable.

She draws a large rectangle in front of her with her hand the way Mom taught her. A plane of air detaches and folds itself into an origami Black Forest cuckoo clock. The transparent, crystalline structure floats before her eyes. Its pendulum swings back and forth and the skunkworks fills with the sting of an offstage chorus whenever the pendulum stops at the peak of its arc. Light diffracts through leaves lining its sides. Color sprays across the pipes and Daniel. The egg tart still sits in his outstretched hand and he looks sillier than Ellie would have thought possible given his "I am deadly if you come within five paces" body.

The clock unfolds itself back into a rectangle, marked with creases where it had been folded. They divide the plane of air into facets that refract pipes behind them into something Syncretic Cubist. She grabs the newly retrieved blueprint. Its hard edges dig into her palms. She warps it, at first, into a dome, then into a sphere that seals her in.

Daniel splinters into "Man with an Egg Tart," a Braque that Braque never painted. He's all shards of black, gray, and brown flecked with grains of yellow. This piece of the skunkworks, however, resolves into something uniform and regular.

The multiple perspectives merge into one. Pipes straighten and meet at right angles. Ellie spins along three axes inside the sphere. Her hands and feet work their way up, down, and around the hard, cold sphere for support. Dense knots of machinery explode, laying bare their pipes and gates. The labyrinth of pipes has become now a regular matrix. The hardware matches the blueprints then.

That's one possible issue eliminated. She's not shocked. No problem as straightforward as a mismatch goes undiscovered for days, much less millennia. The sort of things that take forever to discover tend to be subtle. Fundamental constants shifting, even slightly, is not subtle. That implies a recent change. What she has to do now is find it.

The dataflow through the machinery is now perfectly straightforward. Pulses of data bulge from one pipe to another. They sweep in waves across the matrix, each wave a straight line traveling from one side of the matrix to the other. Whoever built this hardware followed the design rules derived from the physics for this universe.

That's another possible issue ruled out. Again, a design-rule violation that makes the kilogram unstable was unlikely to stay undiscovered for millennia. So far, the lack of any mistakes in construction suggests that none of this hardware has changed for the longest time.

The waves propagate, however, faster than she expects. They should be regularly spaced. Each wave should be swallowed by a set of reservoirs that, a moment later, sends out a wave of its own. Instead, waves crash into each other. That's bad. In fact, that's not possible. It does, at least, highlight which paths are violating the hold-time constraint.

Daniel has verified that the design is correct. The hardware matches the design. It follows the design rules derived from the physics of this universe. It's in good shape. There shouldn't be any hold-time violations. It's supposed to work, exactly as it has for millennia.

But it doesn't.

While the skunkworks match the blueprint in construction, they don't match the blueprint in function. She's tempted to give up and just fix the symptom. A few buffers inserted into the relevant paths and the violation would be gone. Anyone with any training as a builder could do that. But she wants to know why a repair is necessary in the first place. Otherwise, she's not really solving the problem.

"Fuck me." She slams a foot against the sphere. It shatters with a chord from the offstage chorus. "The valves are fine. The design is fine. Everything is fine."

She falls face up onto the mesh and thinks horrible things about Chris. Her backpack bounces above her, then lands on her stomach.

Daniel seems to have disappeared. This completely tracks. Ellie was running bog-standard diagnostics. Three seconds of boredom and Daniel wanders off, sometimes to another universe. In this case, almost certainly back to their own, probably the instant she started doing her thing. It's too bad because Ellie could use someone to talk through whatever is causing the skunkworks to fail like this.

Ellie knows the right thing to do. Chris probably has some idea of how to deal with this. Ellie should ask Chris for help. However, Ellie dismisses the idea almost before it crosses her mind. She can already hear exactly what Chris will say. Ellie doesn't need a helping of "How can you be so useless? I ask you to do a simple bit of maintenance and you can't even do that by yourself. And you wonder why I don't want your help with Mom" before Chris finally deigns to offer a suggestion.

Instead, Ellie closes her eyes. Mentally, she ticks off entries on the checklist that builders follow when they troubleshoot. Mom walked her through it every time they were in the skunkworks together. Usually, though, they don't make it as far as checking for design-rule violations before they have some clue of what's going wrong.

There's one entry on the checklist left, she realizes. Something happened that shouldn't have in the skunkworks one universe out. That is, the skunkworks that generates the universe she is in now, which contains the skunkworks that generates her own universe. The recent change is there, not here.

In other words, she needs a verifier, say Daniel, to check out whether that skunkworks is working right. She keeps her eyes shut and listens to the valves around her clack open and closed with metronomic precision. Maybe a moment or three to clear her mind would be a good thing.

"I'm back." Daniel's rumbling voice shocks Ellie's eyes open. "Did you miss me?"

Daniel looms over her, his hands behind his back. He smells like soy and ginger. An amused expression sits on his face.

"Egg tart?" He crouches, then places the pastry on the backpack. His other hand is still behind his back.

"I don't need to study the equivalence report." She pushes herself up by her elbows. "I trust your analysis."

"I meant to eat. It's a functional mismatch but still edible." He nudges the backpack toward her head. "You haven't had dinner yet, right? You'll feel better with something in your stomach. Personally, I think that's just a story my boyfriend tells me, but maybe eating really does clear the mind."

She sits up. The backpack and egg tart slide to her lap. "Don't you want your mind cleared?"

"Nyah. I don't believe in emotions." He notes her skeptical gaze and a grin lights his face. "I had a protein shake and a banana before I showed up."

"I've checked everything else, so there's only one thing left that can be wrong." She takes a bite of the egg tart. It tastes sweet, sour, and . . . gamey. "Turkey and cranberries?"

"Hey, I said the report was a mismatch. I do what I can." Daniel rolls his eyes. "So what's wrong, cuz?"

"This entire universe." She finishes the egg tart. It's not bad if you know what's coming. "It's like someone secretly added lots of helium to the air and now we all squeak. Except less resistance rather than higher pitch. The skunkworks wasn't designed for data to flow through pipes this easily. The properties of this universe can't have changed much. Most of the skunkworks still works right or we'd be seeing—I don't know—people diffracting through fences or something, but a few paths are now too fast."

"Which is why we're seeing functional failures even though what was built matches what was designed then functionally verified." Daniel nods. "What next?"

"Check whether the skunkworks one universe out is working properly. I want to know whether just fixing the violating paths will solve the problem for good."

"I popped out to check while you were assessing equivalence here. It's fine." From behind his back, he brings out a plate made of compressed, deep-fried rice that he must have been holding all this time. He puts it onto her backpack. Pieces of pan-fried fish coated in brown glaze sit on the plate. That's why he smells of soy and ginger. "Also, I went to an archive and pulled a copy of the latest changes made to the skunkworks that generates the universe we're in now."

He digs a small, clear, iridescent dodecahedron out of the right, front pocket of his jeans and tosses it to her. Its facets are numbered. You could make an attack roll in an RPG with it. Fractures appear and disappear inside the die as Ellie rolls it around in her hand. She rotates the die from 20 to 1 and reads the shifting cracks. Her eyes widen at the sheer scope of some of the changes. These are not mere parts replacements or surgical bug fixes.

"So the maintainers of this universe intentionally changed their own physics? Why would anyone do that?" This goes against everything maintainers are supposed to stand for. "If you already knew that, why bother asking me what's wrong?"

"I didn't already know. Speculative generation." He smiles. "You were busy and there was no reason not to check before you asked. I know what the builders' checklist looks like, and it wasn't impossible that you'd make it all the way down to the bottom. Sooner we get out of here, the less likely we'll have to deal with any troublemakers. I saved us some time. And if it turned out you didn't need me to do anything, no big deal."

Ellie breaks off a shard from the plate to test the fish. The glazed fish's crispy skin cracks against the deep-fried rice. She sniffs at this equivalence report. Then again, the egg tart smelled normal too.

"Is this going to taste icky sweet like 八寶飯 or something?"

Now Daniel looks annoyed. His gaze is sharp and his hands rest on his hips. "No, it's going to taste like a deconstructed garlic fried rice paired with a soy-and-ginger-glazed tilapia. The skunkworks one universe out is fine. Eat."

She lances a piece of fish and tries it. The tilapia is mild. Its triumph is that it doesn't sit like cotton in her mouth. The glaze is lovely. Garlic, shallots, and a little brown sugar round out the soy and ginger.

Daniel simply shakes his head when she offers to share. She hasn't had dinner yet, and she doesn't have time, so it all disappears quickly. The glaze never cloys even when it coats her mouth. The plate made of rice clears the glaze away in any case.

"Show-off." Ellie smiles before letting sparks flit from finger to finger on her left hand. She can show off, too.

The air becomes gauze that scatters the pipes, valves, reservoirs, even Daniel into mathematical points that then recombine. The machinery that generates the universe shimmers. When the gauze coalesces, it becomes cool, metallic, and malleable, not coincidentally the stuff that thickens into pieces of the skunkworks.

Her right hand extrudes a delay element out of the gauze. In time with the omnipresent clacking of valves, her left hand strikes the pipe in front of her twice. Sparks fly. The pipe splits into three pieces. Clean, parallel scars separate a ring from the pipe on either side of it. She removes the ring and replaces it with the delay element, her left hand sparking again to fuse the delay element into place.

One by one, she inserts extra delays to slow the paths that have become too fast. Click. Insert. Clack. Insert. She can only repair the skunkworks in the moment when the pipes are settled. It never halts. The skunkworks that lives in the innermost universe generates the outermost universe, whatever "innermost" and "outermost" mean when the universes are arranged in a loop.

Stopping one skunkworks stops all of them.

How you start them back up again is something she hopes she never has to figure out.

She dismisses the gauze and the skunkworks sharpen. The pipes grow and shrink in sync with the clacking of valves. Data no longer skids through paths causing pipes to expand or contract when they should be still.

"OK, Daniel, show me where to go. We need to flush out any speculative state before it's committed, or we're stuck with the results of a faulty skunkworks."

The skunkworks is constantly speculating multiple possible futures. Ideally, only the correct one is committed to become the present, which becomes the past and what the skunkworks uses to speculate possible futures. The rest are all flushed away. Those futures never happen.

They, of course, are already stuck. Some mistakes of a faulty skunkworks have already been committed. Say a bug in the skunkworks causes fundamental constants to go out of whack. As a result, a beach ball tunneling through a brick wall is committed as the present instead of being flushed out. That's now the state of the universe. Within the universe, whoever was looking at the beach ball saw it glitch from one side of the wall to the other. There's no point to letting those errors compound, though. The universe should be generated correctly from as early as possible.

Daniel shifts his T-shirt across his back and ties it around his neck. It might look like a cape except it's way too short. He appraises her, his face pensive.

"Anyone else might declare it close enough and leave. You really are Aunt Vera's child."

Ellie rolls her eyes. Mom's reputation precedes her. "Considering how long you lived with us, you might as well be, too."

Daniel looks annoyed again. "No, I mean her attitude about the skunkworks and the generated universe . . . Never mind. You have to see it yourself. Come on. Follow me."

He leaps to a thick pipe way overhead. From there, he swings to a swath of mesh, he bounces, and off he goes.

"Hold up, you big lunk. You have over a foot of wingspan on me." Ellie sighs too loudly, then follows him.

CHAPTER 3

Whether or not it's truly hotter, the skunkworks' interior is definitely more humid. Rust covers every pipe. Sometimes, it flakes off as the pipes grow and shrink. The farther in Ellie and Daniel go, the faster the skunkworks expand and contract. The transparent mesh that spans pipes goes taut and slack. It's as though the skunkworks is breathing. A faint hiss precedes the near-unison clack of reservoir valves.

Daniel points out which valves she needs to wedge open and for how long. That will force the skunkworks to flush out its speculative state, then regenerate the universe anew from what has already been committed. By now, that's not error-free. She's already missed that first train arriving at South Station, but nothing left to do about that. He looks up for a moment, nods, then leaps for a pipe above him.

"Now that you've finally made changes to the skunkworks by yourself, you may be marked. Some people might assume you take after your mom." Daniel treats the pipe as a high bar and executes several one-arm giants, swinging all the way around each time. "Guess I should have said something earlier, but I don't see the big deal in this case. A straightforward fix that makes the universe behave correctly is literally what we're supposed to do."

Mom repaired the skunkworks quickly. At some point when Ellie was a kid—she doesn't remember when—Mom started dragging Ellie into the skunkworks with her. Chris, already halfway out the door to university, always demanded to be brought along anyway. Mom always put her off, saying she and Ellie would only be gone for a moment and they wouldn't be doing anything Chris hadn't already mastered. Ellie's presence slowed things down a bit, though.

On these short trips, Ellie had two jobs: pay attention to Mom's lecture-demonstration and keep an eye out for anyone coming for them. Mom always dodged the question of who. Ellie had to resort to asking Chris, who told her they were the isolationists she was always warning her about.

"Daniel, have I ever told you that when I was a kid, Chris used to ambush me in my sleep to see whether I'd wake up in time?"

Ellie climbs onto a pipe and stops, for a moment, to get her bearings. She has no idea where she is.

"No, you don't talk about Chris much." He hesitates for a beat before continuing. "Ambushing you sounds excessive and in your sleep seems utterly unreasonable, by the way, if you don't mind me saying."

It feels like every couple of months, Daniel tests Ellie to see whether she's ready to talk about Chris yet. That Ellie became an adult before she stopped defending Chris to him is so embarrassing that Ellie doesn't know whether she will ever be able to admit it to anyone, even him.

"She told me that she was trying to prepare me for attacks in the skunkworks and, you know, eight-year-old me didn't know any better. She didn't use real knives back then, of course."

"But, like two decades later, you know better now, right?" Daniel hangs still on the pipe. "She doesn't ambush you anymore, much less use real knives, right?"

"Not exactly. It's complicated."

Daniel looks at her, expectant. She's wrong about being ready for this conversation, it turns out, so she doesn't elaborate. There's still some tiny part of her that believes Chris will change. She has to hold on to that hope or else she'll fall into pieces. After an uncomfortable silence, he shrugs and sighs.

"It's funny. No one except me thinks of Chris as a black sheep. She's so nice to everyone. Maybe a little too nice. She was even nice to me, once upon a time. Everyone thinks of me as a black sheep, though. Maybe I deserve it." Daniel swings around the pipe again, releases it, flips through the air in a layout position, then bounces off the mesh toward another pipe. "In theory, I'll verify that any design will work as intended as long as it's well-specified and backward-compatible. Not only bug fixes."

"Architects must really love you." She projects where Daniel is about to land and jumps after him. "One look at you and I'm sure they all ask very nicely. Isn't it better in the long run if we all implement the correct physics correctly?"

"Hey, I have my standards. Change the laws of physics, no. Discover a more general formulation of what we already know, as long as there are no unexpected side effects, why not?"

This time, it's Daniel who stops, to Ellie's relief. It's going to take a moment for her to catch up to him. He's rock steady as the pipe he landed on swells and contracts. Ellie spots the look on his face. He's about to expound on something, strutting and waving his arms like some tent-revival preacher. Daniel has to physically restrain himself from explaining literally anything in excessive detail to strangers or casual acquaintances. Ellie, unless she stops him or he realizes what he's doing, tends to get the full show.

"Look, there will always be architects with clever ideas of how to generate the universe more efficiently so that it can be more detailed or more expansive. There will always be builders who enable them, if nothing else, because they have cool ideas themselves for new valves or better ways to connect pipes. Someone has to make sure they don't destroy the universe—all of the universes, in fact—in the process. So that, on occasion, someone can tell them 'no' and they'll listen. Of course, even then, there's still the occasional unauthorized change."

Ellie finally catches up to Daniel. Her lungs burn. Daniel's probably do too. His breath is calm, though, but metronomically steady.

"That's a nice speech, but I'm my mom's child, remember? How much convincing can I possibly need to remove something that generates incorrect physics?"

Daniel glares. His expression screams "That's fucking flippant" and she wonders whether she's made him angry. Daniel, though, doesn't scream. He's so soft-spoken, Ellie isn't sure he can. In any case, the angrier he gets, the quieter he becomes.

"Cuz, I've known you since before you could walk." To her relief, his voice isn't any softer than his normal quiet. "Just wanted to confirm where you stood before I showed you this."

His gaze shifts to the skunkworks as he points overhead. The tangle of pipes looks like any other in the skunkworks. It expands and contracts, however, to a beat slightly skewed from the surrounding pipes. Rather than clack, its reservoir valves hiss when they shut. Otherwise, the skew would be obvious to anyone listening. The miniature skunkworks within the skunkworks is tied directly into the pipes that commit state, the machinery that declares, out of all the possible things that might happen, the one that actually does. The skunkworks may speculate that a plume of smoke billows across a room, that the plume of smoke rushes underneath a table in that room, that it coalesces into a panting Rottweiler happily wagging its tail, but only one of these things is committed and happens in reality. This miniature skunkworks is connected directly to the machinery that decides that the plume of smoke billows across the room.

"What does it do?"

"You need to see for yourself before I tell you." Daniel holds his hands palms-out, toward her. "Won't make sense otherwise."

Ellie looks up and focuses, but the plane of air above her doesn't fold into anything. Blueprints don't exist for the mechanism Daniel pointed out. Ellie looks puzzled. Blueprints always exist. Otherwise, what did the architect work on? What did the verifier simulate? What did the builder work off of?

She jumps, catching the mechanism's lowest pipes, then flips herself inside. Shadows fall across shadows. The chiaroscuro drains everything of depth. She contorts from pipe to pipe, tracing out paths to build a blueprint in her mind.

Cool, smooth pipes breathe in her grasp. Rust doesn't sand her palms. The air feels thick but doesn't smell metallic. Nothing here can be more than a year or two old, but pipes twist and jag around each other. Builders have inserted subtle fix after subtle fix after subtle fix. She writhes around the pipes and reservoirs, studying the joins, working out the order in which they must have applied each change. Pipe by pipe, reservoir by reservoir, she works out what this contraption does.

Those who designed, built, then kept tinkering with this must have tracked Mom's treatment history. A set of pipes tweak electron orbitals, changing the shapes of chemical compounds, specifically those pumped into Mom. To make them more effective against Mom's tumors, Ellie guesses.

She's stunned, the breath knocked out of her lungs. Mom would be appalled, as should the community of maintainers as a whole. No one should make changes to physics for personal benefit.

A skunkworks generates an entire universe. Physical laws don't apply to only three specific chemical compounds. This mechanism changes the universe she lives in so much more than they intended. It's like making mashed potatoes when all you have is dynamite. They wanted mashed potatoes so much they blew the potatoes up.

The newest bits try to pull a similar electron orbital trick, but on the chemicals inside Mom's brain. Ellie crawls through those paths three times before she can convince herself she's right. This is why, every once in a while, Mom seems to wake up. Ellie gasps. Days seem to pass before she can breathe again.

The mechanism might heal Mom eventually. Well, it needs some more tinkering first and she has some ideas. If she understands things right, it may also, bizarrely, cause a species of migratory bird to go extinct and any of a number of other things that are also not supposed to happen. She has no idea how to avoid any of that. This mechanism wasn't designed to be subtle. It was designed to save Mom's life.

She doesn't have the time to work out everything else it will also do. The isolationists will find her and Daniel soon.

"This causes a lot of collateral damage." Ellie hangs by the mechanism's lowest pipes, then drops onto the pipe Daniel's standing on. "No wonder you want me to get rid of it."

"My feelings about it are complicated." His voice blends into the hiss and Ellie strains to separate it out. "Aunt Vera took me in when no one else would."

"Of course." She fixes her gaze hard at Daniel. "Then why even show me this?"

The thud of bodies—isolationists, she assumes—hitting mesh, the creak of pipes buckling and unbuckling surrounds them. Daniel spins around, his gaze pinpointing their swinging through the skunkworks.

"OK, apparently just coming here with a builder causes the troublemakers to show up." His voice has reverted to merely quiet. "Look, everyone loves Aunt Vera. Constructing this violates pretty much everything anyone who can access the skunkworks stands for, but some number of architects, verifiers, and builders all worked on it and no one has removed it. I'll buy you time to do whatever you decide to do. And whatever you decide, we won't speak of this again."

"Do you need any help with them?"

"You're joking, right?" Daniel puffs himself up. His chest expands, his back spreads and, scarily, he manages to look even bigger. "I can drown them in boiling oil whenever I want. Cuz, you have arc welders for hands. I'm not worried about you. I'm buying you enough time to do your thing before more of them show up."

"You really get off on this whole service and protection thing, don't you?"

"Hey, don't judge me." Surprisingly, he looks a little wounded. "At least I'm taking care of the skunkworks, even if it's for the wrong reason. Plant you now, dig you later, cuz."

Daniel bounds away. The smile on his face is scarier than any weapon.

All Ellie can think of is Mom lying in bed. Mom's head lurches up, staring at Ellie in a simulacrum of life that one day may be the real thing. Hope flares through Ellie, leaving her both empty and wishing it would flare again.

Mom needs her own universe in order to heal without trashing the one Ellie lives in. Of course, a new universe would need too many people over too much time to create a skunkworks that takes up too much space. That's why they kludged this mechanism instead. It may work eventually, even if it also causes birds to migrate at the wrong times to the wrong places. Even if it has other countless side effects that will take lifetimes to map out.

It's built to be dismantled. The pipes that commit state are the only bits of the skunkworks it is connected to. It can be removed at any time. She can wait. She can let this universe be too haphazard to understand, much less document, be the new normal until Mom is cured. The tides will be wrong and the foundations of physics will crack, but Mom will live.

She can have all the mangos and soup dumplings she wants. She and Ellie will chat deep into the night. Mom will tell Ellie stories about growing up on a farm in southern Taiwan. Ellie will tell Mom about holding it together in Boston. When Ellie finally finishes her dissertation and can afford it, she will bring Mom back to Taiwan. They can hike through the country Mom loves, misses, and could never afford to return to. Ellie can't help thinking Mom is worth any number of spontaneously combusting reefs and erratic planetary orbits.

Valves clack and pipes shrink and swell in time. From end to end, they jog and twist around each other at wild angles. Data travels through pipes too long and too hard to trace. No builder would route them this way except to work around pipes already there, all the other possibilities being even longer or harder to trace. Or functionally wrong.

Once, as a teenager, Ellie had found a truly elegant fix. By then, Mom let Ellie make repairs herself, but only after Mom approved them. This one was just a few short pipes connected at right angles installed in an easily accessible place. Piece of cake. They'd be done in no time. She rushed to show Mom, who slowly shook her head and pointed out the one case in billions where data would not reach the reservoir before its valve closed.

Instead, as the people whom Mom refused to name bore down on them, Mom and Ellie threaded pipes through the existing tangle. The fix was time-consuming and ugly. They had to use their arc-welder hands not only for cutting pipe but also for self-defense. Mom drew their fire and kept them occupied, so Ellie could stay focused on the work. Not unlike what Daniel is doing now, she supposes, except they were close enough that she felt the pipes and reservoirs shake as she tried to fix the skunkworks while Mom held the troublemakers off. She and Mom barely escaped with some cuts and bruises. But the fix was also provably correct.

Ellie looks at the valves she needs to hold open to flush out speculative state and the mechanism she might dismantle. She knows what Mom would do in her place. She knows what she has to do.

It's like dismantling her own heart.

CHAPTER 4

The gastropub where she's meeting Daniel and Belt is fancier than Ellie's usual haunts. She leaves all things food-related in Daniel's capable hands. He does things with a knife and a wok that most people wouldn't even dare. Predictably, he's more familiar with restaurants in the South End than she is and she's the one who lives in what a friend in Framingham calls "the city."

Bamboo lines the walls. Planks of aged wood cover the ceiling. Branches and twigs form nests around the light fixtures overhead and hang down in artful ways. The place is bright and inviting. A row of banquette seating lines one wall. On the other side, a set of cream-colored pillars separate the space from the chef's table. A row of round tables sit between the two.

The gastropub isn't empty, but it isn't full either. Ellie's escorted to one of the round tables before she has a chance to tell anyone who she is. The table is set for three. The napkins are impeccably folded into tents, and chopsticks sit next to each one. A server sets a cocktail in front of her, compliments of the house, while she waits for Daniel to show up. This is unexpected, but considering Daniel is involved, not that unexpected.

Daniel is busy collecting his boyfriend Belt, who has just sung Enoch Snow in *Carousel.* Ellie thought the production was fine, if the show itself is a bit problematic. Daniel had some sort of ecstatic religious experience, his face fixed in a broad grin, while tears streamed down his face for most of the show. By intermission, he was barely holding it together. Ellie went to the lobby so

Daniel could contemplate the first act in private. At the end of the show, he suggested she go on ahead and he would catch up with Belt. She didn't argue.

Ellie takes a sip. It's vodka, lime, simple syrup, with a kick of heat. She's not sure where that's coming from. Maybe the vodka is an infusion. In any case, she loves it. Daniel knows her tastes well. Clear liquor with citrus is more or less what she always orders when she wants a cocktail.

A man is escorted to the table. Having seen him onstage for three hours, Ellie recognizes Belt right away. Even out of costume, he looks like if not precisely a herring fisherman from Maine then a lobsterman from Gloucester. He exudes the hardness and solidity of someone who has spent the nineteenth century picking up heavy cages and throwing them onto the deck of a ship. A tall, lean man with a sharp but grizzled face, he's at least a notch too generically handsome to be plausible. No doubt he gets double takes in the supermarket, but no one ever outright stares.

When Belt booked the gig, it would be another nine months before Mom would fall into her coma. Ellie expected this would be one of the occasional weekends she took off from going down to DC. She'd stay in Boston, Daniel would come up, and they'd catch Belt's last matinee and have dinner together. When Mom died two weeks ago, Daniel asked Ellie whether she wanted to beg off.

Daniel didn't say it, but he was absolutely coming to Boston either way. This is a geographically not inconvenient production of *Carousel* with top-notch opera singers, the original orchestrations, and, most importantly, every last note of the score. On top of that, his boyfriend is the second male lead. If, say, evil opera-hating prokaryotes encased Boston in an impenetrable dome and levitated it into the sky, Daniel would have found a way to climb up and punch through.

Ellie couldn't imagine Daniel coming to Boston and not seeing him. So here she is, finally meeting Daniel's boyfriend in person. He books gigs wherever he can find them, and she's only in DC on the weekends. They chat and text on occasion, but this is the first time their schedules have lined up and they've been in the same town at the same time.

"Hi, you must be Ellie. I'm Belt." He waves as he sits across from her. "Daniel'll join us in a moment. He's friends with the chef. They worked together at a previous restaurant or something."

"Of course he is." It became obvious the instant Belt said it.

A server sets a drink in front of Belt. His involves a tawny liquor.

"I'm sorry about your mom." He takes a sip. His eyebrows rise, and he takes a second sip. "How are you doing?"

"OK, I guess." Ellie swirls her glass. "I've been distracting myself with research, playing lab traffic cop, and course-correcting the newer grad students. Deadlines don't really care that your mom died."

"You're doing grad work in, if I remember correctly, some sort of engineering?"

"Yeah, engineering physics." She stops playing with her glass. "I basically run my advisor's lab at this point."

"Isn't that a little on the nose?" Belt unleashes a massive grin. "Given what you and Daniel do."

Daniel will introduce everyone within a fifty-foot radius of him to the real cosmology of universes and teach them the fundamentals of maintenance given half an opening. The odds are fifty-fifty that Daniel described the skunkworks and gave an intro lesson to Belt before he even bothered to mention his own name.

"No, well, maybe a little. My day job is all about how to use physics, not how to implement physics. That said, once in a while, a newish grad student will ask me whether I can make physics more 'convenient' for them."

"Do you tell them to go do it themselves?"

"Of course not!" That comes out louder than Ellie intends. "I mean, if they want to learn how to maintain the universe, I'll teach them. They never do, by the way. But our job is to make sure that physics continues to behave sensibly, not change it to suit our whim."

"I don't see how what Daniel does can change physics at all." Belt leans in with interest. "Do you do something different?"

"When Daniel's not cooking, he's all about making sure that physics makes sense and that the machinery as designed correctly generates that physics. It's all kind of abstract." Ellie takes a sip. "I work with the machinery, mostly replacing worn parts, but sometimes building fixes for bugs. Materially changing the physics goes against everything we stand for."

"How's your sister taking it? Older sister, right? Daniel talks about you all the time, but he never really talks about her."

"Oh, Chris doesn't like him. He probably doesn't like her either. If I had to guess, she's always resented him living with us." Ellie fumbles with the folded napkin and chopsticks in front of her. "Probably because she thought Mom was making her take care of another kid."

Ellie immediately wishes she hadn't said that. Somewhere between the very little alcohol she's had so far and the flow of a conversation with someone who seems to care, it slipped out.

"What do you mean?" Belt looks curious.

"My parents ran a restaurant—nothing like this—until I graduated from high school. Daniel is only a few years younger than Chris and he was never around that much anyway. All she had to do was live with him, but there were a few years where Chris basically raised me."

Horror sweeps across Belt's face before he recovers himself. Daniel must have talked about Chris at least a little. Ellie can imagine what awful but true things he told Belt. She and Daniel have a polite disagreement about Chris. Ellie has to believe that

Chris can change. Otherwise, she would stay curled up and frozen in bed most weekends, unable to force herself down to DC. Besides, Chris only got truly horrible after Mom received her diagnosis and she took it upon herself to be Mom's one and only caregiver. Ellie puts up with Chris only because Mom wanted her to.

"Does she also maintain the universe?"

"She's a builder, like me." Ellie forces herself to stop playing with the table setting. "How much do you know about what happened to my mom?"

"Daniel said you saved the universe, and let your mom die her natural death." Belt is absolutely matter-of-fact, as though that is a sentence he tosses off all the time.

"I think 'saved the universe' is excessive."

Daniel finally makes his appearance. He has a hopeful "Are you two best friends yet?" look on his face. His shirt, as usual, would make a better motorcycle tarp. Daniel has never met a shirt that fits properly.

"Not at all." Daniel pulls out the seat next to Belt and sits. "The universe was unstable and now it's not. Or at least much less so. I'm not saying it's bug free, but it's certainly more predictable now."

A server shows up with Daniel's drink. His is inside a smoke-filled glass cloche. The server also hands out menus and says she'll be back in a moment to take their orders.

Ellie scans the menu. On the right-hand side, it has a column of bao. She wants an order of every bao the restaurant makes. They all sound delicious. The column heading "Bao Buns," however, earns a glare of disapproval.

"Yeah, they had to call them 'bao buns,'" Daniel says, reading her expression. "If they didn't, no one would understand what they were ordering. By the way, the bill is already taken care of, so go nuts."

"What?" Ellie sets down the menu. "I can't let you do that. You're the guest."

Etiquette demands that she mount at least a token complaint, but, also, she's not sure how Daniel can afford this. She can't either, but that's not the point.

"Ellie, save the politeness for a relative who wants it." Daniel looks vaguely offended. "I've had a year to plan. Let me have this. Besides, there isn't a bao on the menu you don't want to try."

Daniel's right, of course, but she goes back and forth with him for two more rounds anyway. Belt looks amused as Ellie and Daniel go through the motions. The bill, as Daniel says, is already taken care of.

They order all six kinds of bao, chili garlic string beans, and a whole fried branzino to share. This strikes Ellie as a spectacularly large amount of food, but Belt looks like he spends his days hauling lobsters, and he's practically a waif sitting next to Daniel.

Daniel opens his cloche. Smoke drifts away to reveal a lowball glass with a pink cocktail. He takes a sip. His eyes close as he savors the cocktail.

"So how badly is your sister taking it?" Belt asks. "If you don't mind me asking."

"Her reaction kind of took me by surprise." Ellie's hand grips her cocktail glass. "When I showed up at her house the following afternoon, she already knew what I had done. She said she felt the change in the universe."

"Chris, of course, is a font of pure, unerring truth. Nothing false has ever passed through those angelic lips." Daniel sips from a smoky, pink cocktail that cannot possibly be as dry as his comment. "Some number of people saw you dismantle that contraption. I could keep them only so far away. The news had to have spread quickly."

Ellie doesn't want to get into how Chris reacted. This time, she probably deserved it. Either way, Daniel doesn't need Ellie to tell him that Chris tore into her for condemning Mom to death. Belt doesn't need to know.

"So how did you two meet?" Ellie lets go of her glass when she realizes her hand is a vise locked around it.

Daniel squirms. He hates talking about himself and finds the idea of being talked about mortifying. If a relative stranger talked about him, he'd view it as an attack, she suspects, and bear it. Ellie can embarrass him at will. She only ever does by accident. In retrospect, no one who has endured a childhood with Chris could on purpose. In any case, she wants to know how they met and she's desperate for a change of topic. If Ellie has to talk about Chris, for once, Daniel can talk about Daniel.

"Oh." Belt holds up a hand to Daniel. "I was jogging on a treadmill in the gym when this mountain rushes at me. My life passes before my eyes, and I'm searching for what I've done to deserve an early death."

"Oh, I just *can't* with you." Daniel looks incredulous. "There are sugar-free breath mints more menacing than me. I started jogging on the treadmill next to yours and politely waited for you to notice me trying to make eye contact."

"Of course you did." Ellie expected no less. Her only surprise is that he didn't also arrange for mood lighting and music.

"Anyway, his first words to me are literally 'I'm falling in love with someone.'" Belt hesitates for a moment. "I may have flirted cautiously at first, then shamelessly after about five minutes. In my defense, it did not seem unwelcome. Also, I may have asked him out before I realized he was talking about the song from *Naughty Marietta*."

"While you were jogging on the treadmill?" Ellie eyes Belt incredulously and laughs.

"Look, multitasking is a thing. Also, if you can flirt and jog at the same time, you're not overtraining." Belt is as dry as Daniel. He may be joking, but Ellie never will know unless she asks.

"Daniel's surprisingly adorable once you realize he has not come to reap your soul. At least not today."

Belt grins. He toasts Ellie and Daniel with his glass and takes a sip. Daniel's embarrassment dissolves into a smile.

"He sang Captain Richard Warrington in a production of *Naughty Marietta* I saw." Daniel is in full explanatory-comma mode, which invariably negates any possible discomfort he feels. "He interpolated a fabulous high E-flat at the end of 'I'm Falling in Love with Someone.'"

Plates and plates and plates of bao arrive, along with green beans, and fish. The branzino is still sizzling and the spicy garlicky perfume of the beans fill the air. Servers place steaming bowls of white rice before them.

Ellie immediately reaches for the closest plate, the fried chicken bao with a pickle garnish. Daniel starts to fillet the branzino. Belt surveys the feast in front of him and reaches for the pork belly bao.

"So, Belt, what are you doing after *Carousel*?" Ellie slides a bao and some pickles onto her own plate. "Another musical?"

"He's coming home with me." Having taken some fish, Daniel pushes some green beans onto his plate.

"Bel canto opera." Belt picks up his pork belly bao. "I'm singing Don Ramiro in *La Cenerentola* in DC in three weeks."

"Are you going to be able to make it to Mom's funeral?" She idly picks up a bao. "You don't have a Saturday matinee or something?"

Belt and Daniel exchange glances. Ellie wonders what she's done.

"Ellie." Daniel's voice gets ostentatiously gentle. Ironically, to Ellie, whenever that happens, that's when he sounds the scariest. "The funeral is in two weeks. What did Chris tell you?"

Ellie sighs. Chris told her the wrong date. Ellie has no idea what Chris has in mind for Ellie a week after the funeral. It's entirely possible that Chris has nothing in mind. Making Ellie miss her own mother's funeral is merely yet another bit of spite.

"Oh, I'm sure Chris just got her dates mixed up." Ellie takes a bite of bao.

Ellie doesn't really believe this, but she also doesn't want to deal with it right now. She'd rather have a fun dinner with her cousin and his boyfriend.

Daniel also doesn't believe this, but he's hiding it surprisingly well. Ellie can only see the strain because she's known him for decades. A righteous condemnation is all set to burst out of him. Belt, however, seems to accept it. He also acts so well that he does it for a living. All three of them have chosen to accept this polite fiction for now. No one wants to ruin dinner.

And dinner is not ruined. Daniel settles down, eventually. There is another round of cocktails. When all the plates are empty and they are full, there is no bill, but there is a visit from the chef, who bids Daniel goodbye with a hug. Everyone agrees that they should have dinner together again, and that is not a polite fiction.

CHAPTER 5

Mom's funeral is exactly as awful as Ellie expects. The hundred or so mourning Mom are squeezed into a dull box at the funeral home meant for seventy at best. Even so, a ring of empty chairs pointedly surrounds her like the poisoned space around a mold. Discreet cameras at the edges of the room and a director sitting at a control board livestream the funeral.

August is everything she doesn't miss about metro DC. The odor of flowers, sweat, and, oddly, nutritional yeast form a sweet, heavy blanket that smothers everyone and presses the air out of their lungs. In its defense, the area would be a sauna even on the coolest and driest of days.

The preacher drones on from a dais at the front of the room. An interpreter stands next to him interjecting English into the pauses between the Mandarin. The English is adequate. However, it bears only an incidental, maybe accidental, resemblance to the Mandarin. Ellie has to restrain herself from shouting, "Yes, that's what he said but that's not what he meant." Her only experience interpreting is Mom pressing her into service, as a child at the supermarket, for example, and eventually as an adult with the oncologist. Even she, however, can do better than this. Certainly, Mom deserves better.

Two giant stands of flowers trap the preacher and interpreter on the dais. One stand holds a tasteful wreath of white and green. The other holds a paisley explosion with the words "From Ellie" scrawled in black on a red ribbon that splits the arrangement like a gash.

Ellie sighs. If she'd thought to send flowers, maybe Chris wouldn't have sent some for her. Because of course Chris sent flowers in Ellie's name. And, of course, those flowers have to be garish and inappropriate. There's no point asking Chris why she did this. She'd say, innocently, that she simply bought the flowers she thought Ellie would want to send. Now that Ellie thinks about it, what Chris would really say is a daughter who loved her mother—or at least one who didn't kill her mother—would have thought to send flowers herself. Ellie is willing to admit Chris has a quarter of a point. Then again, even if Ellie had sent something, they would have shown up next week. Chris takes it as a given that Ellie must have simply misheard her. After all, why would she give Ellie the wrong date? Ellie will grant Chris another quarter of a point, but she won't like it.

One after another, eulogies render her mother into an undifferentiated mass of pity and saintly suffering. Mom asking for a slice of mango before she fell into a coma is mentioned. Chris, who didn't want Mom to get fat, hiding food from her in what turned out to be the last few months before the coma, is not. Mom grinding away for minimum wage at Taco Barn is mentioned. Mom diagnosing and repairing the workings that create the universe when everyone else was stumped is not. Even the Chief Architect of the skunkworks falls into platitudes. Why the universe keeps working is something most of the mourners don't even know to think about. If clean water always comes out when you turn on the spigot, you don't care about the infrastructure that gets the water from the reservoir to the tap and makes sure the water is safe to drink. A funeral is neither the time nor place to tell them.

As Ellie withstands the eulogies, her hands grip the seat of her folding chair and she clamps her mouth shut or else she'll scream. By the time they're done, her mother is a pathetic figure diminished and neatly secured within the bounds of the audience's polite grief. Ellie is livid.

The reception grinds away in another dull box down the hall. This one seems larger but only because there are no chairs. Long tables are pressed against the wall. Platters of indifferently piled cold cuts, crackers, and cheese fill half the tables. Bottles of soda, tubs of ice, plates, and cups fill the other half.

People chat in tight circles throughout the room. Most of the circles are either maintainers or family. The intersection between the two groups isn't huge. Chris is working her way from one circle to the next. Ellie supposes she should too. She knows it won't go well, but it's still her job to thank everyone for coming and for paying their respects.

Ellie avoids Daniel's parents. They abandoned Daniel as a kid. She doesn't need a lecture about betraying Mom, and definitely not from them.

Daniel makes a beeline past his parents toward a tidy-looking man in a faded gray shirt and slacks, who is very clearly the focus of his circle of conversation. They occupy an otherwise neglected corner of the room. Daniel approaches him with the reverence one reserves for a god, or in Daniel's case, an especially talented Broadway or opera soprano. Their conversation is a good deal friendlier and more personal than that, though. Daniel twirls around showing off his suit and, in turn, the man appears to be giving him both praise and tailoring advice.

Ellie decides not to intrude. Daniel didn't sit with her at the funeral. Maybe he has his own reasons or maybe he, too, can't be seen in public with her. Either way, she doesn't want to know right now.

In the middle of the room, an aunt from Taiwan chats in a circle with some cousins from the US. She is telling them stories in Mandarin about Mom as a kid when Ellie walks up to them. Ellie is not unconvinced that at least a few of her cousins are merely nodding along, catching maybe one word in ten.

She lurks outside their circle, learning about Mom's childhood in Taiwan. Mom rarely talked about it, unless there was some point she wanted to make. One story Mom told was about how some kid who kept stealing her soup eventually left her alone when she started giving the soup to him. Her point was that she expected Ellie to appease Chris, to figure out how to be her sister. As a kid, Ellie truly believed that if she was nice enough, Chris would leave her alone. As an adult, Ellie can't escape Mom's expectations.

Her aunt, however, has very different stories of Mom. She was someone who hiked across the mountains and slaughtered the pigs herself, not someone who would surrender her soup to anyone. Listening to her aunt, Ellie is pretty sure Mom flat-out lied to keep peace in the house.

They don't let her into their circle. It's not because they don't notice her.

"My little sister must have been so disappointed in Ellie," the aunt says, not looking at Ellie. "She didn't do one thing to take care of her. Didn't visit her even once—"

"You know I can understand you, right?" Ellie cuts her off in perfectly respectable Mandarin.

The surprise on her aunt's face is worth the disrespect of interrupting her. Ellie will pay for this eventually, but she was already screwed to begin with.

"Chris said you couldn't understand Chinese." Her aunt's arms fold across her chest, squeezing herself tight.

"Maybe you shouldn't believe everything she says."

With that, Ellie flounces away. There's no point waiting for an apology her aunt will never make.

Her next conversations go about as well. The maintainers accuse her of killing her mother. The relatives accuse her of neglect. This is when anyone acknowledges her presence at all. To her surprise, she's philosophical about this. Not having to deal with any of them is a relief. She will be everybody's scapegoat, if it makes everybody's lives simpler, including hers. No one seems to care which of Mom's dear friends bent the rules for her. If Ellie never thinks about that contraption again, it will still be too soon.

The respite won't last, of course. Chris's reckoning still looms. There's no running, no hiding, no escape from the wrath of Chris. That said, it's not like Ellie hasn't thought about taking the next train home. Unfortunately, she bought the cheap train tickets. No changes allowed, and she can't afford another ticket.

Ellie stands in a deserted corner watching Chris harvest the love everyone lavishes on her. Her sister's grief is undoubtedly real, but the way her eyes glisten but aren't teary, how her voice threatens to break but never does, make their sympathy practically Pavlovian. Chris moves from one clump to the next. She'd love to talk more, but there is still so much work left to do before the funeral ends.

She's so bound up into Chris's not-a-performance performance that she doesn't notice Daniel until he taps her shoulder. The walking mountain has been standing right next to her for who knows how long. The sight of him knocks Ellie out of her mental spiral.

Involuntarily, she takes a half step back and her eyebrows rise. There's how the clothing industry believes men are built and then there's Daniel. There are weddings of mutual cousins where he's a giant, formless shadow looming at the side of photos. He's a guy who desperately needs the intervention of a good tailor. Or, rather, needed.

Nothing will ever fit him as well as the suit he's currently wearing. It has room for his chest and back without exaggerating his already broad shoulders. There's a taper to the waist, but it's tasteful rather than excessive. The understated belt, she suspects, is functional as well as decorative. A tailor can only do so much. Right now, he's either the leading man in some spy movie or a waiter at some extremely fancy restaurant. He's holding a paper plate, which spoils the illusion. Still, if Ellie forgets that this is her goofy cousin, his intentions would look perfectly balanced between "kill you" and "feed you." Neither is out of the question for Daniel, she suspects.

"Yeah." He shrugs, then gestures at his suit. "I figured I should try to look good for Aunt Vera. That's why I'm late. I got stuck in traffic on the way from the tailor."

Ellie instantly feels guilty for ever doubting Daniel. At least she didn't accuse him of anything.

"You didn't miss much. The eulogies were . . ." Ellie heaves a deep sigh. ". . . syntactically correct sentences in both English and Mandarin."

"Oh, I wasn't that late. Just stuck in the crowd at the back. Otherwise, I would have sat with you." He offers her the plate. "Roast duck?"

His plate was empty a moment ago. Now, it's filled with bite-size roll-ups, each one a perfect little pancake smeared with hoisin sauce and wrapped around a piece of duck and a sliver of green onion. Their savory, peppery, sweet scent perfumes the air. Any moment now, someone is going to notice something delicious in the ignored corner of the room. Assuming Daniel making food appear out of nowhere hasn't already freaked someone out.

"You're checking the state of the skunkworks?" She stares up at him incredulously. "Now?"

"Oh, this isn't an equivalence report. This tastes like whatever I make it taste like."

He inhales a roll-up. No one should be able to eat anything that quickly.

"I mean the whole food-from-thin-air thing."

"Oh please." Daniel rolls his eyes. "No one's paying any attention to us. Definitely not anyone who might be freaked out by this. Being the family black sheep has literally only one upside. Besides, so what if they are?"

What the extended family makes of Daniel faithfully changes

between family gatherings. This is the first time the extended family has turned on Ellie. All they know about Mom's death is what Chris told them. She said nothing about Ellie removing the monstrosity that both trapped Mom between life and death and threatened to destabilize physics. To the extended family, all that matters is that Mom is dead. Somehow, that's Ellie's fault. Also, Mom died on a Wednesday. Ellie was at school, not by Mom's side, since she only visited every weekend. Chris will never forgive her for that.

Ellie takes a roll-up. The duck skin crackles when she bites into it. The duck is rich but not overwhelming. The hint of sweetness from the smear of hoisin and something acidic keeps it all under control.

"Wow." For a moment, she's happy and sad all at once and can't find any words. "This is the first good thing that's happened to me in weeks. Thanks."

"So." Daniel braces himself, and he looks set to be punched. "Have you talked to your sister about your mom yet?"

"No." She doesn't go for another roll-up.

"Ellie . . ."

A reproving Daniel is quite the sight. It's as though gravity were disappointed in you. It'll still attract things to each other all the same, but the protest will be palpable.

"Have you talked to your parents?"

"Ouch, but fair." The mountain heaves a sigh. "We're back to them not speaking to me. Like I wasn't going to bring Belt with me. They think I'm embarrassing them."

Belt and Daniel have been together for a couple of years now. Ellie thought Daniel's parents, her aunt and uncle, had finally made their peace with Daniel because he is their son or maybe out of sheer exhaustion. Apparently not. It must take so much time and energy to be so petty for so long.

"Well, yes, being them is embarrassing, but it's not because you brought your boyfriend." Ellie looks around. "Where is he anyway?"

"Making my parents uncomfortable by having a thoroughly respectable, if somewhat one-sided, conversation with them where he expresses his genuine condolences over Aunt Vera's death." Daniel holds a hand up in surrender. "It was his idea. I just didn't stop him."

A man steps into their ignored corner. He's not a relative. She knows all of her relations in the US by sight and, in any case, they're all Taiwanese. He looks kind of familiar, so he's probably a maintainer who worked with her mom. Honestly, though, it's not like there's a shortage in the world of solidly built white men with blond hair who are about a head taller than her.

The man's face is stern. He holds out an envelope, staring expectantly. Ellie has no idea what this is about. She meets his gaze and takes the envelope. The man turns to leave, but immediately turns back.

"You know." The pressure keeping the man's voice level could transform rocks. "They could have done it. They could have changed the universe into one where Vera could be cured."

"Yeah." Ellie keeps her gaze locked with his. "I can tell from the way she stayed in her coma."

"You didn't give them a chance." His face flushes. "Maybe they needed more time."

"Because she was all about perverting the universe for her own benefit." Ellie crosses her arms. "What might have gone wrong in the universe to save her?"

"Do you see her?" He points to Chris, across the room, accepting condolences and barely able to hold back the torrent of tears. "You did that to her."

"But you, of course, wouldn't know anything about being an asshole to someone who's recently lost her mother."

The man grits his teeth. His face hits full boil.

"You don't deserve to call her 'mother.'"

Daniel takes the tiniest of steps forward. He waves at the man.

"I think this conversation is over." Daniel's voice is this quiet rustle that nevertheless fills the room. "Don't you, Tom?"

Tom stumbles back a step. His gaze widens and his face pales. He's only now realized Daniel is right here.

Looking at Daniel or, rather, Tom's reaction to Daniel, Ellie suspects she sees Daniel differently from everyone else, or at least differently from Tom. She can't help but see Daniel as big and affable. They've known each other since they were kids. He's the guy who makes food appear out of nowhere and jokes about the workings of the universe. Based on the panic smeared across Tom's face, the man who barged in then insulted her sees someone else entirely. Daniel's presentation has clearly shifted from "feed you" toward "kill you." To Ellie, it's subtle. To Tom, maybe not.

Tom stammers something about reading the note from the Chief Architect. He backs away a little too quickly and nearly trips as he turns to flee.

Ellie stares up at Daniel, disapprovingly. Daniel stares back, puzzled.

"What?" Daniel's puzzlement dissolves into a grin and his gaze sparkles when it shifts to the envelope. "Aren't you curious what the Chief Architect has to say?"

It can't be business. There's a hierarchy to the folks who maintain the universe. There's a small list of people the Chief Architect delegates to and Ellie is not on it. Maybe she's going to express her condolences. Or maybe she's going to insult her, like Tom, but more formally.

Ellie takes a deep breath before she rips open the envelope and takes out the note inside. It's some subtle shade of cream with few sentences written with a precise hand and an unmistakable signature. Her heart pounds, and she forces her hands to steady.

Apparently, it is business even though Ellie has never met the Chief Architect. Unless getting annoyed at her eulogy counts.

"The Chief Architect wants to talk to me. In half an hour at her house."

"Have you been there before?"

"No, the first time I've even seen her was at the podium during the funeral."

"So, with traffic, you need to go now." The roll-ups disappear and the paper plate crumples as Daniel claps his hands. "Can I come with?"

"Sure."

"Really?"

The surprise on Daniel's face is a guilty pleasure that Ellie enjoys a little too much. Very little catches Daniel off guard. Or if something does, he rarely shows it. She half wishes Daniel had been drinking something. The spit take would have been epic.

"Yeah, she says to bring you along if you ask without me prompting you."

She shows him the note. The disdain is obvious on Daniel's face.

"Why is 'big lunk' in scare quotes?"

Ellie sighs. The big lunk can be so predictable.

CHAPTER 6

Ellie knocks, and the front door opens. The Chief Architect is shorter than Ellie expected. After seeing her on the platform eulogizing Mom, Ellie expected someone taller. Maybe watching Daniel fold himself into and unfold himself out of the driver's seat of his ramshackle subcompact has warped her sense of scale.

"Ellie." The Chief Architect offers her hand. "My condolences about your mother."

"Thank you, Chief Architect." Ellie shakes her hand.

"Oh, please. Call me Mary."

Daniel steps out from behind Ellie. The Chief Architect's gaze grows wide, and she takes an involuntary half step back. He leans in and offers his hand.

"Hi, I'm—"

"Oh, I know who you are, Daniel." The Chief Architect's hand is swallowed in his. "Your reputation precedes you."

She knows him well enough to call him "Daniel" rather than "Dan" or, even worse, "Danny." He can be rather particular about some things.

"You have a reputation?" Ellie looks up at him. "For what?"

At first, Daniel looks befuddled and shrugs. Not that this means anything. Befuddled is his go-to facial expression. Maybe it's a resting expression, but he seems to do it a lot, especially around people he doesn't know. If he's trying to play dumb, though, he's pretty bad at it. His insatiable urge to be helpful inevitably kicks in. Ellie questions whether anyone truly believes Daniel is as dumb as the expression on his face misleads you into thinking.

"Why is 'big lunk' in scare quotes?" Daniel crosses his arms over his chest.

The Chief Architect rolls her eyes as she ushers them through the door. Both Ellie and Daniel stop, expecting to take off their shoes. The Chief Architect, oblivious, strides past them into the family room.

Ellie and Daniel exchange glances. Ellie freezes for a moment. When her host blithely tromps through her own house with shoes on, Ellie's never sure whether taking shoes off before entering is rude or not. Maybe taking shoes off is Just Not Done or maybe her host just doesn't care.

Ellie slips off her flats. It'd feel weird otherwise. Daniel, of course, has already taken off his black, light hikers. Not even looking good for Aunt Vera can separate him from all-terrain footwear. He simply stands there waiting for her with serene patience.

The tight pile carpet that covers the family room floor is an "I hide dirt well" brown. Scratches and dents mar the coffee table and the arms of the sofa. A particularly rambunctious kid must have lived here. Either that or a tornado made of tiny knives. A rusty railing with cracked white paint divides the family room from the kitchen. The refrigerator and stove are both avocado green and tinged with stains that have survived decades of scrubbing.

The Chief Architect opens a door next to the kitchen counter. A set of stairs descends into the dark. She flips a light switch just inside the stairwell and enters the basement. Ellie and Daniel exchange another glance before they follow.

The Chief Architect still hasn't said a word about why they're here.

Ellie gasps at the bottom of the stairs. It feels like they've stepped into another universe, but they haven't. She would have noticed.

Tasteful chairs and tables ring the room along with the occasional cabinet and chest of drawers. All of it is on the impeccably executed side of Scandinavian Modern. Crafted with clean lines and natural materials, they are the furniture equivalent of the multi-hundred-dollar T-shirt. The tornado has obviously never made it here. If the workroom of an architect isn't another world, though, it's the next closest thing and that makes it all the more unexpected.

Folded planes of air fill the tables. They refract the walls behind them, chopping and warping wood grain and scattering it throughout the room. The patterns rotate and twist as the structures on the table flow from one impossible shape to another. When Ellie focuses on one of them, she can work out the machine, the chunk of physics, it is meant to represent.

Daniel taps Ellie's shoulder. He lowers his head next to hers.

"Close your mouth, Ellie." His voice is a gentle wave lapping a beach. "You know you've seen this sort of thing before, right?"

"Yes, but not in someone's basement."

"Architects have to work somewhere."

The Chief Architect pointedly clears her throat. Ellie snaps upright. Daniel subtly shifts his gaze upward, and becomes extremely aware of the basement ceiling. He straightens, gingerly, not quite to his full height, leaving a few inches of clearance.

"This is not a magic trick." The Chief Architect puts a key in her left fist and holds both fists out to Ellie. "Which fist has the key?"

"Seriously?" Ellie ignores the wince on Daniel's face.

"Hey, I'm in charge of maintaining the machinery that generates the universe." The Chief Architect flashes a quick smile. "Humor me."

Daniel nudges Ellie. Obligingly, she points to the Chief Architect's left fist.

"You should get used to this." The Chief Architect reveals the key lying on her left palm before closing her hand into a fist again.

"We'll be doing a total of thirty trials before you take the key and open that drawer over there."

It isn't even the fifth trial before Ellie starts pointing to the Chief Architect's left fist out of reflex. As advertised, this is not a magic trick. Each time, the Chief Architect reveals the key in her left fist before hiding it again. Ellie's mind drifts to thoughts of asking what this is all about. Instead, she keeps her mouth shut and iterates through trial after trial on the slim hope that, eventually, there will be a point. Anything else would be disrespectful.

Daniel, of course, has checked out of the "not a trick" completely. He's working his way around the room, examining the planes of air one by one, turning and prodding them. His face contorts in a symphony of downturned lips, widened eyes, and extended tongues. He moves from one to the next like some chess master winning against several dozen players at once. Not that doing this doesn't take effort, but he is both making a show of how hard this is for him and breezing from one to the next. Tiny jewels of folded air emerge between his gesturing hands. They're counterexamples, cases where the mechanism in question would fail. He attaches them to the planes, occasionally digging inside them to balance them against the right fold. Every once in a while, between trials, the Chief Architect throws a glance Daniel's way. It's invariably impressed or dismayed. Daniel's oblivious to her reactions, even when the glance becomes a glare.

"That's an obscure corner case," the Chief Architect says, referring to the counterexample Daniel is delicately attaching to some hidden, inner fold.

"But I'm not wrong." Daniel, focused intently on his self-imposed task, steps back to inspect the plane of air.

"No, you're not." The Chief Architect nods. "That's going to be annoying to fix."

On the thirtieth trial, Ellie reaches for the key. When the Chief Architect opens her left fist, though, the key isn't there.

"Whoa." Daniel shivers and the floor vibrates in sympathy. "Something's very wrong. Dangerously wrong."

A boule materializes in his hands. The crust is dark and ragged with coarse flecks of wheat germ. He taps it. His brow furrows at the muddy sound.

"Wow, that's not even enough time to blink." The Chief Architect reveals the key is actually in her right hand. "Your scan dump, however, is a loaf of bread? Seriously?"

"Sometimes, it's soy-braised oxtails or Brussels sprouts with a ginger-balsamic reduction glaze." Daniel's tone is deadpan but with an undercurrent of annoyance that Ellie is positive the Chief Architect doesn't notice.

"I've never seen anyone else do that," the Chief Architect says.

"I'm not anyone else." Daniel sounds ever so slightly self-defensive. "Maybe other verifiers could, too, if they wanted. I dunno. This works for me."

Daniel pops a pinch of bread into his mouth. He chews slowly, nodding as he savors the flavor.

"Can you two do that again?" He's ripping open the boule and examining its crumb. "The failure caught me by surprise. I only caught vestiges of it."

"What are you on about, Daniel?" Ellie's gaze shifts from the Chief Architect to Daniel. "It's just sleight of hand."

"Yes, I know that. Her manual dexterity is not the sign of a bug in the skunkworks." Daniel turns to face them, then rolls his eyes. The boule disappears as he clasps his hands. "Have you looked at what's in your hand?"

Ellie looks down and gasps. A white ceramic disk is now in her left hand. It wasn't there before. When she holds it level to the floor, a complex wireframe structure emerges from the disk and levitates about a centimeter above it. It is both physically substantial and weightless. It looks like a 3D image but is unquestionably material. The iridescent wires are both lines in the geometric sense and thin, laser-like struts. They are both evanescent and absolutely sturdy.

The structure is a model of a skunkworks. Mom showed her one of them when she was a kid.

These models are the direct reification of complex systems of mathematical equations. They operate billions of times slower than reality, but they also don't have any of the limitations of actual machinery. You don't have to worry about how long it takes for information to travel from one point to another. Gates open and close in zero time. Information never leaches away from the reservoirs. The deviations from the ideal, the physical realities that any implementation of a skunkworks must engage with, are all abstracted away.

"This skunkworks model used to be in that drawer." Ellie is absolutely certain of this. "You created it thirty years ago. It was your first."

Architects generally build them to see their bug fixes work in context. They hand them off to verifiers to check their work. Builders take them and figure out how to turn this ideal into working machinery. Ellie can't shake the sense, though, that Mary did not build this for a bug fix.

"Do you know anything else about it?" Mary prompts as she heads toward the drawer.

"You created it to try out a novel 'toy' physics for a class project years ago. It generates a physics that's incomplete and somewhat inconsistent. You didn't have to simulate the creation of a universe, so this physics doesn't deal with singularities at all, only steady state or near steady state. But the model already has a universe in steady state preloaded into it."

Ellie feels for a switch on the edge of the disk. It clicks when she touches it. An orb materializes above the wireframe, a toy universe generated by a toy skunkworks. Individual atoms, visible as tiny dots, crash into each other at great velocity for this universe, like pearls sinking into clear sludge for anyone watching.

The Chief Architect unlocks the drawer. She pulls it open. Ellie and Daniel peer inside. It's empty, except for a thin layer of dust. There's a hole in the dust the size and shape of the disk in Ellie's hand.

"How did I know why you created it?" Ellie turns back to the Chief Architect and Daniel, showing them the toy skunkworks.

"Well," Daniel says. "Picking the left fist again and again biased which future the skunkworks speculated—"

"But the key was in her right hand, so I never took it." Ellie shakes the toy skunkworks at Daniel. "The speculated future where I took the key from her left hand and unlocked the drawer got flushed out. It never happened. There shouldn't be any vestige of that in this universe. I shouldn't know anything about what was in that drawer, much less have this model in my hand or understand why she created it."

"Yes, that would be the bug." Daniel's gaze is as narrow as his tone is dry. "Obviously, picking her left hand over and over again and the key being there all those times biased the skunkworks toward guessing you will take the key so much that when it didn't happen, its recovery was incomplete. Not everything from that incorrect future got eliminated."

Daniel has his own annoying definition of "obviously." Either it's so broad that it's useless or the word is its own antonym. Ellie has long since given up trying to get him to find a better one.

"The consequences of that would be awful." Ellie turns off the toy skunkworks and the orb vanishes. "You don't need to know anything about maintenance to exploit this, so literally anybody can make anything happen, at least in part, by making it seem plausible enough for long enough. Why is the skunkworks behaving like that?"

"How should I know?" Daniel looks incredulously at her. "That's why I need you two to do it again. I need more data."

Ellie offers the Chief Architect the ceramic disk. The Chief Architect studies Daniel, sizing him up. The man is an avalanche waiting to crash down a range. Daniel straightens to his full height. Surprisingly, at least to Ellie, there is still a little clearance between his head and ceiling. His gaze suddenly wide and his mouth open, he's just realized he's ordering around the Chief Architect, someone who has probably resolved more problems with this universe than Daniel will ever find.

The Chief Architect smiles. Ultimately, the urge to be helpful always beats out any attempt, intentional or not, for Daniel to play dumb.

She takes the disk from Ellie and locks it up in the drawer. The two play their not-a-trick again and again. As they do, Daniel samples through a banquet, one bite of everything before it disappears. Steamed fish appears. It rests on a plate composed of fried rice in his hand. The scent of ginger perfumes the room. He savors the broth, prods at it to test its texture, then makes it disappear. He slurps a bevy of noodles: thin, thick, stir-fried, floating in a rich beef broth, cold and tossed in a chili sauce that makes everybody's eyes tear up. Crispy slivers of pork tossed with thin strips of oil-slicked carrots and celery appear on a bed of steamed rice. He digs through with chopsticks that he didn't have a second ago, then makes it all go away.

Ellie's mouth can't help watering. Everything smells as perfect as Daniel can make it when he's just doing it for fun. That doesn't say anything about what is going wrong with the universe, at least not to her. Daniel only hums and makes odd grunting noises. The Chief Architect's eyes look ready to jump out of their sockets. Her mouth stays open, always about to interrupt Daniel's work except she never does. For all her experience, she's clearly never seen Daniel when he's determined to figure something out.

Finally, after a few iterations of a ceramic disk mysteriously appearing in Ellie's left hand, he gestures at them to stop their not-a-trick. The air in the room becomes crisper and sharper. For a moment, the first sting of winter bites them. A fluffy, white ice coalesces inside a wafer cone he's suddenly holding. He breaks off a bit of the cone and scoops a bit of the ice. He savors it, his head slowly nodding.

"Here, try this." He offers it to both of them.

"Are you kidding?" Ellie's hands remain resolutely by her side. "You want me to taste something you made while working out the root cause of something, in your words, dangerously wrong?"

"Would I ask you to taste something truly inedible?"

"Yes."

"No. Come on, just try it." He pulls the Chief Architect into his gaze. "I'm making a point."

Ellie sighs. She stretches her exhale like some sort of contortionist of breath. With a twist of her wrist that radiates "against my better judgment," she digs out a little ice with a fragment of wafer cone. The Chief Architect scoops out her taste of ice with far less petulance.

It tastes like the cold respite from a blistering summer day she's been craving ever since coming down to metro DC. The pucker from the lemon is pleasant, rounded out by a hint of sweetness and a little bitter pith. Ellie involuntarily reaches for another taste but stops herself. The Chief Architect simply takes a taste then levels her gaze at Daniel, waiting for him to make his point.

"I don't get it." Ellie chews and swallows the bit of wafer cone. "It tastes exactly like what it is, a lemon ice."

"That's my point." He clasps his hands and the cone of lemon ice disappears. "If any subsystem isn't behaving the way it's intended, it's beyond me."

"It's not just you." The Chief Architect finishes off her wafer cone. "So you don't understand the problem—"

"Oh, I can sketch out for you the sequence of events that lets anyone get access to shards of unrealized futures left lying around in the skunkworks. That's what I've been spending the past who knows how long working out." He stops for a moment in concentration. "It's kind of involved and subtle. I can't talk at the same time. Gimme a sec."

He spreads his hands and cleaves a plane of air from the room. His face contorts, as if a twisted mouth and scrunched eyes would make the air more compliant. Ellie can't tell whether he's back on his "I'm not that competent, really" game or whether this is genuinely hard for him. A metallic shriek echoes with each fold. His chest and arms bulge as he wrenches the plane into shape, bending and twisting in directions that otherwise don't exist. Sweat drips down his face and his tongue peeks out of his distorted mouth. All sorts of food manifests on a whim, but these planes of air apparently need to be wrestled with. Both Ellie and the Chief Architect stare as Daniel studiously ignores them.

The entire ordeal takes a few minutes or so. A spiky, mirror-like structure with faintly glowing folds bobbles right above Daniel's palms. He runs his hands over the imaginary sphere that surrounds the structure. It rotates slowly in sync with his hands. Deconstructed faces and furniture shift from one facet to another. The structure settles down, and Daniel looks positively smug.

"So this is what is happening: Each sub-subsystem is behaving exactly as you'd expect it to but—" The smugness fades when Daniel spots a structure under a table. "Oh, you're already working on a fix."

The Chief Architect plucks the structure from Daniel's hands and sets it under a table next to the one he noticed. Her gaze sweeps Daniel's structure up and down before she turns to face Ellie and Daniel again.

"And I thought I shouldn't take the rumors about you too seriously. It took us weeks to work out why this was happening." She folds her hands across her chest. "Now I'm wondering whether everything else they say about you is also true."

Daniel's face is a mask of panic and horror. He waves his hands in front of him as if to ward off an oncoming steamroller.

"Who is 'they' and what else do 'they' say about me?" His words rush out oddly high-pitched and loud relative to his usual rumble. He takes a deep breath. His voice drops to its normal octave, volume, and pace. "It's so much easier when the bug is so obviously reproducible like that."

"Oh, please, Daniel." The Chief Architect's grin is far too wide. "You made more progress in the past hour than two teams of verifiers have in several weeks. You really can't help yourself."

"No." Daniel scrunches up his face. "I am just a completely harmless, moderately competent verifier."

Ellie's gaze darts back and forth between the two of them. It's absolutely possible that Daniel believes this the same way he believes that he's not that much stronger than anyone else. The Chief Architect is pretty clearly needling him. Ellie doesn't see the point. He's not usually particularly needled.

"There's a vast infrastructure of maintainers who find and fix bugs. It seems to have a handle on this one." Ellie gestures at the work under the table. "Why did you ask us here?"

"Because I need a favor." The Chief Architect takes a deep breath. "As bugs go, this one seems suspiciously exploitable. It's a side, or worse, covert channel that lets anyone who knows how to use it funnel out whatever they want—"

"Well, not whatever they want. Technically, it's only stuff from an alternate present that almost but not quite happened," Daniel says as he raises a hand. "Ellie couldn't have learned anything or gotten anything from the hypothetical present where you had put gardening shears or a rabid ferret in the drawer three years ago, for example."

"Thank you, Captain Pedantic." The Chief Architect's tone is dry. "My point is that not only is it suspiciously useful, it also leaves the physics of this universe basically intact. If you don't search for it, you're unlikely to stumble across it. I'm not saying that it isn't just an extremely unfortunate bug. I've seen my share. However, this is also the sort of thing that, if it were deliberately installed into the universe, would require a team of expert maintainers with sufficiently dubious ethics."

A side channel is unintentional. Someone opens their refrigerator and cold air comes out. It does whether anyone wants it to or not. To steal the cold, a hypothetical cold thief only has to know how to open the door. A covert channel is intentional. It's as if the cold thief has surreptitiously drilled into the refrigerator and added a camouflaged system of pipes and pumps to sneak the cold out. Ultimately, the only real difference between a side channel and a covert channel is whether whoever built the thing that lets the cold air out meant for the cold air to escape.

Ellie bristles at the idea of a covert channel in the universe. That goes against everything anyone has been taught about being a maintainer.

"So there's some secret cabal of maintainers?" Ellie lets her arms fall.

"*We're* part of a secret cabal of maintainers." Daniel raises his hand again. "That each universe is generated by machinery in the surrounding universe is common knowledge—at least among some physicists—but who maintains that machinery or even that the machinery needs maintenance doesn't exactly make the evening news."

"You know what I mean." Ellie punches him in the arm and it's like punching stone. Pain shoots up her arm. "Secret even to us. Maintainers willing to change the physics of this universe for personal gain."

"Exactly." The Chief Architect shoots Daniel another look. "Exploiting this is straightforward. Anyone who knows about it, including those who don't even know that maintenance is a thing, can take advantage of it. Some secret cabal sneaking covert channels into the universe will wreak havoc in ways I can't even begin to fathom. That's why I need you to make sure there isn't a cabal. And if there is, find out who they are."

"No, no." Ellie holds her hands up. "I have to be back in Boston by Monday if I want to keep my grant funding."

It's bad enough that she's stuck here until the Sunday-night train. Being forced to talk to a bunch of people who already hate her is the only way it can be worse.

"That gives us today and tomorrow." Daniel's rumble is aggressively good-natured. "With the both of us, that seems doable."

Ellie shoots him an exasperated look. Daniel ignores it. He pulls chairs over for the three of them. As he sits, he stretches his back.

Once in a while, rather than being his usual agreeable self, she wants Daniel to shout "Fuck you and the horse you fucking rode in on!" instead. That the only way either one of them can refuse is to offer an extremely respectful excuse makes the thought all the more satisfying.

"Why me?" Ellie lets her hands fall. "There have to be any number of more experienced maintainers you can ask."

The Chief Architect takes another deep breath. Slowly, the air escapes, her cheeks puffed out, in an exaggerated sigh.

"I didn't know about the mechanism keeping your mother alive until the uproar after you dismantled it." The Chief Architect sits and gestures for Ellie to sit, too. "What do you think that means?"

Daniel's eyes widen and his jaw drops. It's a bit curious considering he did know about the mechanism.

"There wasn't a ruckus when it was installed so I assumed everybody above my pay grade knew and approved. Then it kept getting modified and no one seemed to care." His composure restored, Daniel's voice regains its usual sand-shifting-on-a-desolate-beach demeanor. "Someone who is not me had to have noticed. How do you hide something like that? The blot on the design of the skunkworks and the generated universe was so blatant."

"Did you notice, Ellie?" The Chief Architect's voice is as pointed as her gaze.

"Well, no." Ellie stiffens and the words rush out of her. "But I, I'm not a—"

"Relax. Practically no one, not even verifiers, noticed. Or, honestly, could notice. Daniel is just being Daniel."

"What is that supposed to mean?" Daniel jumps up in protest, forgetting about the ceiling, flinching only at the very last moment.

The Chief Architect pays no attention to him, pushing on with her speech. Daniel sits back down.

"The maintainers who designed, verified, and built it did very careful, subtle work. Everyone who knew was involved and hiding it from me, excepting the tiny handful who weren't involved and didn't bother to tell me." The Chief Architect gives Daniel a pointed glare before shifting her attention to Ellie. "I'm amazed they strung your mother along like that. It seems cruel."

Ellie struggles to find anything to say. Declaring that even the slightest chance of saving Mom was worth the very real chance of wrecking this universe is awful. Declaring that Mom's life was not worth the work to save is just as awful. How Ellie feels, though, lies somewhere in between and would take hours to explain. To her relief, the Chief Architect forges ahead without waiting for an answer.

"The point is, out of all the maintainers in the world, you are the one who has clearly put your money where your mouth is."

"I don't understand." Ellie shakes her head.

"Maybe there is no cabal and what I demonstrated is simply a bug, a disastrous one but unintentional. The idea of some cabal out to pervert physics for their own personal gain, however, is now absolutely plausible. We all say we'd never do anything of the sort, but some of us did and you put a stop to it. You dismantled the mechanism installed into the universe intended to heal your mother."

"All I did is what any builder who knew about it would have."

"If that were true, you'd still be on speaking terms with them." The Chief Architect's voice is warm and kind. "There may not be a plot to subvert the integrity of the universe. If there is, though, one person who I know can't be involved in it is you."

"Then why am I here?" Daniel looks vaguely offended either by the implication that he can't be trusted or that he can. "Maybe I'm a deep mole trying to gull you into thinking the covert channel is really a side channel."

"No, you are not a deep mole." The Chief Architect's eyes cannot roll back far enough. "You are the smart fool who thought it was a good idea to make Ellie confront the monstrosity forcing her mother into some state where she's neither truly dead nor alive."

"But it worked out." Daniel spreads out his palms. "Ellie stabilized the universe."

"Exactly." The Chief Architect smiles. "Vera took you in when your parents kicked you out. Ellie might as well be your sister. What you did to her was unconscionable, as cruel as what they did to her mother. You care more about the stability of the universe than about your favorite relative. You are constitutionally incapable of working for that sort of cabal."

Daniel pouts. Being petulant because someone has told him that he is incapable of something he doesn't even want to do is so very on-brand for him.

"Fine, I'm not." He folds his arms across his chest, which expands his upper torso into an overfilled parade balloon. "But, remember, I am capable of unconscionable things when necessary."

"How are you older than me?" Ellie shoots a look at Daniel, who lets his arms fall but only under protest, before turning back to the Chief Architect. "Can't Daniel do this by himself?"

The whiplash between those two questions catches Ellie right in the throat. The second question barely makes it out of her mouth before what a bad idea it is chokes her voice off. The Chief Architect snorts.

"Your cousin is known for many things, but a kind bedside manner is not one of them. And, as he says, he is capable of unconscionable things. I'd like for there to be some maintainers still alive after the investigation."

She smirks long enough for Ellie to think she might be joking. Daniel opens his mouth then shuts it with a resigned sigh. The Chief Architect's expression grows serious as she continues.

"Ellie, I noticed the empty ring of seats around you at the funeral. Not even your cousin here wanted to be seen with you."

"Hey!" Daniel leans toward her. "I got caught in traffic, and I didn't think Aunt Vera's mourners wanted me to plow through them."

"Fair enough. I apologize." The Chief Architect holds up a hand to ward him off. "My point is, the maintainers angry at you might come around if you look into this. Certainly, you would have *my* gratitude."

Daniel rumbles. It is low and soft, even by Daniel standards. Ellie doesn't hear his voice as much as she feels it shiver through her body. If Ellie wasn't sure that the Chief Architect's gratitude meant something before, she is now. It means freezing Ellie out would have consequences. Ellie can't hate that. Navigating Chris is hard enough. No one has the energy to navigate an entire community of Chrises.

"Has anyone actually used this exploit?" Ellie asks. "Besides us, I mean."

"I don't know." The Chief Architect spreads her palms. "We found it by inspection."

"This was found by inspection?" The words explode out of Daniel. "*Really?*"

Ellie jabs him in the ribs. Daniel gives her his patented "What?" face.

"After your mother's death, I asked Jerry for an in-depth audit of the skunkworks. It would have been surprising if they didn't find something."

"Jerry?" Ellie gets the impression she's supposed to know who that is.

"Jerry Neeson. He got in at the ground floor of some tech start-up bent on disrupting aglets or whatever and now he's vice president of product development or something." Daniel adds, not helpfully, "More to the point, he's the Chief Verifier. In his copious free time, he's in charge of that vast bug-finding infrastructure you mentioned."

"It's a bit more than that now." The Chief Architect nods. "He's been wrangling the verifiers, architects, and builders needed to inspect the skunkworks. It's a work in progress."

"Oh!" A candy-like lightbulb glows over Daniel's head for a moment before it disappears. "That's why there have been so many maintainers popping in and out of the skunkworks."

"You're not involved?" The Chief Architect looks surprised.

"No, he doesn't like me." Daniel's face darkens with a grimace. "I don't know why. I mean, I'm not incompetent, and I'm basically innocuous."

Daniel with a grimace, as it turns out, does not look remotely innocuous. At best, he is that full-grown buffalo, some fifty yards away, minding its own business that you desperately do not want to charge at you. As though this has just occurred to him, he casts the grimace off his face. He reverts to his baseline expression of vaguely befuddled.

"Basically innocuous." The Chief Architect side-eyes him. "Really?"

He holds his hands up in surrender and mock pain. "Hey, I am a ripe heirloom tomato. I bruise easily."

"No. You're Jerry's worst nightmare." The smile on her face is radiant. "Can you design and install whatever you want into the skunkworks and get away with it for a while? With a team of builders, sure. How hard would it be for you to scare some builders into doing what you want?"

Daniel bristles at her insinuation. His eyes bulge but, for once, his muscles don't.

"I thought I was supposed to be trustworthy." His hands go back to his waist. "With all due respect, pick a lane."

"You would never do it." The Chief Architect's tone is conciliatory. "Frankly, anyone who tried, there's an outside chance you'd calmly break them down the way a soldier does their rifle."

"Excuse me?" Ellie leans forward in her chair. "What does that even mean?"

"Nothing. Jerry is convinced this is simply a bug. That's why I need you to look into it." She hands Ellie a list of names, numbers, and locations. "Most of them are working on the audit. Maybe they'll tell you something they won't tell me. I'm sure Daniel will be on his best behavior. Or maybe it'd be more productive if he isn't."

"We should get going." Daniel hovers over Ellie, scanning the list. "Most of them are staying in hotels. We should catch them before they go home."

"One last thing, kids." The Chief Architect holds up a hand. "Try to keep this quirk of the universe a secret. Yes, whether there is a group of maintainers wantonly rewriting the laws of physics is more important but, as Ellie pointed out, nothing about this exploit requires any knowledge of or skill in maintenance. If it becomes public knowledge, anyone will be able to use it to grab or learn whatever they want. Security through obscurity is all we have until we design, verify, and apply a fix."

"Yes, ma'am." Daniel straightens and clicks his heels with a vigor too enthusiastic to be genuine.

With that, the meeting is over. If only because Daniel is already gone. Ellie didn't even hear him sprint up the stairs. She shrugs at the Chief Architect before she starts up the stairs herself.

CHAPTER 7

Keys jangle with a steady beat. Sharp thumps alternate with metallic clangs in unerring precision. That exactness is the only reason Ellie thinks Daniel is waiting for her, as opposed to having bolted off to another universe. When she turns the corner out of the basement, she spots Daniel just outside the front door, leaning—not slouching—against the doorjamb with an exaggerated casualness. Daniel does not slouch. His car keys flip twice before they land in his hand, and he throws them up for another double flip.

"What was that all about?" Ellie nabs the keys in mid-flip to stop the noise. "What is going on between you two?"

"I have no idea. We've never met." Daniel stands up straight. "I had no idea she even knew me. Maybe Aunt Vera mentioned me."

"*Daniel* . . ." She starts to play with the keys in her hands, then stops herself, her fingers wrapped tight around them.

"I. Don't. Know." For three words, Daniel is as loud as Ellie has ever heard him. "Maybe she really is pissed off at me for not telling her about that contraption. I'm hardly the only one who didn't. Or maybe she's having some fun with me. You know, big guy. Must be dangerous."

"Sure." Ellie nods, deliberately not pointing out that "must be dangerous" is basically everyone's first impression of him.

"Come on. There's a list of folks we have to talk to." He holds his hand out for the keys.

She hands him the keys. They don't make it ten steps toward his car before she stops.

"Wait." Ellie reaches for Daniel's arm to stop him. "Someone has tampered with your car."

"How do you know that?" Daniel winces when Ellie's eyes bug out and her face blasts "Are you fucking kidding me?" at full force. "Oh, right. It's any machine in front of you, not only in the skunk-works."

If Daniel has been trained to be at one with the workings of the universe, Ellie has been trained to understand mechanisms, to take them apart in her head. It's impossible to fix them if you don't understand them first.

She walks to the hood. The driver's door and the hood release check out. This close, however, the changes to the ignition are unmissable. By now, they are also quite familiar. This is not her first car bomb. These changes, however, are a little too familiar.

"I always check." She waves Daniel over. "It should be safe to pop the hood. I'll take it from there."

"You always check?" Daniel unlocks the door and eyes her skeptically as he presses the hood release. "Why?"

Ellie silently berates herself. Talking about her relationship with Chris will never not be embarrassing. Whether she's ready for the conversation she keeps postponing with Daniel or not, she's about to have it now. At least Daniel will believe whatever Ellie says about Chris. He's the only person Ellie knows who doesn't think Chris is some perfect, helpful angel.

"Chris hasn't tried to kill me since Mom died, so now it's just force of habit." She props open the hood and looks for the ignition switch. "Ah, there it is. A bomb is wired to your ignition. Odd, this looks like Chris's work, but I don't think it is."

Ellie studies the situation. What's under Daniel's hood is very recognizably an ignition-car-bomb-shaped thing. The ignition sparks an explosive. A slapdash framework holds everything in place. The idea is to blow Ellie up, not for the bomber to show how clever they are. It's not that Chris never repeats an element now and then between attempts. There are only so many ways to kill Ellie. Chris, however, never makes an attempt where all the elements are repeats, even from several different bombs.

"Does she car-bomb you a lot?" Daniel pokes his head in next to hers under the hood. "Do you even own a car?"

"Sometimes, it's a land mine or some other explosive. Once, she trapped me in a moving van with a player piano snapping its strings, a giant mechanical metronome jabbing its pendulum at me, and a bottle of olive oil trying to slice off my head." Ellie studies the ignition switch for anything that might identify the bomber. "Another time, it was a swarm of nanobots carrying polonium."

Daniel stares agape at her. She stares back with a look that retorts "You asked!"

"Why would she plant a bomb in my car?"

"If it's her, it's because I would be sitting in it." Ellie rolls her eyes. "You're collateral damage. Like you said, making changes to the skunkworks has marked me. For an embarrassingly long time, I convinced myself that she wasn't lying when she said all she was doing was preparing me for the folks who'd kill me for maintaining the skunkworks."

"But now you finally realize she's been lying to you all this time?" Daniel sounds positively hopeful.

"I mean, for the first decade or so, her attempts were more like deadly puzzles that ramped up in difficulty over time. My death had to look like a horrible accident, not murder. For at least the first few years, maybe she really was trying to prepare me, and if she happened to kill me in the process, well, at least she tried."

The explosive, a gray, gloppy goo held in place by a crystalline containment chamber, is unusual. It comes from several universes out. There's enough here to vaporize Ellie, Daniel, the car, and some amount of the Chief Architect's front yard in a dazzling but silent light show the neighbors would remember for ages.

"Daniel, do you think you can create this explosive?" Ellie points at the containment chamber.

"Why would I bomb my own car?" Daniel's befuddlement looks genuine this time. "Never mind why, when could I have?"

"That's not what I mean," Ellie snaps. "Just answer the question."

"Well, if you describe it in enough detail, I guess." Daniel reaches for the containment chamber, but Ellie blocks his hand. "That's a lot of explosive, though."

Ready access to an explosive from another universe narrows the suspects down, barely. It can still be Chris. Ellie has no idea how Chris sourced the explosive the first time.

"Do you seriously think she was training you at first?" Daniel clearly does not.

"Either way, you either got real good at surviving right away and kept getting better, or you died. Whether she intended it or not, I got a lot of practice with all the builder skills, which came in handy whenever Mom took me to the skunkworks."

"So what made you finally realize she wasn't training you in the most passive-aggressive way possible?"

Ellie hesitates. This is all too embarrassing to admit. She's come this far, though, she might as well go all the way. If she's going to come clean about this to anyone, it's Daniel.

"I don't know. For the longest time, I didn't let myself think about it." A tiny blade of light juts out of her left index finger. "Maybe it's the way she took care of Mom. Generous and giving in a way that also limited Mom's autonomy. But, before, the only person in danger was me. Once she wanted me to move back, she tried to take out my Boston friends and classmates as collateral damage. And now you, too, of course."

"I'm flattered." He flashes a sardonic grin.

"When she stopped, I hoped that maybe she'd changed." Ellie studies the mount holding the bomb in place for any signs of who might have built it. "This doesn't have to be her. It's been over a month. Before, it was like twice a week."

"Who else could it be? How can there be anyone already trying to stop us? We haven't even started yet."

"Chris never repeats herself. Why would she try to kill me with anything I've dealt with before? Maybe the bomber doesn't realize I've dealt with lots of these by now."

Burrowing down to the molecular level to make the explosive stable and noncombustible takes some effort. The goo turns red and solidifies into putty. Likewise, demagnetizing mounts holding bombs in place isn't what gets Ellie out of bed in the morning. She's much happier dealing with gears and switches. Even one too small to see is better than this. Still, she gets it done.

Disconnecting the bomb is the easiest bit. She loosens the solder joins with the light blade and pulls the bomb away. The light blade retracts into her finger. She tosses the bomb at Daniel, who catches it reflexively.

"Here, a memento of what I'm sure, for you, is yet another brush with death." She doesn't expect the unreadable expression on Daniel's face. "How many brushes with death have you had?"

"Not once every couple of days. Definitely not enough to be as blasé as you about it." Daniel stares at the bomb as if he expects it to go off at any moment. "What should I do with this?"

"Daniel, relax." She pushes the hood shut. "It's harmless now."

Daniel gingerly places the bomb in the backseat, then gets in the driver's seat. Ellie buckles herself in on the passenger side and pulls out the list the Chief Architect gave her.

The name at the top is Jerry Neeson. She taps his number into her cell phone. They can chat, he explains, only if she and Daniel drop by right now. His flight home is in a few hours.

"Jerry Neeson." Daniel buckles himself in and pauses for a moment before he starts the car. "Should be fun."

The car does not explode. It purrs down the street, exactly as it's supposed to.

CHAPTER 8

It's been a couple of years since Ellie has lived in metro DC during the summer. After she moved to metro Boston, she convinced herself that summers in metro DC couldn't possibly have been as bad as she remembered. It's the second day of her visit home, and she's convinced that it's worse.

The area is one gigantic crab boil. There are sections of the skunkworks where the air is even thicker, but they have the excuse of literally being in another universe. The sheer heat of metro DC could be comforting, but the air presses down on her and blocks her way no matter which direction she walks. A wave of humid heat overwhelms and drowns her as she leaves the desultory air-conditioning of Daniel's car.

Daniel, of course, is oblivious to the weather. His beautifully fitted suit still looks freshly pressed from the tailor. He doesn't so much walk as glide through the late-afternoon heat, as if the air were thirty degrees cooler and fifty percent drier. Compared to him, she's swimming through the muck.

The hotel, on the other hand, is aggressively arctic. The harsh cold slaps Ellie when she makes it through the automatic revolving door. Daniel takes several tries to find the right stride length. His natural one is too long for this door. It halts after each of his first few steps. His exasperation grows with each try. If pressed, Ellie would admit that walking through revolving doors may be one of the few advantages of being at most half his size.

The hotel bar diffuses into the lobby in three ragged layers.

Tiny square and round tables are scattered in a vague grid next to the bar. People sit around them, sipping their expensive cocktails and eating their overpriced burgers. Long tables stand off to the sides. People sit in front of them on tall stools, typing on their laptops. Stuffed chairs surround tiny circular tables that are likely a little too far away for Ellie to set down or pick up a drink.

Daniel explodes out of the revolving door, as if it has swung him around and ejected him into the lobby. He rushes directly at a man sitting in one of the stuffed chairs. Ellie follows at a walk, like a reasonable human being. The man is leaned back, his feet propped on the tiny circular table, reading an ebook. A roller bag rests next to the chair. Ellie side-eyes the bag. It probably only fits in an airplane overhead with a lot of vigorous encouragement. It must be a couple of inches too large in every dimension for what an airline calls a carry-on.

For a split second, Daniel looks like he'll run through the man. In the space of a step, though, he goes from full tilt to dead stop in front of the tiny circular table. If it were anyone else, Ellie might wonder whether momentum was truly conserved and how he didn't face-plant into the table.

"Hello, Daniel." The man looks up from his e-reader with aplomb. He shifts his gaze as Ellie walks up. "You must be Ellie. Call me Jerry. My condolenccs about your mother. She was a dear colleague."

Neeson stands and offers Ellie his hand. Like Daniel, he's in a tailored suit, although Neeson clearly has a bigger budget for this sort of thing. It fits so flatteringly that it was probably patterned and cut specifically for him. Unlike Daniel, Neeson belongs in a suit. It doesn't make him look like a waiter or anyone who might have a license to kill from a covert state organization. It is his skin. He carries himself like the prince of a foreign land who deigns to accept your presence but who is so magnanimous he would never insist your presence is something anyone needs to deign. Ellie forces a smile.

"Thank you." She accepts his hand, which squeezes hers as though it were Jell-O.

He sits down and gestures at the other stuffed chairs around the tiny circular table. Ellie sits next to Neeson. Daniel sits in the chair opposite him.

"So what can I do for you?" Neeson leans back in his chair but doesn't prop his feet up on the table.

"We were wondering about the side channel uncovered in the audit."

"Yeah." Daniel hunches forward, resting his forearms on his thighs. "How are you so sure that it's a bug and not sabotage?"

Ellie shoots Daniel a look. Daniel looks puzzled back at her, mouthing "What?" Neeson grins.

"I don't know that I can drill down to the level of detail that will satisfy Daniel." Neeson side-eyes him. "The car I hired to take me to the airport is coming and, besides, I haven't done any meaningful verification in years. All I do is oversee the folks who conducted the audit that found the bug. What would a manager know?"

The way Neeson stresses the word "manager" makes it a bullet. Not one, however, aimed at Ellie. Despite looking at her, he's obviously resuming some protracted conversation he's been having with Daniel. Knowing Daniel, Ellie would guess that Neeson has been having that conversation mostly with himself. Either way, if the bullet hit its mark, Daniel doesn't seem to notice.

"Daniel will survive." Ellie doesn't roll her eyes, no matter how much she wants to.

Daniel, to his credit, stays silent. He's still hunched forward but a vague if genial smile rests comfortably on his face. Then again, rising to the bait would require Daniel to realize he's being baited in the first place. Ellie isn't sure whether he's being magnanimous or oblivious.

"There's nothing about this bug that hasn't been part of how the skunkworks operates for over a century," Neeson says simply.

"Pretend I've only ever been in the skunkworks once." Ellie is not above underplaying her experience.

Neeson starts to walk through how to expose the bug. It's like the Chief Architect's not-a-trick except in words. More words, but not any more detail. His lecture probably has a structure and a direction. It's also boiled chicken breast in the form of sentences and paragraphs. Ellie manages to get it down but she'll be shocked if Daniel can withstand anything this boring for more than a minute or two.

A whole two minutes, an eternity in Daniel time, go by before his left hand starts tapping the table. From pinky to index, each finger hits the table one after the other in a steady rhythm before the process starts again. Neeson drones on. He either doesn't notice or, more likely, is ignoring Daniel.

It's only a few minutes more before Daniel excuses himself. He paces the lobby in a giant oval, looking less agitated with each circuit. Neeson forges on like an intrepid letter carrier pushing through not only rain but also snow and sleet, not to mention hail.

Ellie lines up Neeson's words with the Chief Architect's actions. The skunkworks speculates possible future states of the universe even as some state is committed as the present. Representations of the futures that never come to pass may still be lying around in the skunkworks somewhere basically unfindable. The exploit games the skunkworks into calculating the possible future you want and leaking it so it manifests in the universe.

Neeson winds up his explanation. Daniel, looking much more settled, returns with suspiciously perfect timing and sits across from Neeson.

"So, as I said, none of this is new." Neeson's gaze acknowledges Daniel's existence for an instant before it returns to Ellie. "The idea of speculating future states came in with quantum mechanics over a century ago. The notion of temporary transient-state storage is older than that. This bug is the accidental fallout from a bunch of decisions, many of which are decades, if not a century, old. The architects say it's removable, so there's that."

"Thank you for the explanation." Ellie sounds as sincere as possible under the circumstances. "So it's a bug. A side channel isn't great but it beats the alternative."

"Listen, your reputation precedes you. Vera must have trained you as well as she's trained her other daughter. Chris is always going on about how annoyingly good you are at all the things a builder has to do." Neeson leans in ever so slightly. "I can use another builder like your sister in my organization. She has been invaluable to me."

Chris has never mentioned working with Neeson. Then again, Chris told Ellie the wrong date for the funeral. If Chris ever mentioned working with Neeson, that might have been the surest sign she isn't. Conversely, that she's never even uttered the name Neeson around Ellie may be the surest sign she is. Along the same lines, though, Chris has never complimented Ellie to Ellie, but apparently has to Neeson. Ellie had no idea Chris ever said anything good about her to anyone. Maybe Mom is right. Maybe Chris can return to Ellie the love and respect owed to family that Ellie tries her best to give Chris. Maybe they can have the relationship that Mom always told Ellie to have with Chris. She sets the thought aside for later.

"Why does Verification need builders?"

"For issues like that hold-time violation you found and fixed last month. We need builders to study the actual physical structures, to rule in or rule out damage or a bad build or that the laws of physics have changed out from under it. That's a good chunk of the inspections we're doing now. Architects and builders have to be involved or else we'll never figure anything out. The dirty secret is no one completely understands how any universe works."

Neeson's cell phone chirps from a jacket pocket. He takes it out, clicks a side button, and stares at the screen.

"My car is here." He slides the phone back into his jacket. "You don't have to answer now. If you have any other questions, you know how to reach me."

He shakes her hand again and gives Daniel a nod so slight it's practically subliminal. A large black SUV pulls up to the hotel door. Neeson drags his roller bag behind him out of the hotel. The driver puts it in the trunk as Neeson gets into the backseat. The SUV pulls away.

"Well, he seems nice." Ellie turns to face Daniel.

Ellie isn't sure what she expected but it wasn't a relatively reasonable explanation and an invitation back into the community of maintainers. She can't say she isn't tempted. If both the Chief Architect and the Chief Verifier vouch for her, everyone else might not welcome her back with open arms but at least they might feel forced to stop whispering unfounded rumors about her. Whatever is happening between Neeson and Daniel groans like a dull alarm in the distance. Honestly, though, being too boring to hold Daniel's attention is not that hard.

"Yes." Daniel nods slowly. He's still watching where the SUV disappeared from view and he squints as though if he stares hard enough he can still see it. "It's weird. He's not normally this nice."

"Wait." Ellie holds up a hand. "Why do *you* think this? He barely acknowledged your existence."

"Exactly. He acknowledged my existence." Daniel nods as if he's made a point. "He even called me 'Daniel.' Something's off."

"So you don't believe him?"

Daniel's gaze shifts to the floor. He takes a deep breath before facing Ellie.

"I'm sure he said a bunch of things that are technically true, although I doubt Aunt Vera ever nontrivially worked with him. We knew he'd explain to us why it's just a bug. He's simply telling us what he told the Chief Architect." Daniel shrugs. "I don't trust him. There's a difference."

"Daniel, did you tell anyone the physics of the universe our skunkworks lives in changed?"

"No." Daniel shakes his head. "There wasn't a bug in the logic as designed, so I had no report to file."

"I didn't either. Neeson brought up changing the laws of physics, though." Ellie shrugs. "For something that's never supposed to happen, it's come up a lot."

Ellie pulls out the list of people the Chief Architect said to interview. Most are the maintainers doing the auditing, so it's not like the Chief Architect wants them to take Neeson at his word. Ellie pulls out her cell phone and, one by one, she works her way down the list.

The calls don't go well. Ellie barely gets past "hello." Everyone makes a point of expressing their condolences. Some of them immediately go on to claim they know nothing about the contraption that kept her mom alive. A few sidetrack her with one reminiscence or another about some obscure bug or difficult construction issue or something that her mom solved.

Once Ellie is allowed to explain why she's calling, though, it's shocking but unsurprising how they all have to get off the phone that very moment. Many of them simply must leave for the Smithsonian immediately or have a dear friend whom they hadn't seen in years they need to visit right now on the Maryland side of metro DC or, less believably in, say, Gaithersburg or Towson. The latter is on the other side of Baltimore and about an hour and a half away before you even think about traffic.

Everyone she calls nails that mode of politeness that is both performatively obsequious and, honestly, the least they could do. She can hear "Besides, I'm sure you're too deep in grief to discuss an obscure bug" only so many times before she hurls her phone across the lobby. It's not their business how she deals with Mom's death, and the way they throw it in her face makes it obvious how little they care whether she's grieving or not. She shouldn't care what they think of her, but each phone call is another tiny cut, prodding open a wound she desperately wants healed.

Halfway down the list, she can't take it anymore. Maybe it's not them. Maybe it's her. She hands the list to Daniel.

Daniel doesn't fare any better. Based on his side of the conversation, no one likes him either. Unlike Ellie, however, Daniel reacts with an apparent obliviousness, a refusal to be insulted, that Ellie hopes burns them and lets him live rent-free in their heads at least for the rest of the weekend. Eventually, Daniel shrugs and places his phone back into a pocket, and the two head back out into the sauna of the DC summer.

"You know, maybe we should call it quits on this whole interview thing." Daniel crosses a name off the list, carefully folds it into a well-creased quarter, then slides it into a pant pocket. "I hate to admit Neeson may be right about anything but, sometimes, obscure but dangerously exploitable behavior is just a bug."

"There's only one left, right?" She holds out her hand and, reluctantly, Daniel obliges with the list, now unfolded. "Yes—"

"We don't need to talk to him."

"But he's only about fifteen minutes from here with traffic."

"Ahdi taught me everything I know about the architecture of the skunkworks and how to verify it." Daniel takes back the list, folds it, and eases it into a pocket. "He's as likely to be involved with a covert channel as I am."

"I thought he was a builder." She veers toward Daniel's car, now mere steps away. "Mom used to hold up his handiwork as examples to live up to and made me analyze them."

"Oh, he is. I mean, he is, too. Maintainers from every universe call on him to sort out issues that no one else can figure out. I doubt he has anything to do with Neeson, but he can't have anything to do with this." Daniel hesitates for a moment, as though the next words need to be shoved out of him. "I've known him since I was a kid. If I'm sane, Aunt Vera and Ahdi are the reasons why."

Ellie stops at the passenger-side door. She turns to Daniel and, for a moment, she wonders whether he can really be that naive. He stares back at her, curious.

"So, of everyone on the list, he's the one who can design and build a covert channel all by himself?"

Daniel looks utterly betrayed. He tries to speak, but his jaw hangs open. The tiny cry that comes out is wrenching, a dull blade that rips and tears into Ellie. Daniel snaps his jaw shut and swallows hard.

She has never seen him like this. After Daniel moved in, he wasn't home very much. It hasn't occurred to her until now where he must have been when he wasn't home, who must have raised him at least as much as Mom. Ahdi must have been the man Daniel tried so hard to impress with his suit at the reception.

"I'm sorry, Daniel. I didn't mean it." The inadequate apology rushes out of Ellie. "All I meant is we should talk to him."

But Daniel has already composed himself. He's once again the guy who is utterly unflappable, who refuses to let anything live rent-free in his head. Jauntily, he strides to the driver's side of his car.

"It sounds so incriminating when you put it that way." Daniel unlocks the doors. "Besides, there's a matter of scale. Well, I doubt he'd need an entire team. Maybe just one accomplice? A builder to install the covert channel with him."

"This is a maintainer you know well. Why don't you call him up and invite him to dinner? No one is accusing him of anything. He sounds like he'd be helpful in sorting out exactly what happened."

"Sure." He shrugs, resigned. "Why not?"

Ellie fiddles with the car's air-conditioning while Daniel stares at his phone. "Indifferent" isn't an actual setting but if the air out of the vents is no longer hot, it's not cold either.

Everything about Daniel's expression screams "The only way out is through." He takes a deep breath, taps his phone, then puts it to his ear.

"Hey, Ahdi." Daniel's voice, still ridiculously soft, starts an octave too high in excitement before it plummets. "Good to— . . . She's here with— . . . When— . . . OK, we'll be right over."

"Well?" Ellie has given up on the air-conditioning and slumps into the passenger seat.

"He's invited *us* to dinner."

CHAPTER 9

Ellie can't tell one house in this neighborhood from another. They're all gable-roofed single-story structures with an attached single-car garage. Black railings line the steps to every front door. A big window covers the rest of the street-facing side of every house. The only things distinguishing one house from another are color and house number. Even then, there are perhaps only five colors, distributed randomly, and the numbers go up by two with each house.

Daniel pulls his car into one of the many interchangeable driveways with confident ease. The two climb the cement steps to a forest-green metal door, and Daniel hits the doorbell. The door opens and a broad-shouldered man appears. He's tall—but not Daniel-tall—and burly. Dressed in a tidy faded gray shirt and tan slacks, the man Daniel showed his suit off to at the reception is as neatly put together as a puzzle box.

When his gaze locks on Daniel, a broad grin unfurls across his face and his arms stretch for a hug. Daniel grins back and full-on tackles Ahdi, finally throwing his arms around the man. This probably worked better when Daniel was smaller. On the other hand, Ahdi is still standing and none the worse for wear. If Daniel is the unstoppable force, Ahdi is the immovable object.

The man untangles himself from Daniel and offers Ellie both his hand and his condolences. Ellie accepts the latter with a tremor in her voice she can't quite iron out. Her mind is crammed with her mom's stories of Ahdi as a builder's builder, the times he delicately manipulated subatomic particles to precisely the correct energy levels, the times he reconstructed gigantic switches through raw force. His grip, though, is as gentle as his condolences.

"Come on in, kids. You must be hungry." Ahdi heads into the house. "Make yourself comfortable in the dining room. I'll be in the kitchen."

Ellie and Daniel set aside their shoes. Ahdi has gone far ahead of them. Ellie follows Daniel in.

The house is as well put together and as tidy as he is. It could be a feature in some architectural magazine. Ellie half expects a photographer in the corner preserving an ideal too impractical for real life. Bookshelves filled with books cover the walls of every room Ellie passes through. The book bindings meld into a motley wallpaper that should be at odds with the sleek, clean furniture but for some underlying unity. Ellie wonders if he built them himself. Maybe there is a basement that doubles as a large woodworking shop.

His furniture is a model of spare elegance. The joins on tables, ottomans, and sofas could not be more precise. They can't be what they are with even one bit less material. She sees the furniture for what it is almost reflexively, of a piece with the books in a way that's just beyond the edge of her senses.

The smell of dinner wafts through the house. It's warm and savory and mouthwatering. Daniel walks with an eager bounce. Even before the first bite, dinner already feels impossible. It's only been about twenty minutes since Ahdi invited them and food out of nowhere is an affectation that's, as far as Ellie knows, unique to Daniel.

More stuffed bookshelves cover the dining room walls. The Platonic ideal of a table fills most of the room, surrounded by the Platonic ideal of chairs. They're all built from something glass-like, and Ellie can only see them by how they function. They distort the floor, bookshelves, and ceiling when she looks through them. Slight and delicate looking, they're also built out of more tiny gears than she can count. The table and chairs give her the sense that even after both an earthquake and a nuclear bomb, she would be gone, but they would still be intact and usable.

Three place settings sit on the table along with a tea service. They're the sort of thing a good restaurant-equipment store might sell, but they seem to float rather than rest. She's not sure what the Platonic ideal of a chopstick would even be. Then again, she wouldn't have had a clue about the Platonic ideal of table or chairs until she saw these.

She isn't sure this is a room one would sully by, say, having a meal in it until Daniel sits in one of the chairs. The grin is still pasted on his face, but he doesn't so much bounce as vibrate. He practically blurs.

"Yeah, he's a lot," Daniel says, catching the awe on Ellie's face. "The house is more or less always like this."

Ellie eyes warily the chair next to Daniel. The contradiction is hard to take. Gossamer struts look like they should shear and collapse the instant a mote of dust lands on the chair, but the math checks out. There may be bridges with less load-bearing capacity. Besides, Daniel is sitting comfortably, his chair easily supporting his weight. It'd be rude to just stand there.

When Ellie sits, the chair adjusts, its gears spinning and struts telescoping and contracting. Her body bobbles and pitches as she shifts her weight against the thing. It makes weirdly comforting purring noises as it morphs below and behind her.

"Ellie, sit like a normal person, not like someone who can sense every stress on every one of its joints. Pretend it's a typical chair. Don't try to help it out. Sit and let it do its thing."

She forces herself to stop. For a split instant, it feels like the chair will buck and shove her into the table. In the time it takes to think that, all the stress and strain leaves her body. The chair is clearly supporting her weight but it feels like she's levitating.

"Wow." She turns toward Daniel and her chair fluidly adjusts to her shift in weight. "This explains so much about you."

Daniel is exactly the man who grew up in a world where Platonic ideals are the norm. Putting every detail in its proper place is a matter of habit.

Ahdi walks in with a tray of small plates. He smiles when he sees Ellie comfortably seated. The plates are filled with spicy smashed cucumbers, pickled radishes, and thinly sliced pig's ears braised in soy sauce. They smell the way you want to remember better days of the past. She hasn't had anything like this in years. Either she has been in Boston or Mom has been too sick to cook. Ellie forces her breathing to steady.

"Why don't you two get started?" Ahdi turns back toward the kitchen. "I'll join you in a moment when I bring in the noodles."

Daniel pours a cup of tea for Ellie and pushes a cup to the other side of the table for Ahdi before pouring a cup for himself. Ellie savors the steam and the earthiness, as well as the hints of ginger and ginseng that hit the back of her throat. Daniel attacks the appetizers, piling chili-flecked cucumbers next to thin slices of radish next to tangles of sesame-specked pig's ears with the precision and grace someone else might save for a particularly difficult tap combination or a roundhouse kick. He empties his plate one sliver at a time, working from one side to the other, as if each sliver were worth a life.

Ellie picks at her plate. It's not that Ahdi's cooking is bad. She could bear that. The man has to be incompetent at something, although it's apparently not cooking. What she can't bear is how the cooking reminds her of her mom's. The cucumber is crunchy, spicy, and garlicky. It's both cool and hot sliding down her throat. The radishes are sharp and sour and lovely. They cut through the chili oil in the cucumber. If the pig's ears are beautifully gelatinous with a crunchy center, she may cry. She leaves the pig's ears alone.

Ahdi enters carrying a tray with three large bowls of noodle soup. Ellie finally places the savory smell. Meatballs, some made of fish, others made of pork. Aldi catches the glint of recognition on her face.

"There's more in the kitchen." Ahdi sets the tray down and places a bowl before Ellie, then a bowl before Daniel. "Eat up."

"Fishballs!" Daniel's face glows with joy. "You know, Ellie, the first time I tried to generate an equivalence report, it came out unintentionally as a piece of fish."

Ellie has never seen Daniel volunteer anything about himself unprompted. Usually, the idea of being the topic of conversation causes him to beat a strategic retreat.

Daniel and Ahdi exchange glances. Ahdi's eyebrows rise and Daniel responds with a grin.

"Your cousin spent the next several minutes singing 'Tilapia, I just made a piece of tilapia' and so on."

"I was, like, twelve or whatever!" He folds his arms across his chest but the indignation doesn't quite play. "And, for the record, I sang 'ate' at first but you insisted that I had to make a tilapia before I ate it and so I should save 'ate' for the second half of the quatrain."

"He improvised several choruses and a bridge. I thought he'd never stop singing 'tilapia.'" Ahdi sits across from a momentarily appalled Daniel. "I was impressed."

Ellie sees what they're trying to do. Daniel has made himself deeply uncomfortable in order to make Ellie laugh, and Ahdi is going along with it. In Ahdi's defense, watching Daniel squirm is a rich, indulgent dessert made with too much butter, sugar, and chocolate. Too much of it is a horrible idea, but a morsel is divine. Daniel tries to make himself as small and as unobtrusive and as harmless as possible. Hurricanes have done better pretending to be gentle breezes. She smiles despite herself.

Steam from the bowl drifts to her face. She stirs the rich broth with her spoon. Thick, flat, glutinous rice noodles swirl like galaxies marked with giant fishball and meatball star clusters. She takes a bite of a fishball. Her eyes well up with tears. They sell frozen fishballs in Asian groceries, but nothing in this bowl has ever been anywhere near a freezer. She recognizes the bouncy texture, how they soak up the broth, the flavor that's both delicate and pronounced. They take her to her mother's stories of living by the ocean as a kid. It is both delicious and not quite what her mom would have made. She has never been both so near and so far away.

"Oh, Ellie, I'm so sorry." Ahdi leans forward and offers his hand. "I was hoping you'd find this comforting."

"No, it is. This is exactly what I wanted for dinner." She's surprised to realize how true the words are as they tumble out and she takes his hand. "It's just . . . I miss her . . . so much. I haven't had this since she . . ."

"I know. I try but it's never what your mom makes. Made." His smile is warm and he gives Ellie's hand a gentle, reassuring squeeze. "I'm sorry."

"I can show you. Or at least I can try." Memories of her mom patiently teaching her how to cook flood her mind. "She would want that, I think."

"Yes, I'd like that. Thank you." He twists a long, flat noodle into a spoonful of broth. "For what it's worth, I think you did the right thing. I'm not saying saving your mother was possible—I don't think it was—but nothing they did seemed to even try. Stringing your mother along like that seems to me more cruel than kind."

Ellie and Daniel exchange glances. The latter looks triumphant. A single sentence from Ahdi justifies what he did or, rather, didn't do.

"See? I knew I wasn't the only one who didn't tell the Chief Architect." Daniel is jubilant. He recoils a bit at Ellie's and Ahdi's glare in response. "What?"

"I know why Daniel didn't tell her, but why didn't you?" Ellie twirls her chopsticks idly in the broth.

Ahdi stares down at his bowl for a moment before he meets her gaze again. When he speaks, he's picking his words carefully.

"Everyone grieves in their own way." Ahdi sets down his spoon. "I figured whoever was involved needed it."

"You don't know who?"

"Very little is changed in the skunkworks without me noticing. I kept an eye on and adjusted the skunkworks to make sure the universe didn't grow too unstable. They needed to do this to cope. It would have been impossible for pretty much anyone to convince them to stop."

"It doesn't matter who did this to my mom."

"*Really.*" Ahdi holds Ellie in his gaze for a moment before he swallows a spoonful of soup. "Having torn down their abomination, I might want to give them a piece of my mind for torturing your mom like that, or at least find out why. She would have found perverting physics, even for her sake, unacceptable. How did you find out about it, anyway?"

"Daniel showed it to me." She sets her chopsticks across the bowl. "He led me to it and explained why it was there."

"Daniel . . ."

Ellie sees who Daniel learned his reproving look from. Daniel, however, can only muster gravity, the weakest of the fundamental forces. Coming from Ahdi, it's six thousand trillion trillion trillion times stronger. It's as though the strong force is disappointed in you. Ellie half expects Daniel to disintegrate because his quarks will refuse to bind together to form his protons and neutrons.

"What?" Daniel looks scandalized, absolutely undeserving of disintegration. "She did the right thing. There were only two people with the moral authority, and Chris was never going to be of any help."

Ahdi relents. His gaze softens and he sighs.

"I suppose I should be happy you didn't simply go to every builder you could track down and insist they remove it for you."

"You didn't, did you?" Ellie wouldn't put it past him.

"Ellie." Daniel's appalled expression is epic.

"So, if it's not to find out who designed and built that contraption, why did you call me?"

Neither Ellie nor Daniel react. At least, that's what Ellie thinks until Ahdi speaks again.

"I see. There's a serious problem with the skunkworks. You're trying to get to the bottom of it."

"How did you do that?" Ellie tilts her head, studying Ahdi the way she might a complex set of gears.

"I've known Daniel since he was a kid." Ahdi shrugs and picks up his chopsticks again.

"So have I."

"But you were an even younger kid when you two first met." Ahdi slurps a noodle, chews thoughtfully, and swallows. "It seems to me you need an architect if you're going to fix it. No, you're not here to ask me to help fix it. You're wondering whether I created the problem in the first place."

"You didn't create a covert channel in the universe." Daniel rushes his words as though if he said them fast enough, they could reach Ahdi before any accusation can land.

Ahdi drops his chopsticks. They clatter on the table. His gaze widens and either the man is also an excellent actor or this is the first he's heard of it.

"Covert channel? Have you looked into it? Yes, you clearly have, Daniel. So, of course, you've worked out the mechanism." Ahdi's words are an expectation, not a question. "Show me."

A structure of folded air materializes on the table, a theoretical construct resting on a Platonic notion. It is a giant, translucent sea urchin in desperate need of a haircut and designed by an impractical urban planner who has a thing for spires but no sense of proportion. The sea urchin barely has a body, and its spikes jut out in all directions. They vary in height, and their widths range from gossamer to Polish sausage. Each spike is built out of folds upon folds, forming facets that reflect the room this way and that.

Daniel's theoretical construct is nestled among the small plates scattered on the table. Sparks dance from one teetering spike to another as the construct settles. It rolls for a few inches before it finally finds a stable configuration.

Ellie infers the construct's existence the same way she recognizes the table is here. The folds refract the surroundings. From where she's sitting it is a portrait of Ahdi deconstructed into triangles from too many incompatible perspectives.

"Do you know when these changes were made to the skunkworks?" Ellie asks. "We need to find out who did this."

Ahdi stands over the structure. Occasionally, he prods at a fold. It vibrates, emitting a noise that's a cross between a squeak and a chime. He unfolds sections to expose deeper folds. The structure sings out not as much in agony as in counterpoint with itself. Its elegantly prepared dissonance resolves into glorious consonance again and again. Ahdi buries himself in its internals. It fragments the image of his head, scattering the pieces across the room. A nose turned at one angle juts up against an eye turned at another. Ellie has no idea what he is gleaning. Judging from Daniel's expression, he's not exactly keeping up either.

Ahdi's analysis only takes a minute. When he's done, he folds the structure back together. It sits on the table, looking exactly the way it did when Daniel first created it. Ahdi rubs his hands, as if he were trying to scrape some powder or residue from his palms.

"Well. That was interesting. It's not going to be easy to work out who did this." He sits down. "If all of these changes were put in specifically to create this behavior, your conspiracy would need to have been around for at least a hundred years."

"Wait." Ellie bobbles in her chair before it recovers her balance. "Are you saying there is a real shadow cabal of maintainers working over the past century to sneak a covert channel into the universe piece by piece?"

"No. There's nothing here to rule that out, but odds are we implemented quantum physics incorrectly over a century ago. Everything that creates the behavior we didn't intend is also part of what creates the behavior we did intend."

A cookie crumbles out of Daniel's hands. Dribbles of oatmeal and raisins fall onto the table. Daniel, of course, didn't have a cookie a second ago. He tamps down the grin on his face, shrugs innocently, and makes all evidence of the cookie go away as Ahdi gives him the mildest of reproving glares and presses on.

"Being able to grab fragments of highly probable realities that almost existed is a side effect of how we implemented quantum physics. It didn't have to be this exact way, but no one could have foreseen all the ramifications back then or, for that matter, now. This unwanted behavior is much more likely to be an especially unfortunate bug than a deliberate attempt to subvert the universe." Ahdi holds up a hand. "Listen, this will take a while and dinner is getting cold. We should eat while I explain."

They eat as Ahdi goes through his analysis, Ahdi eventually having seconds and Daniel thirds. The way he keeps peering at his empty bowl, Daniel clearly wants fourths, but no amount of gentle encouragement can get him to fill his bowl or let Ahdi fill it for him. Daniel mutters something about maintaining an optimal strength-to-weight ratio.

Ahdi digs into the structure between swallows of soup and slurps of noodles. Thick, agile fingers pry folds apart to reveal yet more folds. Methodically, he works through every fold, explaining how the side channel co-opts the mechanisms that make the universe work. As he does, he complicates the model Daniel created. It sprouts extra spikes and facets that put the fold he's explaining in context, to show how it participates in creating the universe they intended. Those spikes and facets go away and others take their place when he moves on to the next fold.

The model morphs from one configuration to another with the grace of a dancer's muscles flexing under taut skin. Ahdi does this so easily that it doesn't even occur to Ellie to be impressed until the bowls are empty, the analysis is complete, and the structure is restored to its original configuration. Now static, it reflects the walls, Ahdi, Daniel, Ellie herself, and the reflections of their reflections in scattered triangles. When the scope of what Ahdi has done with such ease finally hits her, her mouth works soundlessly for a few seconds before she gives up.

"That was a bit dry. I think we need a field trip to the skunkworks." Ahdi meets Ellie's and Daniel's gazes. "Are you two up for that?"

They both nod, Daniel eagerly, Ellie less so. Ahdi nods back.

"Good." He rubs his hands. "Leave the travel arrangements to me. It's faster that way."

CHAPTER 10

Ellie expects Ahdi to dissolve and to lay a trail for her and Daniel to follow. Instead, the world shatters around her into tiny flecks of light that scatter, leaving her hanging in a black void. In the next instant, the world coalesces again and the three of them are together in the skunkworks. She hadn't realized being taken anywhere was even possible. Even when she was a child going to maintainer school, Mom led her there and back but Ellie still had to travel for herself.

The trip is so fast that Ellie slams into the syrupy air like a wall when she arrives. Ellie grabs on to Daniel for support. Daniel, who looks as though Ahdi takes him from place to place all the time, wraps an arm around Ellie in turn.

"How did you get all three of us here by yourself?" Ellie eases her grip on Daniel.

"I guess the process *is* a bit more involved than bringing just yourself." Ahdi looks vaguely embarrassed. "Not right now, but I'd be happy to show you how."

How Ahdi got them here does nothing to erase Ellie's doubts. On the defense side of the balance, Daniel trusts Ahdi implicitly. On the prosecution side, if there is a maintainer who can change the skunkworks in a way everyone swears happened a century ago, Ahdi is blasting on all frequencies that he is that maintainer. No one who did, though, would be so open about it, she suspects.

The three of them are standing on a dais. Beneath them, tiny switches form a grid that stretches out in all directions, farther than she can see. The switches click and clack in a way that feels like it ought to be a pattern. She can't find it, though.

Or maybe she's wrong. It's not like she's ever been in any of the skunkworks' caches before. She only recognizes that it is a cache from her mom's descriptions.

"What we store and where we store it is kind of a mess." Ahdi gestures at the grid below them. "Even when everything works as it's supposed to."

"It looks like a well-formed array to me?" Ellie's not sure what he's referring to but, as the words leave her mouth, she realizes it isn't this.

"Oh, sorry, I don't mean the structure. Yes, caches themselves are perfectly regular. I mean their contents. See that possible traffic accident there?" He points down at a set of switches immediately below them. "Different outcomes for the same cars. Only one of them will make it into the committed state of the universe, but all of them are still here."

She doesn't see it until he points it out. Then she can't miss it. What's encoded into the vast field of switches below them is a hodgepodge with no rhyme or reason she can see.

Shards of discarded and potential futures litter the caches of the skunkworks. The graveyard of what almost happened and what may still happen is tossed in with what did happen, the state of the universe. Stars going nova lie jammed up next to coffee-splattered spoons, next to the vain struggle against the ennui of the one thousand thirty-seventh grilled cheese in a row, and a shower of sand that lands on a piece of particle board to form an exact re-creation of Hiroshi Sugimoto's portrait of Voltaire. The graveyard is ever-shifting. A tea-stained cup in a sink is shuttled away, replaced by a positron and electron annihilating each other. A shifting of sand on some alien world is ruthlessly overwritten by a plume of smoke doing the jitterbug.

Ellie shakes her head and, for a moment, shuts her eyes. Maybe there is a pattern to the data, but where it is parked and when it's retrieved, if it is at all, seems haphazard.

"And the skunkworks can find the data it needs in that mess?" Ellie looks up at Ahdi in blatant disbelief. "It can tell what might still happen from what it hasn't gotten around to overwriting."

"Kind of amazing, right? There's a pile of hardware whose sole purpose is to keep track of the stuff in the caches." Daniel grins the way he does whenever he engages with an especially clever bit of engineering. "Believe it or not, this is a performance optimizer. That is, we don't need it for correctness. It makes everything go faster."

"Yes, the future never recapitulates the past exactly, but it rhymes more often than you expect. It's faster to find it and fish it out than to create it again from scratch." Ahdi echoes Daniel's grin. "As maintainers have complicated the physics of this universe, we've had to deploy more and more tricks to keep the universe stable and operating fast enough to allow conscious beings. Speculating potential presents and caching, though, came in over a century ago."

"Your point is that no one today put in some mechanism to keep around discarded futures so that they can fish them back out. That mechanism was already there." Ellie sighs. "Mr. Neeson said the same thing."

"Neeson?" Ahdi arches an eyebrow. "He and I agree about something. Will wonders never cease."

The skunkworks shatters into myriad points of light. In the next instant, Ellie is back in Ahdi's dining room, seated next to Daniel and across from Ahdi. She didn't even see the universe coalesce around her.

"You and Mr. Neeson agree. So, that's it? Are we done?" Ellie pushes Daniel's hand aside as he tries to get her attention. "This is just a side channel and, so, a bug? A serious bug but not some nefarious attempt to corrupt the universe."

When Ellie finally turns to Daniel, the agitated, anxious look on his face makes her jump in her seat. Once she remembers that it's Daniel making that face, she realizes that the universe is not about to implode on itself. Instead, it's that she said the wrong thing.

Sure enough, she turns back to Ahdi and his expression is stern. There is still a bit of softness, though, a kindness in his gaze, steel covered by the idea of padding.

"No." Ahdi's word is almost a whisper, but it feels like a shout. "There's a reason why Mary asked *you* to look into this. And I'm sure she wanted you to keep it a secret until it is removed." He shoots Daniel a look. "Neeson is a fool, but I may be complicit and spinning a plausible but misleading tale. You need to go to the archives and see if my story checks out. No, you are not done."

Ahdi nods to himself and his expression returns to friendly. Ellie takes the speech, though, as her cue that dinner is over.

"It's getting late." She slides her chair away from the table. "We'll hit the archives in the morning."

"Oh, one more thing." Ahdi holds a hand up. "Are people trying to kill you?"

"Not as far as we know." Ellie stands and the chair slides itself back in.

Daniel almost falls out of his chair. He steadies himself and looks oddly at Ellie.

"Excuse me." Daniel stands. "Your sister planted a bomb in my car earlier today."

"Interesting." The look on Ahdi's face is curious. "Chris tried to blow up Daniel's car?"

"That wasn't Chris." Ellie looks annoyed at Daniel, who rolls his eyes as he sits. "She hasn't tried to kill me in over a month."

That seemed like a winning argument when it was only in her head. Now that she's said it out loud, she realizes how wrong she is.

"But she's tried to kill you before?" Ahdi's gaze grows not incredulous but worried.

Ellie sighs. She doesn't want to get into a humiliating conversation about how Chris played her, not that there is any other kind of conversation about her and Chris. Ahdi, however, took the idea that Chris has been trying to kill her seriously. Daniel did, too, but he's at least seen a bit of the Chris Ellie knows. She sits down, as it may take a moment.

"Maybe a couple times a week since I was a kid." Ellie pushes the words out, seething at herself more than anyone else. "At the time, she told me it was for my own good and, like a fool, I believed her."

"You trusted her. What little kid wouldn't trust their big sister?" Ahdi says simply. "And, as a kid, you didn't know any better. She probably scared you with stories of what happens to maintainers who don't behave."

Ellie does a double take. This is not the conversation she expected. It's a relief to be believed.

"I never really questioned it until after I left for university." Ellie slumps and the chair slumps with her. "My friends with older siblings all had ones who were . . . I don't know—nicer."

"Chris is everybody's cheerful, helpful, caring friend." Ahdi spreads his arms, his palms facing up. "Everyone loves her, except Daniel here."

"I've been trying to tell everyone she isn't as nice as she seems since I was twelve." Daniel leans back in his chair, his hands folded across his chest. "You believed me right away, but you're the only one who ever did."

"I talked to Vera about Chris. It didn't go well." Ahdi presses his lips into a flat line. "I wasn't surprised. After all, she was fiercely loyal to her brother, who abandoned his son. I don't know that she was ever able to accept that family could ever do anything truly bad to family, even if she did practically adopt his son.

If Vera ever thought Chris—or you, Ellie, for that matter—was anything short of an angel, she'd never let it show. Not to anyone."

Daniel remains curiously silent through all this, except to squirm a bit at being talked about. Then again, it's hard to imagine Daniel ever confronting his aunt about his parents or having anything bad to say about her, regardless.

For an instant, Ellie hates her mom, but Mom never knew the Chris that Ellie knew, at least not until her last days. Ellie checked for herself a few months after diagnosis, after Chris swooped in and took over Mom's life. She left Chris's house then sneaked back in. Ellie didn't know what she expected, but what she found was a stranger in Chris's body. A solicitous Chris cooked Mom's lunch. She wouldn't let Mom do anything for herself, not even change the channel on the TV. It was like that old Chinese folktale about the son who, in the midst of a famine, fed his own flesh to his father. Both Chris and Ellie were raised on that story and ones like it. This is what parents expect of their children. Mom was cool and reserved, but Chris was warm, chatty, and too eager to demonstrate her filial piety.

"Chris never behaved badly around Mom. Well, not until what turned out to be the final months. As far as Mom knew, she was the perfect daughter. For the longest time, Mom probably thought Chris and I had only the ordinary sorts of squabbles between two sisters. Nothing could have been as bad as I made it out to be." Ellie stares down at the table. "Mom always told me to humor her. Even after Chris wouldn't let anyone else take care of her, she still told me to humor her."

"What's important, Ellie, is that you know better now." Ahdi leans forward, his arms pressed against the table. "If you ever need help, you know where to come."

"I honestly think she's stopped for good." Ellie sits back up. The chair slowly rises with her. "We've run out of parents for her to impress. There's no one left for her to show how much better a daughter she is than I am. Like I said, it's been over a month. Maybe now we can be the normal version of two sisters who don't like each other."

Ellie really wants to believe this. However, Chris has been Chris for as long as Ellie can remember. Once, Chris caught Ellie reading a Chinese newspaper. Chris badgered her and badgered her and badgered her, claiming Ellie was illiterate and faking it. The campaign was nonstop. She chased Ellie from room to room, forcing Ellie to admit the "truth." Eventually, Ellie confessed just to make her stop. In retrospect, she realizes she's done an awful lot of relenting in her life to make Chris stop. As usual, the only thing Ellie was faking was the confession. Nevertheless, she had never seen Chris so triumphant. Ellie never let herself read Chinese around Chris again. Another time, Ellie was jogging on the sidewalk when Chris's school bus passed by. The kids on the bus made fun of the way Ellie ran and, in the guise of "watching out" for her little sister, Chris made sure Ellie knew.

Chris is the only direct relative Ellie has left. It shouldn't matter. Ellie doesn't want it to matter, but it does because of what Mom wanted. You have to love your sister even if you don't like her. Mom was insistent about this and Ellie can't deny her. That Mom's dead is beside the point. Ellie has to leave the door open for Chris and find a way to get her to walk through. Otherwise, she doesn't know how she gets out of bed every morning.

Ahdi looks pensive. His gaze narrows. He's clearly weighing his options of how to react. His gaze softens and he grunts.

"If it's not Chris, you two may want to reevaluate whether you made any other enemies then." Ahdi pushes himself away from the table. "Your car has been booby-trapped again while we were out. They tried to hide it, but I expect you, Ellie, would have noticed when you got closer."

He's already done several seemingly impossible things just in the past couple of hours. Ellie's not surprised he can sense, from the dining room, something added to Daniel's car in the driveway. Distance doesn't seem to be an issue for him.

"Dismantling it will be a good exercise for the two of you," Ahdi says as he sees them out.

CHAPTER 11

Ahdi sticks around by the front door as they approach Daniel's car. At first glance, Ellie doesn't notice anything unusual about the car. In her defense, neither does Daniel. She gets within touching distance of the driver's-side door and realizes this car bomb is much more sophisticated than the last one. A good exercise for the two of them is a triumph of understatement.

"Daniel, tell me you can make some sense of the mechanisms involved and can model them."

"Already on it." Daniel is sitting in the driveway, very focused on the ceramic disk in his hand.

Ellie manages a small sigh of relief. They need a model of the thing, if they want to test their plan to disarm the bomb before they try it out for real. Building a model isn't generally a part of a verifier's bailiwick. A test harness around the model, yes, but not the model itself. That's more of an architect's thing. Given who mentored Daniel, though, Ellie is not exactly shocked that Daniel is building the model with aplomb.

He fiddles with the wireframe that floats above the disk. With a few deft gestures, he shifts a wire here, creates a new join there. This process goes on for a while before he finally nods at it, pronouncing it good or at least good enough. It's a model like the toy skunkworks in the Chief Architect's basement, except vastly smaller in scale. It only has to simulate a car bomb.

"We can make it more accurate as we go." He stands and shows

Ellie the model. "By the way, we have to figure this out because I refuse to die disarming anything this inelegant."

Ellie studies the model and compares it with the bomb inside the car. Daniel has an exacting standard for elegance. Either way, the model is as faithful as it can be without any data about how the mechanism responds under stimulus. For obvious reasons, there are some responses Ellie does not want to see firsthand. They are going to be very careful with stimulus.

The extraction goes slowly. It's past dusk and the car is lit only by light from the house and a flashlight Ahdi handed Daniel about an hour ago. They still haven't done anything to the bomb. All they've done is probe it, iterate on their model, and simulate attempts to extract it.

Ahdi's gaze presses against Ellie's back like a gentle but unyielding wind, as it has since this ordeal began. Assuming she survives this experience, she half expects an assessment from Ahdi out to at least twelve decimal places. His gaze must press at least as hard against Daniel, but he doesn't notice. Or if he does, it doesn't show. Daniel both all but bounces from excitement about the job and grouses from disgust about how clumsily conceived one subsystem or another is, redesigning it on the fly.

Ellie doesn't join in on the "we should be killed more elegantly than this" discussion, except to steer Daniel away from designing the car bomb they should have built to kill them and toward analyzing the car bomb they did build to kill them. In any case, it's a car bomb, not a weapon known for its precision. From what little she can glean about the explosive, when it goes—if it goes—the result won't be pretty. They will be splattered all over the driveway.

The model is more complicated now, denser with wires and cross-links. The test harness is a thin, shimmering web that surrounds the wireframe. The simulated bomb floats in the harness, exploding for the thirty-seventh time. Ellie has lost count, but Daniel has been his assiduous self.

"Any other ideas, Daniel?" Ellie sits in the driveway, surveying the simulated wreckage.

"Can you do anything to the explosive?" Daniel, sitting across from Ellie, grazes the edge of the ceramic disk, resetting the model.

"No." She stares flatly at Daniel. "I don't understand why it hasn't ignited itself."

"So, it really is a matter of 'figure out how to trick the meta-bomb' then."

Nestled in the undercarriage is an infrastructure that checks that the bomb is still a bomb and blows everything up if it detects any interference. Daniel has taken to calling it the meta-bomb. Ellie has a couple of other names for it, none clean, that she's keeping to herself.

Throughout the entire ordeal, Ahdi has remained frustratingly silent, which Ellie takes as a good sign. Anyone who would let them blow the car up and themselves in the process wouldn't have warned them about the bomb in the first place. If they were on the wrong track, she thinks he'd give them a helpful nudge. That said, he's kept them well supplied with pens, paper, and, eventually, snacks.

Ahdi sets exquisite, thoughtful bowls of shrimp chips and salted duck egg salmon skins next to Ellie and Daniel on the driveway. They are clearly homemade and even more irresistible than the commercial stuff. Ellie could wolf them down in handfuls, but she limits herself to one chip at a time as she watches each simulation. Daniel nibbles on the occasional chip or three, savoring each one.

As she snarfs yet another salmon skin, Ellie wastes three seconds wondering whether they should leave Daniel's car here. She's positive this has not occurred to Daniel. Leaving, though, would be admitting defeat. She doesn't want to admit defeat, especially if the bomber turns out to be Chris. As insufferable as Chris is already, she can always be worse.

Simulation #41 turns the car into a rhinoceros, albeit one with a bomb plastered to its underbelly. Daniel and Ellie stare at each other. Ellie is stunned, but Daniel wears a grin that screams "We should try this!"

"No, Daniel."

"The data we would collect would be invaluable for correlating the model to the real thing."

That he's absolutely right is not the point. Ellie is more worried about what if, after all this work, the model is still too wrong in a way that matters and she detonates the bomb instead.

"I am not getting blown up because you want to see your car turn into a rhino."

"What if we find a way to turn it back into a car first?" He withers under Ellie's incredulous gaze. "Fine."

They both retrace their steps. Scouring the model and gently probing the car's undercarriage with this stimulus points out only minor mismatches. They update the model of the bomb and the car. It changes the number of horns the rhino has from one to two.

Still, that counts as progress. This behavior has to be a bug. No one designs a car bomb that intentionally turns the car into a rhinoceros. They can exploit this.

Simulation #65 makes the car explode into a mix of multicolored confetti and cranberry-lime seltzer. Being soaked and splattered with wet paper is embarrassing, but it wouldn't kill her. Dusk has become night and Ellie wants this to be over. It's been hours. This might be as close as they get.

"No, Ellie." Daniel's voice is surprisingly stern. "We are not blowing up my car."

"You were fine with turning it into a rhino." Ellie stands and stretches.

"There would still have been a bomb. We would have figured out how to change the rhino back." Daniel gestures Ellie to sit. "If we're not going to turn my car into a rhino, we are going to figure out how to extract the bomb."

Not for the first time, Ellie is grateful for the concept of grammar. This is how Ellie can hear Daniel say yet another sentence that has never been said before in the history of the world and understand him. She sits back down but in a particularly protesting way. Or at least that's how it seems in her head. Daniel probably just sees her sit.

Simulation #81 causes the bomb to detach from the car and drop, unexploded, onto the driveway. Both Ellie and Daniel turn to Ahdi, who does not react. He is a judge in one reality-TV cooking competition or another. No one will find out from him whether bread flour was the right choice or whether they should have gone with all-purpose.

Ellie and Daniel double-check everything that can be checked. They create a list of what Ellie will have to do. Miniature switches need to be jammed. Circuits need to be opened and components need to be replaced with a harmless load before they are closed up again. She rehearses the list again and again.

Ahdi has tire chocks, a jack, and four jack stands ready for them. Ellie's relieved that Ahdi didn't expect them to build those from scratch. They could have, but now they don't have to. Ellie wedges the chocks under the tires. Daniel adjusts the height on the jack stands.

"We don't need the jack," Daniel explains as he sets the jack stands down next to the car's jack points. "It'll be faster if I pick up the car and you slide a stand into place."

"Pick up . . . the car?" Ellie eyes him critically.

"It's a subcompact." Daniel looks vaguely defensive. "It's not like it weighs anything."

Daniel goes to the driver's-side front, reaches underneath, and lifts. The only giveaway that it takes him any effort at all is that he lifts the car with exquisite form. The legs take most of the weight, not the back. Otherwise, it's like watching someone pick up a piece of paper.

A tiny part of Ellie wants to take her sweet time getting the jack stand into place. The rest of her is happy to never be in a situation where she sees the limit of Daniel's strength. That probably doesn't go well for either of them. She swiftly slides the stand in, and Daniel gently lowers the car with absolute control. The other three go quickly and the car is ready for Ellie to work on. Daniel's right. It was faster this way.

Ellie's fingers light up with thin, laser-like beams. She slides under the car. Steadily, she picks apart the mechanism sprawled in a microscopically thin layer across the underside of the car. Methodically, she does what she rehearsed.

"Ellie, is there any chance you can do this faster?" Daniel never panics, but his voice can become urgent.

Ellie now notices what Daniel has noticed. They missed a deadman switch. It set off an alternate chain of events that will cause the bomb to go off. The chemical reactions play out in her mind. Her work has slowed it down, or else they'd be dead already. She has about six seconds, she estimates, to finish before it catches up. She needs at least two minutes.

"Not bad." Ahdi's voice feels practically subliminal, a scratch in the back of her mind. "You two got about ninety-five percent of the way."

There's a change in the air. Ellie can't put her finger on what. The air is perhaps a little thinner. The chemical reactions have slowed drastically.

"Wait." Ellie stops working. "What just happened?"

"I've given you some more time, Ellie." Ahdi sounds much closer now, perhaps right next to the car. "We'll go over everything later at the postmortem, if you'll excuse the expression. For now, you have work to do."

Given the two minutes she needs, Ellie's work goes smoothly. The bomb detaches from the undercarriage and glides past Ellie. It's not what they simulated, but it's not not what they simulated. Ellie rolls out from under the car only to find Daniel lowering it off the jacks.

The bomb, a vast sheet cluttered with hundreds of writhing tendrils, sits next to the car. The car is now solidly on the ground. Both Daniel and Ellie are drenched with sweat. The two stare at each other, unsure of what to do next. They've gotten it off the car, but it's not like it can't still explode.

"Now, step away—carefully, Daniel—and pull your car slowly out of the driveway when you leave." Ahdi walks toward the bomb. "I'll take care of this once you're clear."

"Well, it was good to meet you." The bomb writhes between them, so Ellie merely waves her goodbye.

"Good to meet you, too, Ellie." Ahdi holds a hand up. "Remember, you are a maintainer. What you do either repairs the universe or breaks it. Up to you."

Ellie has no idea how to respond. A honking car horn breaks the silence. Daniel waves from the driver's seat. Ellie waves at Ahdi again, then gets in the car, and they leave.

Daniel turns the car onto the road. A bright light fills the driveway and he immediately slams the brakes. Ellie stifles a cry. The only reason she thinks Ahdi might still be alive is that there wasn't any noise or a compression wave.

She and Daniel both look out the passenger window. A large glowing vortex looms over Ahdi. He spreads his arms wide. The light dims, the vortex shrinks, and its swirling slows. Only a few seconds pass before it becomes a dark, inert rock, falling harmlessly to the ground. Ahdi spots the car and waves goodbye at

Ellie and Daniel, backlit by the light from the house. Daniel zooms down the street.

"I feel like I just took a surprise exam." Ellie sinks into her seat. "Did I pass? I did pass, didn't I?"

"I don't think that was intentional, at least not on his part. The bomb isn't tidy enough to be Ahdi's work. Like Aunt Vera, he can't be anything but exquisite even if he tried." Daniel checks his blind spot before he changes lanes. "That said, he somehow always manages to give me homework whenever I visit."

"What you do either repairs the universe or breaks it." Ellie echoes Ahdi's solemn tone.

CHAPTER 12

Chris's house is a massive, multi-gabled hulk set by itself in a cul-de-sac. Even by the standards of a neighborhood filled with big, expensive houses, this is a big, expensive house. Ellie has always wondered why there isn't a perimeter and a gate.

The house is already dark when Daniel pulls into the driveway. Ellie's seat belt retracts to the passenger-side door.

"I can walk you in?" Daniel unclips his seat belt in turn.

"No, that's OK." She opens the passenger-side door. "I'll be fine."

"I should give my condolences to Chris."

As excuses go, from Daniel, this one is particularly unconvincing. Ellie can't remember the last time Daniel volunteered to talk to Chris.

"Daniel, it's literally midnight. She's probably asleep." Ellie steps out of the car. "I'll be fine. See you tomorrow."

She closes the door behind her. Pavers laid in an intricate pattern create a walkway that arcs from the driveway to the stoop and front door. It's no longer hot, but the air is still thick and heavy. Each step feels like pushing through a slurry.

The high, vaulted atrium still takes her by surprise. Anyone walking in is immediately confronted with an ostentatiously high ceiling and a long sweeping staircase that curves up to the second floor on her right. Before she can acclimate to the grandeur, an emptiness takes its place. It's not that the house is cold, but a chill grips her. Something has sucked the air out of the house. The sense of phantom structures that should exist, but don't, screams in her mind.

When she arrived from the train station this morning, she noticed it the instant she walked in. It was the first time she'd been in the house since Mom died, and she thought she imagined it at first. When she extends her senses, she feels the structure surrounding her. The house, of course, is exactly like it always has been. Without Mom, though, it is also nothing like what it was.

Chris's home office is on the left. Like all the rooms, it has a substantial, carved hardwood door. Ellie doesn't need to check to know it's locked, and she suspects it'll never be unlocked for her ever again. It's the room where Chris stowed Mom once she became too weak to navigate the sweeping staircase, the room where she slept in her coma, and the room where she died.

They'd made arrangements for hospice care for Mom. Chris even made a point of it because, Ellie assumes, Chris felt Ellie wasn't taking Mom dying with the appropriate level of gravitas. In the end, the idea that someone who knew what they were doing would take care of Mom in her final days was a pipe dream. The dutiful daughter wouldn't let anyone else, especially the relatives in Taiwan, think she was shirking her duty. Ellie knows this for certain because she heard Chris saying it again and again.

Every time she walks past, she half expects to walk in and see Mom. Every time she remembers that, no, Mom cannot be in there. It's like being told Mom has died all over again. It rends her heart every time the way it did the first time.

The atrium leads straight to the kitchen. Chris sits there, waiting. Gray light through a window splashes Chris's shadow across the kitchen table. The expression on her face is taut and angry. Of course it is, because Chris is always angry at her and Ellie rarely knows why. Chris is still, as if trapped within a sliver of time, left to seethe at the kitchen table for hours, waiting for Ellie.

Ellie suppresses a sigh. Not only is this not her first rodeo, it's the latest in a circuit she wanted to retire from years ago. Her freshman year, when she came home for Thanksgiving break, she went to a party to catch up with her high school friends. Chris, by then, had already gone to university, gotten her degree, and been back for years. In a triumph of restraint, it took an entire half hour before Ellie's friends became Chris telling her to come home right this moment. How dare Ellie worry Mom and Dad, who—not that it mattered—were not worried at all. They had given Ellie the car keys and told her to have fun.

Coming home to Chris patiently stoking her anger for hours has been an inevitable part of Ellie's life. This is how Chris shows her love, Mom had once told Ellie. By the time she was certain no one else came home to someone inescapably waiting to take a piece out of them, she had not only moved to Boston but passed her qualifying exams and had her dissertation topic approved by her committee.

If she had a choice, Ellie would tear off her shoes and fly up the sweeping staircase. She's tired and the last thing she wants is to have The Conversation again. However, a brother-in-law and a nephew are asleep upstairs, and a determined Chris is not to be denied. The clamor of Chris demanding Ellie come down to the kitchen is out of the question.

Instead, Ellie slowly pries off her shoes and sets them in the closet. She can't escape the punishment coming to her anyway. Avoiding Chris now only makes it worse in the long run. Ellie has learned that the hard way. Never let yourself be dependent on Chris for food.

They will have The Conversation. It never changes.

Chris will tell her she's a terrible daughter to their parents. She will do this in exhaustive detail. She will then exact retribution. Sometimes, it's petty. Chris will force her to sleep on the floor or Chris will serve her rotten meat for dinner. Of course, only someone who loves Ellie would treat her this way. Anyone else would just let Ellie be the horrible excuse for a human being that she is. Chris always insists this.

They've had The Conversation so many times that Ellie wonders what the point is. Honestly, she would avoid invoking The Conversation in the first place if she knew how. Maybe there is a right way to behave so that Chris doesn't fume. Ellie hasn't found it yet. She sighs and makes her "walk of shame" into the kitchen.

Chris sits up. Her arms rest on the table, her hands clasped together. The expression on her face is pleasantly neutral. She might be a news anchor waiting for her cue. Ellie's not fooled.

"Where have you been?" Chris, as usual, fails to sound casual, her cadence too measured and contained.

"I'm not a kid anymore." Ellie leans against a counter.

"You left in the middle of the reception." Chris's words get even slower, leaving no vowel or consonant unmolested. "How were you ever Mom's favorite?"

Ellie straightens up. Chris has gone off script. She's never said anything like this before.

"Why would you think Mom played favorites?"

The look Chris gives Ellie is one of pure contempt. Usually, Chris tries for some sense, sincere or not, of sisterly concern.

"You can't be that stupid." Chris is matter-of-fact, downright casual. "Mom took you with her into the skunkworks one thousand, three hundred and forty-seven times more than she took me."

Of course Chris knew about every trip, even when she was at university. And of course Chris kept count. Not that it matters. Even one trip more than her is too many for Chris, but the number feels goosed up. Ellie suspects Chris is also counting trips to maintainer school. It was like Chinese school, which Ellie also went to. Practically everyone at Chinese school was ethnically Chinese. She knew maybe two kids at maintainer school who weren't the children of at least one maintainer parent. Anyone can go, but no one is interested.

"Why does it matter if Mom brought me along more—"

"I begged and begged. But once she started taking you"—Chris hurls the last word as an accusation—"she never took me with her anymore. Mom loved you more than she ever loved me and this is how you repay her? You leave me alone at her reception and make me wait up for you?"

Ellie takes a moment to do the math. By the time Mom dragged Ellie along to the skunkworks regularly, Chris was probably at university. Certainly, she had finished both Chinese school and maintainer school. By then, she went to the skunkworks without Mom all the time. It's not like she needed Mom to make sure she didn't do anything stupid.

"Well, Mom's dead, so I don't know that she cares one way or the other. Funerals and receptions are for the survivors. And you didn't need to wait up for me even when I was a kid."

Ellie turns on the lamp hanging over the table. The switch on the wall makes a satisfying click. A rough cone of light falls onto Chris. She squints and anger finally seeps through that news-anchor veneer. Something twinkles on one of her fingers. A diamond ring. Ellie has never seen it before.

"You ungrateful bitch. You should appreciate the sacrifices I make for you. What were you doing at the Chief Architect's place?"

Wherever Ellie is, Chris knows or at least can find out. Ellie doubts that if she asked again, this time Chris would tell her how she always knows.

The question sounds like an accusation, as if they were in a cop movie and this is the scene where Chris interrogates the bad guy. Chris deploys the sentence as if expecting Ellie to deny it, so that she could slap down some piece of paper and say, "What would you say if we could make you for the murder of Alberto

Fujimori there this afternoon?" Ellie would be damned for killing the problematic former president of Peru. There would be nothing for her besides the death penalty.

"She wanted to give me her condolences."

"That's all?" Chris does not look the least bit convinced, her hands now flat against the table. "Just admit you didn't care enough to stay."

"If the Chief Architect asked you to come over right away, wouldn't you?"

"I would have made her wait." Chris's voice is the epitome of calm. "Because I love Mom."

Ellie does not take the bait. The reception is yet another cudgel for Chris to beat Ellie with.

"Why didn't you ask the Chief Architect yourself?" Ellie folds her arms beneath her chest. "It's not like you stayed for the whole thing. You left to plant a bomb in Daniel's car."

Ellie still hopes it wasn't Chris. This, however, is as good a way as any to find out.

"Are you serious?" Chris's expression is more mocking than usual. "When have I ever tried to kill you? And even if I want to, are you really so conceited that you think, today of all days, in the middle of Mom's funeral no less, I'd waste time on you?"

That last sentence could be the truth. On the other hand, she hasn't denied it.

She's no longer using the "I'm trying to kill you to keep you on your toes" line. If this is her way of telling Ellie that she's quit trying to kill her, that's good. If this is only more gaslighting, that's bad.

"When did you get the ring?"

A startled expression flashes across Chris's face. Her eyebrows rise and her jaw drops before a calm mask wipes the expression away. Her hand moves to cover the ring, though, like that does any good now.

"Mom gave it to me. Which you'd know if you'd simply quit grad school like I told you to."

Ellie assumes "Mom gave it to me" means "I bought it for Mom, and it just so happens that I get it back after Mom dies." She's ashamed to even think this. Mom wearing a diamond ring, though, is not something Ellie could have missed. Most weekends after Mom was diagnosed, Ellie took the train down from Boston Friday nights and the train back Sunday nights. No point challenging Chris, though. Ellie wasn't here when Mom died. To Chris, that's all that matters.

"Anything else or are we done?" Ellie knows she should end this bit of theater now, walk away, and leave Chris hanging. She's never been able to.

"Do you think you've done everything you could to save Mom's life?"

The trap Chris is setting up is so obvious. Ellie killed Mom with malice aforethought while Chris was the long-suffering angel who did everything possible to save Mom's life. It's a lie, but the tiny grit of truth embedded inside it makes it deadly, the sort of trap that clamps down on you and you have to gnaw your leg off to escape.

"Well, I think we all could have done more." Ellie manages a sanguine smile. "Even you."

"I did everything I could have possibly done." Chris pushes herself to a stand for emphasis.

That's not true, which never stops her from saying it all the time. It drives Ellie nuts.

Mom always told Ellie to put up with Chris. After her brain surgery, Mom recovered in the hospital for a week or so, a giant bandage wrapped around her head. Chris wouldn't let her eat anything besides the gruel she made for her. The surgeon said it would be better for Mom to feed herself. It would stimulate brain activity. Chris, however, simply had to spoon-feed Mom at every meal.

That she was in the hospital, though, gave Ellie some rare moments where she saw her without Chris. Once, Chris had gone to pick up her son from Chinese school. Ellie sat by Mom's side. Mom squeezed Ellie's hand and told Ellie, once again, the stupid story she'd been telling Ellie forever, the one about the bully who stopped once she gave him her soup. When the story failed to convince Ellie, Mom said they both needed to avoid riling Chris, so she didn't get suspicious. She grew quiet when they heard Chris scolding her son down the hall. What Mom said made more sense later, when Ellie started helping Mom sneak out of the house at night.

Now that Mom is dead, Ellie can't live like that anymore. It's not like she wants to rile Chris. She wants Chris not to be so easily riled.

"You never quit your job to take care of Mom full-time." Ellie's voice is steadier than she expected. "So, you didn't do everything you could have possibly done."

"Don't be ridiculous." Chris puts her hands on her waist. "Why would I ever need to do that?"

"You thought I needed to."

"Well, that's different. You live in Boston."

"How is that different? I offered to move here and work remotely."

"Was killing Mom your plan all along?" Chris's mask is finally failing, and Ellie feels every barb catch. "Is that why you never helped me take care of her?"

"I didn't kill Mom." Ellie tries to iron out the wobble in her voice, but it still shakes. "I rectified the physics of the universe. You always went out of your way to prevent either Daniel or me from helping. Half the time, you wouldn't even let me see Mom. The last time I tried to help, you literally told me to go to another universe instead."

"The perfect answer!" Chris throws her hands in the air. "You always think you have the perfect answer, don't you?"

Chris can't say that Ellie's wrong, and to Ellie's surprise, she hasn't. She didn't let anyone help and had to be the one who did anything for Mom. Whenever Ellie made lunch for Mom and Chris caught her, she threw it out and made it again herself. She physically blocked doors and ripped forms out of Ellie's hands.

For countless weekends, Ellie sat at this kitchen table begging for anything she could do. Once, Chris's husband took pity on her and let Ellie pick up her nephew from Chinese school. Chris raced to Chinese school to pick up her son first, then screamed at Ellie because she made extra work for her. Chris never let Ellie do anything and, apparently, that's Ellie's fault, too.

"No, I don't but I'm not wrong this time." Ellie pulls herself away from the counter. "If you'd let Daniel and me help, maybe Mom would still be alive."

The instant it leaves her mouth, Ellie wishes it hadn't. Knowing where the trap is doesn't mean you won't step right into it anyway.

"How dare you!" Chris points toward the door. "Get out of this house!"

Ellie knows she's supposed to be hurt but she's weirdly relieved. Some small part of her knew that this was how the conversation would end.

"Fine." She forces her face into her best neutral expression. "I'll go pack."

"No need." Chris pushes Ellie's roller bag out from under the table. "I've done it for you."

Much as Ellie wants to, she does not laugh. They had this conversation so Chris could manufacture a reason to kick her out.

Ellie unzips the roller bag and does a quick inventory. Clothing, toiletries, tablet, power supplies are all there and she doesn't sense any mechanism that shouldn't be. One never knows with

Chris. Ellie drags the roller bag behind her out the door. She does not say goodbye.

Daniel's car is still parked in the driveway. Ellie almost trips off the stoop from the shock. She hurries over. Daniel pops the trunk and opens the passenger-side door. She stows her bag and gets in.

"Why are you still here?" Not that she minds at all in any way.

"I made it as far as the end of the driveway before I decided you might need a place to stay." Daniel smiles. "I did live with you all for a long while."

"Were you going to wait here all night?" Ellie still can't quite believe Daniel stayed.

"No, of course not." He looks incredulously at her. "I figured if a bedroom light turned on, then everything was all right, or at least you had somewhere to sleep for the night."

"Thank you."

"Don't worry about it." He waves her off and starts to back up the car.

"Daniel." Ellie feels crazy for even bringing this up. "Do you know when Mom gave Chris a diamond ring?"

"Aunt Vera bought Chris a diamond ring?" Daniel stops the car and looks at Ellie, baffled. "While she was in a coma?"

"That's what she made it sound like. Maybe she meant before, but I don't know where Mom would have gotten the money to pay for it."

"Maybe she meant that she'd bought it for Aunt Vera and has now inherited it?"

Ellie sighs in relief. Maybe great minds think alike but they're probably just both making the same assumptions about Chris. That said, Daniel has never been accused of thinking good things about Chris.

"That thought occurred to me." Ellie starts to fiddle with the air-conditioning, then decides there's no point. "But she could have said that."

"It wouldn't surprise me, though?" Daniel shrugs. "I mean, it's a little eccentric, but it's not like she can't afford a diamond ring."

Ellie sinks into the seat. Her body spreads and her arms fall by her side. The seat presses gently against her back. Her shoulders slump, and only now does she understand how tense she was in the house.

This late at night, the highways of metro DC work the way they're intended. Cars roll smoothly around the ring roads. They divert without pause up and down the intersecting highways. It's not always like this. Any weekday morning or afternoon, people are trapped in their metal cages, creeping to work or crawling home five feet at a time.

As she senses the cars humming smoothly down the highway, she turns a thought over and over in her head: For years, she tried to figure out the right things to do and to say in the right order to make everything work out because Mom wanted her to. Mom's gone. She doesn't have to talk to Chris ever again, except Mom died insisting her daughters be sisters to each other. Ellie can't defy Mom and she's sure Chris told Mom what she wanted to hear. It's not fair that instead of some normal contentious relationship between two sisters who can't stand each other, Ellie has this. All she's asked for is something normal, or at least more normal. Maybe without the weight of the filial piety to a fault they've both imposed on themselves, it's possible.

CHAPTER 13

Morning light seeps into Daniel's apartment, painting it in shades of black and gray. Ellie's up because she gets up with the sun whether she wants to or not. Daniel, of course, is already up and out. If she knows him, he's at the gym picking up ridiculously heavy things and then gently setting them back down again.

The kitchen bursts into glorious color or at least tasteful values of metallic when Ellie turns on the light. It, like the rest of Daniel's apartment, is immaculate. If it were anyone else's kitchen, she'd think the owner never used it. But it's Daniel's and, if not in this kitchen, she's seen his deft knife work and his flair with flames in a couple of others. Pans hang from the ceiling in order of size. A magnetic strip on the wall over the rice cooker on the counter keeps all the knives—again, sorted by size—in convenient reach for someone with long arms. She's not about to test them, but she's sure they're all perfectly sharp. The range gleams. The microwave above it isn't splattered with sauces. A tiny table, big enough for two, sits against a wall with two chairs tucked in against the table edge.

The refrigerator looks too perfect to open. It's probably not actually polished to a mirror-perfect sheen—Daniel is tidy, not obsessive—but she still doesn't want to smudge it. Ellie gets over herself. Daniel won't care and it'll take her mere seconds to buff away.

Chinese broccoli and daikon rest in the crisper. Jars of sauces, most of them some variation of spicy, line the inside of the door.

Labeled containers sit in neat columns on the shelves. She picks out the rice porridge, fried dace with black beans, and soy-pickled cucumbers.

The pans clatter and a wind gust buffets her back. She turns around. Belt materializes and crashes to the floor. She didn't realize he learned how to travel like this, not that she's entirely surprised. Given the slightest interest, Daniel will pull complete strangers into a tutorial.

Belt's face is now clean-shaven and any hint of scruffiness has been flensed from him. The effect is less unexpectedly handsome lobsterman of Gloucester and more expectedly handsome fairy-tale prince who has traded places with his trusted valet. His long limbs flail for an instant before he gathers himself.

"Hi, Ellie." Belt picks himself off the floor. "I'm still new at this."

Belt's voice invariably rings. It's high and brilliant. The entire kitchen sings back in response.

"Did Daniel teach you?" Ellie looks around, then puts the containers of leftovers on the counter.

"Do you really need to ask?" Belt rolls his eyes.

"Fair." She opens a cabinet, looking for a bowl. "Tell me you're learning about maintenance of your own free will."

It's like singing. Nothing stops anyone from learning how to maintain the skunkworks except disinterest. Anyone can get better if they learn and practice. Some people, especially if they have been training since they were children, can become great. Ellie imagines Belt can get to the point of doing some easy routine maintenance—whether it's as an architect, a verifier, or a builder—if he wants to spend the years working at it.

"Sure, but I doubt I'll ever do any actual maintenance. It's on my radar about as much as opera is on other people's. I'm happy for some group of people I know nothing about to keep the universe working. I don't need the drama. Well, I guess I know you and

Daniel." He takes a bowl from a cabinet over the range and hands it to Ellie. "After a couple of years of work, I now have two party tricks. I can crash-land here and I can crash-land home. I suppose it's like how Daniel probably would have made a fine professional dramatic basso profondo if he'd spent his first decades tirelessly training to be an opera singer. As if Chinese school and maintainer school hadn't been enough. Instead, he's just this guy with an unusually deep voice. Not that I haven't tried to work on his diction."

"Wait, you have performances next week." Ellie sets the bowl on the counter. "*La Cenerentola*, right?"

"Yeah, hence the shave and haircut. This production wants its Prince Charming as squared away as a marine. I left my score here, and I have a rehearsal in DC in an hour. Otherwise, I'd have taken the Metro, much easier, if more time-consuming."

"It's just occurred to me that you always introduce yourself as Belt, but you're an opera singer."

"Yes." He is absolutely deadpan. "That's the joke."

"You ask everyone to call you Belt Sander and the joke is that you're an opera singer?"

"A name can be funny on multiple axes." Belt exudes a Daniel-like innocent insistence. "Besides, that's not how I bill myself. If you recall, my professional name is Samuel Sander."

"Oh my god." Ellie resists the urge to bury her face in her hands at his nickname's wordplay. "You two deserve each other."

"Yeah, we do." He grins. "I kind of realized that when, for my birthday, he made me a cake that was canned spiced pork interleaved between layers of roasted onions."

It takes a second but Ellie gets it. Her jaw drops. Belt positively glows.

"Oh no." She's not sure why she's so appalled. The pun, a food-based one no less, is totally on-brand for Daniel.

"Oh yes. Say it."

"He made you spam in allium?" Ellie arches an eyebrow at the play on the Tallis motet *Spem in alium*. "He was a wrapped scallion for Halloween once so—"

"Tell me you have pictures."

"Sure. Gimme a sec."

Ellie goes to the living room. She pulls her cell phone out of her roller bag's front pocket. The phone unlocks with a glance. She swipes through until she finds the photo. A book, labeled *La Cenerentola*, and slightly the worse for wear, sits on the coffee table. She takes that back with her along with the cell phone.

She hands Belt both his score and the phone. A smile grows on his face as he takes in the picture. It turns out hiding Daniel's legs in a high-waisted, floor-length pleated skirt focuses all your attention on his massive upper torso. So, if he's wearing a wig of spiky white hair, the shirt is white, the skirt has an ombre from white to green, and he's covered in clingy, tight plastic wrap, the result is more bulbous than your typical scallion but there's no wordplay to groan at if you call him a wrapped spring onion. The eye mask on his face and the foil scabbarded at his waist make him a suitably scoundrel-like wrapped scallion.

"Oh my god, this is perfect. If he still has the costume, maybe I can be some other sort of allium, a plumbing leek or something."

"The spam in allium, did he cut it into forty parts?"

"Of course." Belt looks amused she would even ask. He hands back the cell phone. "Gotta commit to the bit."

His eyebrows rise in shock. His face twists into a scowl.

"How dare you run off like that?" Belt's voice is low and rough. It's lost its ring. "You made me look for you all morning."

Chris. If Ellie were violent and if it weren't Belt's body, she would punch her into orbit around a distant star. The shame Ellie feels, though, takes the edge off the anger. Chris waylaying people has always been disturbing. Ellie doesn't even know how she does it. She shouldn't be more disturbed because Belt is the victim, but she is.

"Let him go." Ellie points away, like she's shooing a dog. "You don't have to do this. You have my number. You can get a hold of me whenever you want. Send me a text like a normal person."

She waves her cell phone at her. Standing up to Chris is much easier when it's not Chris she's standing up to. Maybe Ellie pulled off the stern glare. Maybe her tone was harsh enough. Maybe Chris had an appointment she's late for. In any case, Belt's body relaxes but a puzzled look spreads across his face.

Chris simply left. Ellie expected a few more rounds of argument and insults first.

"What the fuck was that?" The pitch is high and the ring is back in his voice but he's also rubbing his throat. "Did someone take over my body? Is that even possible?"

"Yeah, my sister. She's the only one I know who does that. It creeps the fuck out of me every time— Wait." Ellie pores over him. "You know what happened."

"Yeah, something went wrong in the skunkworks and, for once, I sensed it. Sure, I had to be the one it went wrong in, and I don't want anyone to take over my body ever again, but I'll take the win." Belt grins. "This is like Daniel finally singing a healthy, well-supported G1. I have my hopes."

Sensing bugs in the universe is a very verifier thing to do. That Belt did at least this once has more to do with him learning what Daniel knows how to teach than anything else. As for Chris, exploiting bugs in the universe is not what maintainers are supposed to do. Bugs are supposed to be reported and fixed.

"I'm sorry about my sister." Ellie slides her phone into a pant pocket.

"It's OK. No harm done." He rubs his throat again. "Listen, this is kind of a personal question and you don't have to answer it, but does your sister always gaslight you like that? Daniel said she kicked you out, not that you ran off."

Ellie is caught short. A realization jolts through her. This is the first time anyone else has heard Chris speak like that. Chris was the model daughter around Mom, and all Daniel has ever heard her say could be chalked up to passive-aggressiveness. Not that Ellie wants anyone else to be subjected to this, but having a witness tell you that Chris is gaslighting you is oddly comforting. But, this time, Chris sounded like she genuinely wanted to make sure Ellie was OK, albeit in her own very special way, and, once she knew, she left. Ellie tries to explain, but she stammers instead.

"I'm sorry." Belt takes an involuntary step back. "I shouldn't have said anything."

"No. I'm glad you did. It was the right thing to say. It's just good to have someone else hear her and come to the same conclusion." She gestures him toward her. "Thank you."

Belt waits a beat. He takes a cautious step toward her. The look on his face says, "Are we really doing this?"

"Do . . . do you want to talk about it?" His brow rises and he rushes his next words. "I mean, only if you want to."

"Thanks for the offer, but I think I need a moment to sit with it first." Her gaze shifts to the clock on the microwave. "Besides, I don't want to make you late for your rehearsal."

Belt turns to check the time. He turns back, still looking pensive.

"Yeah, I need go now if I want to be on time for rehearsal. If you need someone to talk to . . ." He waves goodbye to Ellie, who waves back. "Say hi to Daniel for me."

Belt walks into the living room. Ellie doesn't blame him. When she was getting the hang of things, she didn't want anyone watching either.

She stares at the containers on the counter. The one with the porridge is filled nearly to the rim. Gingerly, she pries off the lid. As she spoons porridge into the bowl, the thought she pushed away last night roars back with a vengeance: With Mom gone, she doesn't have to put up with Chris anymore if she doesn't want to.

They've run out of parents. If Ellie cuts Chris out of her life, she's run out of siblings. Unless Daniel counts, which he admittedly does. Still, Ellie's not sure she can cut Chris out of her life. She can still see Mom in bed telling her to smile and placate Chris, do whatever she tells her to do. Ellie making peace with Chris is what Mom always wanted from her.

Ahdi's right about Mom's loyalty to family. Once, in one of those late-night visits where she sneaked into Mom's room, Ellie told Mom about all the things Chris has done to her. Mom pronounced that Ellie would never get her to say anything bad about Chris.

Mom would have wanted Ellie to dismantle the monstrosity trapping her between life and death. She also wanted Ellie to keep putting up with Chris, to keep the family together whatever the cost. Perversely, Chris trying to kill her might be the one stable element grounding Ellie's life. This past month of not knowing when or if she'll start up again has been even more stressful. She doesn't want to go back to semi-regular assassination attempts, though. There has to be some way to make Chris easier to put up with.

CHAPTER 14

By the time Daniel comes back, she's on the dregs of a bowl of hot porridge. The microwave is still unstained, or at least she's wiped it off after accidentally blitzing the porridge for ten seconds too long. The containers of dace and pickled cucumber sit opened on the table next to the half-empty plastic tub of 肉鬆 she grabbed the instant she saw it in Daniel's extraordinarily well-organized cabinets. Sweet and salty, pork but wispy like cotton candy, she loves the stuff. It's not hard to find in Boston, she just never gets around to going to the right stores. Ellie is dumping 肉鬆 into the dregs when Daniel shows up.

Daniel's always even more mountainous after a workout. His uniform of T-shirt and jeans stretches across rather than merely hugs his body. A duffel bag hangs off his shoulder. He's sipping a protein shake out of a shaker bottle.

"Ellie." Daniel tilts the bottle up for a chug. "Is breakfast OK? I can make you whatever you want."

"No, this is great." She sets her chopsticks on her bowl and pushes away from the table. "Do you want some?"

"Oh, no thanks." He shakes his nearly empty shaker bottle. "I'm a protein-shake-and-banana guy in the mornings."

"Belt says hi, by the way. He stopped by this morning."

"Oh, right. To pick up his score. He texted me."

"Daniel." Ellie bites her lower lip. "What do you think of Chris?"

"I don't. She told me that I didn't deserve to help take care of Aunt Vera." He takes a last chug. "What brings this up?"

"Do you think Chris and I can ever have a relationship like two normal sisters?"

Daniel's eyes bug out. They don't pop out of his skull, although they look like they really want to. He takes a deep breath as his eyes slowly retreat back into their sockets.

"I think . . . you must love her very much to put up with her."

"That's not really an answer."

His mouth opens, as if he's about to say something. He doesn't, though, and his mouth closes again.

Ellie's heart pounds. Maybe she hoped that Daniel would have simply said no and that would have been that. Now, she wishes she hadn't asked.

"Guess that answers my question. Thank you, Daniel." She sets the bowl and chopsticks in the sink. "Ready to go to the archives?"

At first, Daniel looks surprised at the turn in the conversation. Then he looks relieved.

"Gimme a minute. Meet me in the living room."

Daniel washes out the bottle, then puts his gym stuff away. Ellie cleans up after herself. When she's done, she heads to the living room. Daniel is sitting on the sofa, crouched over. He's studying a tiny piece of intricately folded air. It floats between his hands, wobbling as its rotation changes axes. His cell phone rings, and he manages to shut it off without dropping what he's studying. When he notices Ellie, the piece of folded air disappears.

"Ahdi's still trying to teach me how he whisks people around like that." Daniel stands as he rubs his hands. "Just follow me to the archives, OK? I promise I've gotten much better at being followable."

Ellie nods. She's never been to any of the archives before.

Daniel dissolves into the air. Individual particles of him go into solution and an ever more translucent Daniel is smeared around the living room. It isn't a second before he's entirely gone. The living room dissolves around Ellie as she follows him. It becomes an impressionist painting that is then smudged into swaths of color. She's following a complex set of equations implying a machine she senses in the void between universes. She's pretty sure it's Daniel.

The colors deepen and darken. Faint clicking in a quasi-periodic pattern surrounds her. Dark browns resolve into two columns of rectangular hardwood tables and chairs, separated by an aisle running parallel to the long sides of a very rectangular room. Each table is parallel to the short sides. Two green-shaded lamps hang over each table. People scattered around the reading room sit hunched, poring over tomes and jotting down notes. A couple of them are bipedal humanoids. The rest are from universes Ellie only knows about from her mom.

The ceiling is a clockwork sky. She senses the mainsprings and movements more than she can see them. Shelves line the walls. Vast windows lie above them. Beams of light spill through, splashing the tiled floor with shadow.

Ellie is about five feet off the ground. Daniel's standing in the aisle between the two columns of tables. He turns and catches her at her waist as she falls. A couple of people look up from their books at them.

"Yeah, we need to work on that." He gently sets her down. "First time I followed Ahdi here, I crashed through a bunch of lamps and a table. Splinters of wood and broken glass all over. Everyone gawked at the clumsy brute. It was great. Not awkward at all."

Daniel is so deadpan that Ellie just stands there puzzled as he saunters past her toward a counter at the end of the room. By the time she realizes where Daniel is, she has to rush to catch up. When she does, she stares for an instant until she realizes what she's doing. Whether the archivist behind the counter is from this universe, Ellie certainly isn't. She's the odd one here.

"Xu, this is my cousin, Ellie." Daniel presents Ellie to the archivist. "Ellie, this is Xu. He's been an archivist for ages."

Myriad tiny insects with iridescent wings form the archivist's body. They flutter in place, glinting like tiny dots as they angle in and out of the light. Daniel opens his arms for a hug and the archivist swarms around him. He arranges his wings into rings of intricate patterns that rotate in alternating directions around Daniel. After he flows back to his side of the counter, his body settles into a standing bipedal form.

"Hi, Ellie." The archivist extends a shimmering hand toward her. "My condolences on your mother."

Tiny wings vibrate against Ellie's skin. The archivist's grasp is firm, though, and when she squeezes back she feels both the heft of his grip and the fluttering of his wings.

"You know me?"

"Oh, please." Xu scoffs, or at least that's how it seems from the way his wings swirl across his body. "I've worked with both your cousin and your mother for years. They both talked, you know."

Chris is curiously missing from that list. She's about to ask when Daniel speaks instead.

"We did?" Daniel looks vaguely appalled. "We said good things, I hope."

"Of course." A row of wings streams from his body, circles Daniel, then goes back again. "I'm sorry there's nothing in the archive about the mechanism installed to hold off your mother's death."

"That's not why we're here." Ellie's words come out a little too quickly.

"No, we're here to investigate a covert channel in our universe." Daniel blanches at Ellie's glare. "What?"

Shock, or surprise, ripples through Xu. The insects of his body scatter and gather from bottom to top. It takes him a second to pull himself back together.

"A covert channel in your universe?" Xu expands to Daniel-like proportions. "Are you sure? Do you know what you're suggesting?"

Ellie and Daniel exchange glances. Daniel shrugs. He is as puzzled as she is.

"What are we suggesting?" Ellie tries but fails to avoid sounding like she's setting Xu up for a punch line.

"Disarray. Secret hardware makes keeping a universe functional harder. Some maintenance work may interact with the secret hardware in a bad way and how would the maintainer ever know?" He shrinks down to a more compact size, his vibrating wings almost touching each other. "Keeping secrets doesn't speak well of the maintainers in your universe."

Daniel looks smug. Unfortunately, it's a wholesome self-satisfaction that reads much more "Hey, it turns out I've been doing the right thing all along" than "I rebuke your baseless glare with the grin of righteousness." Ellie is not nearly as annoyed as she wants to be. That, ironically, annoys her a lot.

"It's bad enough that maintenance isn't part of the standard curriculum in your schools, but the utter apathy about your skunkworks is palpable. It's a miracle there are enough maintainers to keep your universe functioning properly." Xu orients a cluster of insects at Daniel. "Maintainers designing and installing hardware that other maintainers don't know about is beyond the pale."

"That's why we're here," Daniel says simply. "To determine whether it's a covert channel or a side channel. Whether there are maintainers deliberately corrupting the universe is more important than this one exploit."

"And you think the archive will have documents about a mechanism that no one is supposed to know about?"

"Yes!" Daniel smiles brightly. "Most if not all the hardware also creates our universe. We can at least look into how that happened."

"The hardware that generates the covert channel also makes the universe function." Xu sounds puzzled. "That makes it sound like a side channel. Are you sure this isn't a bug? Not that keeping a bug a secret is anything to celebrate."

Daniel spreads his hands. The sculpture of air that describes the side channel materializes on the counter. It is the same giant sea urchin that needs a haircut, with spikes of varying widths and lengths, that Daniel created for the Chief Architect and again for Ahdi. He does it so quickly now that Ellie wonders whether he was playing up the effort for the Chief Architect. Or maybe it's gotten easier with practice. Xu pours his body into the spaces between the folds. They refract and reflect him, painting the sculpture with mismatched wings of every size at every angle. He swirls around inside, his wings rotating as they flutter.

"You want to understand why your universe has quantum mechanics?" The sculpture vibrates, amplifying and reverberating Xu's voice. "I hope you're not in a hurry."

"Ahdi was telling the truth." Ellie can't keep the wonder out of her voice and glares back when Daniel glares at her. "Look, if it was some cover story about how this is the side effect of our specific implementation of quantum mechanics, how would I know?"

"It's not like Ahdi ruled out a secret cabal. All he said was it'd have to be at least a century old." Daniel's tone is final. "He practically ordered us here to double-check all the details."

Xu scatters. Flying dots push themselves into the shelves. The clockwork sky rumbles. Almost everyone ignores the quiet hum making the room vibrate. Besides Ellie, only one person, a bipedal avian, stares up to watch the sky change.

Gears spin. Sections of clockworks slide away. Other sections slide into their place. The sky as a whole slowly rotates clockwise. Ellie feels the library expand. The building with an infinite number of rooms now has an infinite number plus one.

"You want everything. I hope you realize how much data 'everything' is." Xu's voice surrounds Ellie and Daniel. "Follow me."

A mist of wings envelops them. As dots sparkle and fade, Daniel dissolves and fades in turn. Ellie sighs and follows them.

CHAPTER 15

At least the sofa is comfortable. The room Xu ensconced Ellie and Daniel in is surprisingly large. It's the piles of papers and crystalline planes of folded air lining the walls that make the room feel tiny. There's no door, of course, but it's not like they needed a door to get in. They aren't trapped. Ellie just feels trapped. She's lying on a plush sofa with hands folded across her stomach, volleying back answers to Daniel's questions and occasionally turning over hypotheses of how one slips in a covert channel in the first place. If she's stuck here for the time being, at least she's comfortable.

Daniel, naturally, has been dancing from pile to pile from the moment they arrived. He flips through the pages, plays with the miniature planes of air, constructs a few of his own, and mutters a running commentary. Sometimes, the commentary comes in the form of questions. The man doesn't have a huge amount of experience building anything, much less into the skunkworks. Granted, Ellie doesn't either, but she has more than him. She's been fielding his endless stream of questions about the inconvenient details of how one constructs the skunkworks in real life for what feels like hours now.

"Wait. Why do we have two separate mechanisms on opposite sides of the skunkworks for tracking the wave function as it collapses? And why are they ever so slightly different from each other?" Daniel glares at two planes as though he can unify the two mechanisms through sheer disapproval. "Wouldn't it be better to have just one?"

Ellie pushes herself up to a sit. Her gaze sweeps past Daniel to the folded planes of air he is studying. They bobble next to him, refracting the other documents, the sofa, and the table where Daniel has stacked the truly important stuff he wants to review again.

"Sure, but the skunkworks is huge. The propagation delay is pretty awful."

"What do you mean?"

"Get Ahdi to explain it to you sometime. For now, just realize that, unlike in simulation, the farther away something is, the longer it takes for information, for signals, to reach it—"

"I know that." He sounds patronized.

"Let me finish." She crumples a nearby piece of paper into a ball and throws it at him. "A signal may have multiple destinations. The skunkworks is huge. The difference between how long it takes to get to the farthest one and the nearest one can be a relative eternity." Ellie lies down again. "In this case, one centralized mechanism probably can't get all of its control signals everywhere they need to be in time. It's like asking you to run a marathon in the time it takes me to run a hundred meters."

It occurs to Ellie that Daniel might be able to do that. Or at least she wouldn't be shocked to see him blur through twenty-six point two miles. A squirrel trying to swim through a marathon of cornstarch slurry in the same time as a dolphin through a hundred meters of water takes Daniel's athletic prowess out of the equation and might make the point better for him. However, Daniel nods with understanding.

"Fine. But I don't have to be happy about it." Daniel pushes the planes back into their pile with a sigh, his brow furrowing the way it does whenever he studies a less-than-perfect design. "You know, we're never going to find any evidence of wrongdoing if you keep justifying all of the skunkworks' warts."

"Isn't that Ahdi's point, though?" Ellie stands and idly leafs through the pages on the table. "This exploit could have been designed in, or it could be the accidental side effect of a bunch of decisions that seemed practical at the time."

"I can safely say he's not wrong. Then again, I can't remember the last time Ahdi was wrong about anything." Daniel turns to face Ellie. "In any case, we'd need to interview a bunch of long-dead maintainers to tell the difference. I don't know how much that matters. If there is a cabal, all its members should be dead by now. The only thing left to do is what needs to be done anyway, remove the side channel."

A single sheet of paper falls from the ceiling. It teeters and drifts, but finds its way onto the table.

"You know, there's something I don't get." Ellie picks up the paper and studies it. "The exploit is basically 'bias the skunkworks in one direction then make our present go in another—one the skunkworks did not predict.' As a result, the skunkworks' cache has all these artifacts from the alternate present that didn't happen. Then, due to some quirk of design or implementation, we can fish one of those things that didn't quite happen out of the cache."

"Yeah, so far so good." Daniel looks confused. "What don't you understand?"

"Well, speculating alternatives and cluttering up its caches in the process is just what the skunkworks always does, right?"

"Sure, that's fundamental to how we sped up the skunkworks, even before quantum physics."

"The skunkworks speculates in more ways than I can count, and they all leave pieces of what didn't happen lying around all over the place. There are no mechanisms to clean them up and probably countless ways to bias every single one of the skunkworks speculation mechanisms." She turns to look at him. "There should be at least an entire family of exploits like this one."

Daniel's jaw drops. He holds up a finger.

He rushes from one pile to the next. His hands rifle expertly through the papers. His muttering sounds like the swish of a soft white-noise machine. Tiny sculptures orbit him as he works his way around the room. It's odd how precise Daniel can be even as he scrambles in a tight circle.

"Oh no. You're right." Daniel finally stops moving. "We need to tell someone."

"Speaking of which." Ellie shows Daniel the paper. "You're supposed to check your texts."

Daniel pulls out his cell phone. He swipes at it, then swipes, then swipes, then swipes.

"Ahdi." Daniel says the name as though it explains everything. "The highlights: He wanted to warn us that there are multiple families of side channels. Naturally, we now have more homework."

"You may have already done some of it."

"Maybe. Anyway, someone attacked him last night. Don't worry. He's fine. The attacker, not so much."

"What?" Ellie sits up. "Someone attacked him? Who? Why?"

"He doesn't say. It probably has something to do with his next section." Daniel points to his phone. "He doesn't connect the dots but, honestly, I think he did this to test a hypothesis. He altered the skunkworks to eliminate several exploits—"

"Several? Last night? By himself? Is that even a thing?"

"Yes, yes, yes, and yes if you are Ahdi."

"You *knew* he'd pull something like this, didn't you?" Ellie isn't openly accusing Daniel of anything, but she is.

"If I may point out, *I* wasn't the one who wanted to visit him."

"That is so not the point."

"As I was saying, he's telling us to be careful because there really is a cabal of maintainers who, even if they didn't create these side channels—and I'm thinking they couldn't have—don't want anyone to know about them. They certainly don't want anyone to get rid of them." Daniel shrugs. "I keep telling you. He's a lot."

Ellie doesn't dignify that with a comment. She merely sighs and starts going through one of the piles on the table. If she wanted to sort through an absurdly large amount of paperwork and fend off a secret cabal, she could have stayed in Boston. At least no one in grad school has tried to kill anyone.

Not that she knows of anyway.

CHAPTER 16

Daniel's living room comes into focus as Ellie coalesces. It's a TV on the wall, a sofa, and a coffee table on a hardwood floor. The three pieces of furniture are, of course, perfectly aligned and parallel to the walls. Heavy shades cover the windows. Sharp rays of light sneak through. Bright horizontal stripes trisect the room. Coming back from the archive, Ellie doesn't crash into the sofa or through the table. She studied the living room before they left this morning. It's a place she now knows.

She stands at one end of the table. Daniel stands at the other, eyeing a dark corner. A man waits there, not particularly hidden.

He steps toward them, covering them with a gun. Under any other circumstance, he'd probably present as tall and broad. Unfortunately for him, Daniel is standing right there, looming like the cliff he always is. Nevertheless, the man's wide stance and squared shoulders try really hard to make tall and broad happen.

"Hey, Danny boy. This time, I'm prepared for you." The man smirks. "I bet you're wondering how I got in here."

It takes a second for Ellie to recognize Tom, the guy who gave her the Chief Architect's note at the reception. Tom's more puffed up now that he has a gun.

"Not really, Tom." Daniel is pleasantly casual. "You can appear here because once, in some speculated existence, you followed Aunt Vera here."

"Very good, Danny." Tom exaggerates his tone as if Daniel were a toddler potty training. "You *have* been paying attention."

Their exchange makes Ellie's mind reel. It only makes sense if the cabal Ahdi mentioned littered the skunkworks with alternatives from discarded realities where her mom survived. The monstrosity she dismantled kept Mom in an odd sort of limbo. Maybe they weren't trying to cure her. Mom in limbo, combined with some exploit, worked as an engine to generate all sorts of scenarios that involved her, no matter how unlikely. For them, Mom in limbo was better than an actual living Mom. So many more possibilities.

Rage roils through her. Dragging out Mom's death was bad enough when she thought they were trying to cure her. Deliberately trapping her in an unknown state where she could have gone either way is unspeakably worse. The rage feels uncontainable and wants to thrash and shake her body to pieces.

Daniel's gaze locks with Ellie's for an instant before returning to Tom. Ellie forces herself still, for now. Tom is here for a reason. She might learn something if she's patient.

"Flattery will get you everywhere." Daniel deploys a smile so friendly, it's blinding. "You get thirty seconds. I'm impatient."

"I've been briefed. You're not what people say you are." Tom brandishes the gun. "Even if you were, I've evened the odds."

Daniel rolls his eyes. "If you insist."

"I'm not here to kill you," Tom says, despite the finger on the trigger. "Stop—"

"I'm serious. I don't have the patience for this." In a single motion so swift it blurs, Daniel disarms Tom, then traps him in a joint lock with one arm as he holds out the gun with the other. "Ellie, make this useless."

Tom struggles to break Daniel's grip, but he's just doing isometrics. There's a lot of straining and grunting but no actual movement. Daniel's arm might as well be a metal pipe wrapped around Tom's body. Rather than giving any attention to the man failing to worm out of his grip, Daniel levels a gaze at Ellie that's decidedly expectant.

A moment or a day goes by before Ellie can do anything. Daniel has always looked like a long-lost son of some hypothetical war god, but she's never seen him fight like one before. Even with the size difference, she still beats him occasionally when they spar in the gym. Here, Ellie has no idea what happened. The gun seemed to slip from Tom's hand as Daniel pulled at it. Ellie is sure what Daniel did was not nearly so simple. It would all be less galling if, say, Daniel were struggling to keep Tom under control, but the big lunk doesn't even seem to be trying.

"How am I supposed to do that?" Ellie holds the gun gingerly by the grip. "I don't know anything about guns."

"Hey, you're the expert on all things mechanical. Unload it, then make it a not-a-gun somehow." Daniel shifts his attention to the man in his grip. "OK, what's your message, Tom?"

"It's not going to have the same menace like this."

"Nevertheless." Daniel presses his lips into a flat line.

Ellie sits on the sofa. With a little study, the structure of the gun becomes evident. She removes the magazine and sets it to one side. It clacks and swishes against the table despite her best efforts. Now that the ammunition is nowhere near the gun, she starts to disassemble it.

"Stop investigating side channels in the skunkworks. Or else."

"Or else what." Daniel sounds bored.

"That's the bit that would have worked better if I were still pointing a pistol at you."

"I gathered that." Daniel tightens his hold now that he has both arms at his disposal. "Any chance you'll tell us who sent you?"

"You saw them yesterday afternoon." Tom tries to turn his head toward Daniel and fails. "They were at the funeral."

"Can you be a little more specific? There was a crowd."

Daniel tosses Tom over his shoulder and walks to a window. He lifts the blind, and light fills the room. Tom tries to shield his eyes, but Daniel bats his arm away. He opens the window.

Engine hum drifts into the room, along with the heat and humidity.

"Wait." Ellie stands up. "You're going to throw him out the window?"

"Of course not. He's bluffing." Tom sounds incredibly confident for a man helpless over Daniel's shoulder. "Ahdi wouldn't do it. Daniel's not going to do anything his boss wouldn't."

"Wait. What—"

Daniel's "not now" glare chokes off the rest of Ellie's words. Mentor is one thing. Boss is another.

"It's pretty simple." Daniel's voice is the epitome of calm. "Tell us what's going on and you get to leave in whatever way you want. Otherwise, it's the window."

For a split second, Tom is a blur. He snaps back into sharp focus, still trapped over Daniel's shoulder. Given the contact, to leave Tom would have had to take Daniel with him. Maybe Tom tried. If Daniel were willing, it might have worked. As it is, maybe Ahdi could take an unwilling maintainer with him. Maybe.

"This is ridiculous." Tom's words fly out between gasps. "All you have to do is to tell Mary that the side channel she knows about was an accidental side effect of implementing quantum mechanics. I'm not even asking you to lie. Besides, that side channel has been closed. Stay out of our business and we're good. What's it to you?"

"You mean"—Ellie puts her hands on her hips—"why should we care that you made my mom suffer for your own personal benefit? Or that you tried to kill Ahdi for fixing bugs?"

"Puh-leeze." Tom draws the word out. "That's what warning Ahdi looks like. *Actually* trying to kill Ahdi is a far bigger production. As it is, we wouldn't have bothered if he'd fixed only the one side channel Mary knew about. He also took out a couple we still use."

"Look." Ellie gestures at the gun. "I can put the gun back together if that'll make you say something useful."

"Are you threatening me?"

Ellie looks at him oddly. The question is too stupid for words, and it takes a moment before she realizes he genuinely expects an answer.

"Now that you mention it, I guess this would be more threatening." She holds up a hand, and flame arcs from one finger to another. "You haven't exactly been the volunteering type."

"Look, despite your reputation, Ellie, it's mostly potential at this point. We haven't seen any works of genius from you yet. And you, Danny boy, have never killed anyone, much less in seven different ways before their body hit the ground as you explain why their work has a subtle design flaw. You're both in way over your heads." Condescension drips off Tom's words. "Now be the nice kids you are, put me down, and I'll be on my way. No harm, no foul."

"We're in over our heads?" Daniel sounds amused. "And you think you've been briefed on us."

Daniel shoves Tom toward the window. Tom squirms and kicks. A couple of kicks even land, not that Daniel notices.

"We've been renovating the skunkworks for weeks now. The train is already hurtling down the track. You won't be able to stop it." Tom's voice is loud and hoarse. "Interfere and you two are going to get yourselves killed."

"Try again." Daniel squeezes and Tom grunts.

"Why do I even bother?" Tom slumps.

"In that case, give them a message for me." Daniel winds up. "Stop fucking around with my car. I can't afford to replace it."

Daniel hurls Tom through the window. Tom's arms lash out and grasp the window frame, not that it matters. He flies through and screams as he falls.

Daniel slams the window shut, claps his hands together, and

turns to Ellie, his face smug. For a moment, all is silence. Ellie stares at him, jaw slack.

"Oh my god, you did it."

"You doubted I'd do it, but now you must admit that succeed I did?" Daniel smiles at what Ellie assumes is yet another one of his private jokes, inverted syntax and all.

"Yes. No." Ellie sits back down. "Threats are one thing. I didn't think you'd go through with it."

"A." Daniel opens his right hand and taps his right index finger with his left. "I told you that I'm capable of unconscionable things.

"Two." He taps his index and middle fingers at once. "*You* threatened to shoot him.

"Orange." He taps his index, middle, and ring fingers at once. "He has a whole thirty feet or so to get to some other universe or whatever and arrange a safe landing. He'll be fine."

"Because that's something that maintainers do all the time."

"Exactly." Daniel nods with satisfaction. "Ahdi never threw me out of a window or anything, but he's had me practicing stuff like this ever since I was a kid."

"I see." Ellie's words are slow and careful. "I don't think maintainers are typically trained to do that."

"No?" Daniel sputters before he grasps for a desperate ring buoy of a retort. "But your sister tries to kill you on the regular."

"You and Ahdi made it quite clear that that's not typical either."

"So, no."

"No." Ellie shakes her head.

Concern spreads across Daniel's face. His gaze grows wide and his mouth forms a small circle. He shudders.

"Tom's not totally stupid. I'm sure he's thought of something by now." Without looking, Daniel pulls down the window blind. "Can you change the structure of my apartment?"

"Like add a wall or something?" Ellie looks around his postage stamp of an apartment. "Not without some fallout. We're talking about apartment renovation."

"Oh." Daniel looks disappointed. "I just don't want anyone I don't know showing up here out of the blue like that again."

"Speaking of which." Ellie holds up her left hand, and flames dance from one finger to another. "I have a few questions."

"Whoa." Daniel throws his hand up in surrender. "What did I do to deserve this?"

"I've beaten you when we spar in the gym." A realization dawns in Ellie. "Oh no. You let me win, don't you?"

Daniel's gaze softens. Slowly, he lowers his hands.

"No, I never *let* you win. You're far too well trained to not notice." Daniel takes a strategic step out of arm's reach. "Whenever we spar, I pick a set of skills and limit myself to those. That way, I get to practice techniques I don't always get to use, you get practice figuring out an opponent's tics, and it hardly matters that I'm over twice your size. It's no fun for either of us if all I have to do is sit on you."

Ellie decides that this conversation can wait until the next time they spar. She has more important questions.

"Never mind." She grunts in frustration. "Disarming him. I can't even tell what you did."

"I can show you. All you had to do was ask." Gentle is Daniel's go-to move and, right now, he's practically beatific. "You didn't need to haul out the fireworks."

"You are so exhausting." Ellie turns off her flames. "Fine. Let's try it this way. Why does everyone think of you as some sort of invincible verifying assassin?"

"I. Don't. Know." His voice is the sort of quiet that gives Ellie the shivers before it returns to something more genial. "You sound like I want people to think that. I don't want a reputation. I want to be the wind."

"The wind?" Ellie has no idea what he means.

"You know, I breeze in unnoticed and I breeze out unnoticed.

Something happens. Who did it? No one knows. Anyway, as Tom said, I've never killed anyone."

Ellie stifles a laugh. Only Daniel could think he can go unnoticed. Of course, if he is at all successful at being the wind, Tom wouldn't know of any of Daniel's kills. And there may be some kills. Daniel is doing a stellar job of not directly answering any of Ellie's questions.

"So you're not Ahdi's hit man?"

Daniel looks offended. Of course, Daniel also looked offended when she called the *Hamilton* cast album a soundtrack. It's hard sometimes to gauge the level of Daniel's reactions.

"No, Ahdi has absolutely never ordered me to kill anyone." This is the closest to unequivocal Daniel has been all conversation, and he sounds relieved. "If you're going to believe Tom, everyone thinks you're an engineering genius."

Ellie sighs. Daniel is too damn hard to stay angry at. It's impossible to forget that he was also once the teenager who would both trip himself walking across the living room and catch himself with a Hail Mary punch front.

"Fair. But what about how Tom got here in the first place." She puts her hands on her hips. "You went straight to him following my mom here."

"One, apparently, I'm right." Daniel looks slightly wounded anyway. "Two, it can't be me. I hope it's not you. My boyfriend can barely get *himself* here. I don't want it to be Aunt Vera, but there's no one else."

"When would she have done it, though?" The idea of her mom helping Tom at all leaves Ellie a little sick. "It'd have to have been before I dismantled their monstrosity. Are you enough of a threat that they wanted access to your apartment just in case?"

"Well, if you put it that way . . ." Daniel waggles his eyebrows.

He opens his palms. “Or maybe Tom broke in the old-fashioned way.”

Ellie lets out a breath. Her gaze shifts over to the front door.

“Probably not.” She walks over and inspects the door. “You have an absurdly industrial-strength lock—”

“Ahdi made me get that installed.”

“—maybe if Tom is a builder—”

“No— Oh, hi, Ahdi.”

Ellie turns around. Ahdi is standing next to the coffee table. Normally, there’s at least a slight pop or breeze from the displaced air when someone shows up out of nowhere. Adhi looks a bit puzzled, which is exactly how she feels.

“Hi.” Ahdi looks around. “I expected someone to be here threatening you.”

“You missed him.” Ellie folds her arms across her chest. “Daniel threw him out the window.”

Ahdi’s face is a mixture of horror and pride. Ellie arms fall. She tries not to laugh and ends up coughing. Ahdi stares at Daniel with an expression that screams “What the fuck?”

“We’re, like, thirty feet up.” Daniel’s expression is just as disbelieving. “That’s plenty of time to arrange a safe landing, even for Tom.”

Ahdi takes a deep breath. The man is clearly choosing his words very carefully. Ellie interrupts before he has a chance to say anything.

“Have you been here before, Ahdi?”

“No.” It’s a split second before he realizes what question she’s really asking and a split second later when embarrassment is smeared across his face. “Having been here before makes it easier. It is not, strictly speaking, a necessary precondition.”

“Could Tom have done that?” Ellie’s gaze goes back to the window.

"Good god, no." Daniel opens the blinds a crack, peeks through, and whistles. "I've debugged his work. Tom doesn't understand how the universes work anywhere near well enough. He'd have to follow someone who knows what they're doing."

"Tom who?" Ahdi paces around the room.

"Dunham. You know, tallish." Daniel gestures just below his chin. "Rather solid. Blond. Weirdly skittish."

"I think that's only around you," Ellie interjects.

"Oh, Tom." Ahdi's voice is clipped. "I know him."

"It's easier to believe Aunt Vera showed him how to get here."

"That's oddly specific." Ahdi taps the walls as he paces, nodding occasionally. "Oh. Of course that's how he got in. It's not something the Vera I know would do, though."

"I don't think she would either." Ellie presses the betrayal out of her voice. "Maybe in those alternate presents, that monstrosity saved her without saving her, if you know what I mean."

Daniel runs his hands across the tops of his window frames, checking for dust. This is as relaxed and unguarded as Ellie has ever seen him, and yet he still looks like anyone who attacked him from behind would find themselves pinned to the floor before they knew what happened. Even casual Daniel looms like a heavy sword dangling by a thin thread.

"Ahdi, does Daniel work for you?" Ellie takes a deep breath before pressing on. "Tom said that you were his boss, whatever that means."

"Tom is being cute. Maintainers from many universes come to me to talk out their skunkworks issues." Ahdi starts crawling on the ground and pushing at the baseboards. "Daniel, do you work for me?"

Daniel snaps around, looking oddly guilty. He crosses his arms across his chest, but looks like he's trying to squeeze the life out of himself.

"More or less?" He notices his arms and lets them hang. "Things work out better if I just do whatever it is you tell me to do."

"Daniel." Ahdi stops and, for a moment, he slumps in disappointment. "You can't just do whatever anyone tells you to do."

"Not anyone. You." Daniel packs an amazing amount of respect into three words. "Otherwise, what inevitably happens is whatever problem gets more complicated, and I wish I'd done whatever it was you told me to do in the first place. There's like a cadre of us like this."

"A cadre?" Ahdi and Ellie say at the same time, but only Ellie goes on. "That's an interesting choice of word. How many people are in this . . . cadre."

"I dunno." Daniel blows air through his lips. "It's nothing like the numbers Neeson has at his disposal. In this universe, a dozen or so?"

"So, there's a small but impeccably trained group of maintainers who'll do anything Ahdi tells them to?" Ellie asks.

She resists the urge to walk the three steps to give Daniel a dope slap. This seems like something he could have mentioned at any time. Then again, Daniel always gives the impression that he thinks he's pretty typical as verifiers go. Never mind that half the maintainers he runs into treat him like a walking weapon while the other half simply bolt in the other direction.

Ahdi, for his part, simply lies prone on the floor, resigned. His limbs are splayed out, making a giant X on the hardwood. He looks like, despite his best efforts to dodge it, someone has thrown stupid all over him and now he has to wash it off. It's not a huge deal, merely more work he didn't need.

"No, not anything." Daniel looks at Ellie as though she's the one who deserves a dope slap. "The right thing. And we all understand why before we do it."

"How many secret cabals of maintainers are there?" Ellie asks, even though she doesn't really want to know.

"Strictly speaking, Ellie, you're in at least one secret cabal." Ahdi, his composure recovered, starts slithering around the room again. "Just because a group is common knowledge to you doesn't make it common knowledge. And, apparently, you can even run a secret cabal without knowing it."

Ahdi is surprisingly good-natured about discovering that he is the leader of a secret cabal. Daniel looks relieved. Ellie wants to shake Daniel until she's convinced all of his secrets have fallen out.

"And how does that happen exactly?" Ellie's gaze follows him as he inches along a wall.

"You have to understand." Ahdi is now massaging the baseboards. "Maintainers have always come to me for help. We either talk through ways to resolve their design problems, or I explain to them why what they want to do is a terrible idea and why they should reconsider."

"So, you never tell them *what* to do but you do tell them what to *do*."

"Yes, that's the unintended effect." He sounds regretful, not testy as Ellie expected. "I should approach this with more intentionality."

A couple of things about Daniel suddenly make sense. He takes after Ahdi in ways that Ahdi probably does not want or intend. She wouldn't be shocked if Daniel is an accidental assassin the way Ahdi is an accidental head of a cabal. If Ahdi is hard to kill, then Daniel must be nearly as hard. Or, at least, throwing him out a window won't do the trick. Of course, he doesn't let on about that even when it'd be useful for Ellie to know. Daniel is practically her brother, but that doesn't mean there aren't days when she thinks he's too stupid to live.

Ellie stares at Ahdi. Daniel is casual again, leaning against the wall. Apparently, he sees nothing weird about Ahdi circling the room like a giant lizard and feeling the baseboards.

"Ahdi." Ellie pauses to choose her words even though there's no good way to ask. "What are you doing?"

"Ellie, study the structure of this room." Ahdi doesn't look up. "What do you think I've changed about it?"

What's different isn't obvious. It takes Ellie a minute, or maybe Ahdi's question makes time flow like pitch.

"Chirality." She nods her head slowly. "You've rotated the molecular structure of the studs and baseboards."

"I have left-handed wood!" Daniel bristles and glares back when Ellie and Ahdi both turn to him. "What?"

"Anyway." Ahdi grins. "This should stop anyone who needs to understand the structure of a place first. At least until they study this room again. Speaking of which."

He looks pointedly at the two of them. Daniel is tapping on his cell phone.

"Oh, I did that already." He doesn't look up. "I'm just telling Belt what's up, so he'll take the Metro the next time he wants to show up."

Ellie's jaw clenches in concentration. Studying the room is like being dropped into the ocean. The body hits something that should be soft but isn't when you're falling that fast. For a moment, she can't breathe. Chirality is not the only thing that's changing. Uncannily, the room is a rectangular box with eight too many corners before it suddenly has the right number again. Everything snaps into place and becomes something she can contain in her mind.

"How are you doing that?" Ellie lets the wonder fill her voice.

"I can show you." Ahdi gestures for her to come over.

"Is this really the right time?" Daniel puts his phone away. "Isn't there a conspiracy of maintainers rewriting the laws of the universe that we need to unwind or something?"

"I will say"—Ahdi stands up—"the changes they're making are perverse."

It's a moment before Ellie remembers. Very little changes in the skunkworks without Ahdi noticing.

"Perverse?" Ellie asked.

"It's a lot of work for so little effect." Ahdi's words are slow and careful. "They've bolted a lot of machinery on existing mechanisms. A sufficiently high-energy particle collider might reveal a tiny difference in the mass distribution of collisions. No one else would notice any change in the universe at all."

"So they've really 'leapt on' to these changes?" Daniel's jaw drops when both Ahdi and Ellie glare at him. "What? That's funny!"

"After I finish with the apartment, there's a hunch I need to check out with some folks in the universe surrounding ours regarding their skunkworks." Ahdi looks at himself, then brushes off his shirt and pants. "In the meantime, I need you two to do me a favor."

"Sure." Daniel rubs his hands in anticipation. "Anything you ask."

"Daniel, at least wait to find out what I want first." Ahdi closes his eyes and masters himself before continuing. "I need you two to go to the isolationists' archive. It has the most complete change records that exist. They're undoubtedly recording changes right now. Go there and figure out what this cabal is trying to do."

"The isolationists' archive?" Ellie asks, her mind stuffed with her sister's tales of murdered maintainers.

"Drop my name. They'll let you in." A tiny cube of intricately folded planes of air materializes in his hand. "Show them this."

Ellie waits a beat before taking the cube and stuffing it in a pocket. A sharp corner digs into her skin.

"Any hints on what we should look for?" Ellie asks.

"What they're doing is technically somewhat interesting. Their machinery more or less doesn't function given the current physics of the skunkworks. Change the physics of the universe that's one level out—the one that our skunkworks lives in—and their machinery will kick in and the physics of our universe will change. So I'm going to ask around—"

Ellie and Daniel exchange glances. Neither one says anything.

"The physics of that universe has already changed some." Ahdi is stating a conclusion, not asking a question.

"That's the root cause for the hold-time violation I fixed before I dismantled the contraption trapping Mom," Ellie says. "The logic was fine, but the physics of the universe that the skunkworks lives in changed out from under it. Signals propagate a little more quickly in the skunkworks now."

"Then the sooner we find out what they're up to and why the better. No time for any of us to lose." Ahdi points at the door. "Go."

Before Ahdi finishes speaking, Daniel has opened the window and thrown himself out. He breaks into glowing particles. They swirl through the window and disappear in a flourish.

"He knows where he's going, right?" Ellie's gaze is stuck where Daniel had been.

"I've taken him there before." Ahdi sighs. "Wherever he ends up, you'd better be there to keep him out of trouble. People have never been his strong suit."

If Ahdi is trying not to sound resigned, he's not trying very hard. He waves goodbye, then goes to the kitchen. That weird sense of cabinets and the counter changing but remaining exactly the same pervades Ellie.

The living room shatters around her. It breaks into shining particles that scatter in all directions. In the void left in their wake, a slim shimmering thread extends away from her. Daniel, to his credit, when Ellie didn't immediately follow him, thought to lay a trail.

The first time Ellie followed a trail, it was a thick, knotted rope. She was twelve and her mom had laid it for her to follow. There is no "where" in the void between universes, but Ellie felt her mom envelop her, guiding her through the transformations along the trail. She felt like a matrix being inverted or transposed. That odd sensation faded over time, over many trips to the skunkworks.

Following Daniel's thread feels like that first time, except the cold void is where Mom's reassuring presence once was. The system of equations that is Ellie in the void is being transformed in ways she has only ever studied, not experienced firsthand. Wherever Daniel is leading her, it is distant and distinctly alien.

CHAPTER 17

Ellie is suspended in a dim haze. A lattice of bookcases surrounds her. Up, down, left, right, ahead, behind, some number of other orthogonal directions that don't exist in her own universe. The bookcases form a complex, nested pattern that stretches to infinity. She gasps and the air seizes into a solid inside her throat and lungs. It's fluid again in the next instant and she meters it out of her nose and mouth. Faint eddies of turbulence whirl around her.

The haze should be nowhere near viscous enough to support her weight. It does so anyway.

Ellie pushes against the air, like a mime trapped behind a make-believe wall. The air pushes back and holds like a sheet of plasterboard. Her fingers fatten and her palms spread against the pressure. As she lets up, her hands break through. Her body pitches forward. Shc slams into a hardened haze that dissolves into nothingness the instant it stops her only to harden again an instant later.

Her feet lose traction. They slip out from under her. Her body rotates. The haze tenses into a solid and relaxes back to a fluid as she falls. Wisps of haze circle around her as she crashes through what feels like layer after layer of balsa wood. She flails her arms out. As she does, she's struck by a thought. It would have worked so much better if she'd stretched out her arms smoothly and pushed. Instead, she keeps crashing as the haze solidifies and dissolves around her until gravity pushes her directly into the air.

Ellie is upside down, supported by her arms. Blood rushes to her head. An ache works its way from her fingers, through her palm, and past her wrist to her vibrating forearms. The only thing that could make this more humiliating would be Daniel trying very, very hard not to laugh.

Daniel, however, is nowhere to be seen. Not that she trusts her eyes to parse so many dimensions at once.

"Ellie, are you here?" Daniel's sandpaper voice drifts toward her from some direction her brain keeps insisting is impossible.

"Where are we?"

"I think we're in one of the stacks." Daniel's voice does not exude confidence. "I mean, we're literally surrounded by documentation. If so, that would be bad. The isolationists don't exactly invite people to skulk around their stacks without permission."

"Lovely." Ellie lets out a long sigh. "Where are you? Talking to a disembodied voice I can't place is going to freak me out."

"The bookcases are all marked with their coordinates. Let me know where you are. I'll come over."

"You move one inch and I'll flambé you whenever I reach you." Ellie is not going to be defeated by some non-Newtonian fluid in a universe with too many physical dimensions. "Tell me where you are."

Daniel rattles off a long string of numbers. The bookcase next to Ellie is one of who knows how many, all nearly identical. Tall, broad, and deep, they are all gray fastened to equally gray backing. The paint has flecked off the bookcase next to Ellie, exposing the dull, bare metal underneath. Motley collections of books alternate with pristine planes of air on the shelves. A sign with a set of numbers is riveted to one of the sidewalls. Daniel's not that far away. Some of the numbers even match.

One by one, she marches her hands up. Her body cantilevers from upside down toward horizontal. Five steps in, she reaches out and feels nothing but air. Her body drops, then stops as the sudden movement hardens the haze below her. She wouldn't call it falling, but she's upside down again, her weight balanced over her arms.

She stumbles back into the handstand several times before she manages to walk her hands upright. The trick is to move smoothly except when she shouldn't. She hasn't figured out all of the haze's properties. Who knows what's supporting her weight, but she's upright now and can walk. Mostly.

Ellie teeters into a bookcase. It doesn't budge. Magnets and control logic line the sides of the shelf. Magnetic suspension locks it in place, equidistant from all of its neighbor bookcases.

"You're moving away from me, Ellie."

Ellie stops. She clings onto one of the bookcase's shelves. Her stomach sinks and it's not due to the weird properties of the air around her.

"You can see me?"

"Sure. You're not exactly far away."

"So you saw me flopping around."

"Well, I wouldn't call it flopping—"

"And you didn't comment."

"Is there anything I could have said that you'd have found helpful?"

"Fair."

He's seen her trapped inside whatever machine she was trying to construct. She's seen him fill a living room with accidental herring. Still, she gets anxious at the idea of him seeing her screw up. She shouldn't. He's not the one who lords her failures over her. Chris's exuberant flappy-handed glee can be hard to take but, apparently, that's because Ellie can't take a joke.

Ellie grips a shelf for balance, then takes one step at a time. The haze pushes back against her feet as long as she pushes against it first. There's a faint crackle with each step. The nonexistent floor feels thin and brittle, as though it would shatter if she stamped down too hard. Or, rather, her foot would push straight through. Knowing she's wrong is surprisingly unhelpful.

"You're still moving away from me."

"I'm traveling on only one axis at a time."

"Nevertheless." Daniel's tone may be drier than several deserts.

The sign on the closest bookcase hangs with a dejected cast. When she checks it, Daniel's right, of course.

Ellie browses the shelves as she walks. How the stacks are organized makes more sense as she zigzags toward Daniel. The bookcases form a gigantic hypercube. The physical structure of the stacks is practically uniform in every direction. The coordinates are a classification that narrows a document's location down to the bookcase.

The last number in the string clearly represents a date. As Ellie steps closer to Daniel, the folded planes flip by on the shelves. The architecture of her universe evolves fast enough to see. Design fads come and go. Breakdowns in the machinery are either repaired or become the new normal. Maybe it's not a surprise that a group of people who refuse to interfere in the workings of any universe have such a comprehensive record of how it has changed. Still, they have to believe in keeping their archives in good working order. Ellie has never thought to ask Chris about that.

Daniel hovers in the haze next to a bookcase. His arms hang at his sides. A vague but pleasant smile covers his face. In contrast to how he behaved in his apartment, he is now the epitome of calm and patience.

The end of her trip in sight, Ellie bounds toward Daniel. Her feet thump against the haze. Every step strikes stone as it lands.

As she sprints, it occurs to her that maybe this is what she should have been doing all along.

Ellie slams into Daniel. She throws her arms around him and hangs on to his torso. Daniel, for his part, is unmoved. Literally. He is exactly where he was before, which is surprising, and as unyielding as bronze, which isn't. The only real difference between his body and a bronze statue is that the bronze statue is colder.

"Getting around here is easier if you're heavier." Daniel's hand brushes Ellie's back. "Look, you hang on as long as you need to but, at some point, we need to get a move on."

The haze stops Ellie's feet when she stamps. Her body is crouched when she lets go. She straightens and it may be the first time she's seen the top of Daniel's head. He lifts his head to look up at her.

"Listen." Daniel's voice is even softer than his typical sand shifting on a desolate beach.

It takes the eternity of a minute before she hears it. Tiny pinpricks of sound, like fingernails skittering across glass, surround her. Daniel's head turns and his ears perk up on the first click. A few seconds later, everything's silent again.

"That clicking sound. They're looking for us." Daniel barely breaks the silence. "Letting people wander their stacks is really not something they're happy about."

"Well, lead on then." She frowns when she sees him frown. "We could go back to Ahdi and have him show us where to go."

"No." Daniel stares off in a direction that shouldn't exist.

"So you do know where you're going?"

"No, I don't." He turns back to Ellie. "I just don't want to bug Ahdi."

"Daniel." Ellie forces herself to take a deep breath. "Ahdi isn't going to think any less of you."

Ahdi wasn't the least bit surprised when Daniel flew out of his apartment. Going back to ask him to take them to the reference desk is not going to change his mind about Daniel.

"I know. But I think I should be able to find the reference desk by myself." His gaze pivots, and he looks through Ellie rather than at her. "He's probably already gone to talk to the folks who maintain the physics of the universe our skunkworks lives in anyway."

Daniel walks into Ellie. His resting puppy face shows no sign that he's about to plow through her. He takes large steps, and she doesn't have time to do more than throw her hands in front of her. Like that's helpful.

He's a step past her before her hands have stopped moving. A beat goes by before she realizes he wasn't even walking toward her. It's like passing your hand above or below a piece of paper in her own universe. If you're not seeing all three dimensions, it looks like your hand's going to hit the paper. The walking mountain has apparently navigated this many dimensions before.

"Wait." Ellie rushes after him. "Where are we going?"

"I think the entrance is over there." Daniel points in an unhelpful direction. "There should be a trail from there to the reference desk."

Daniel pushes on. It never occurs to him that he takes larger and faster steps than everyone else. Ellie jogs to keep up. In his defense, this is working better for her than walking. The haze stops her feet when she kicks and her body is pushed in Daniel's direction.

"How are you so comfortable with this?" Ellie's head spins with each step.

"Oh, Ahdi would set me on some obstacle course in some universe with a ridiculous number of dimensions."

Bookcases slide past each other, vertices of intersecting cubes that revolve through each other as they meet. They also make Ellie feel like she's spinning as she jogs. Half her footfalls hit in some direction that's almost, but not quite, down.

Daniel stops. Ellie crashes into him. It's like slamming into a slab of steel. He seems not to notice except for one reflexive arm stretched out behind him to steady her.

"Can you hang on to me for this next bit?" The expression on Daniel's face, sheepish and hangdog, is kind of epic. "It's nothing you can't do silently, but you're having issues orienting yourself in this universe, and I really don't want to get caught."

If there's anything Ellie finds frustrating, it's an apologetic Daniel. That she's dead certain he's trying his damnedest to not look like an existential ache racks his soul is bad enough. That he's failing makes it worse.

"Fine." Her tone makes it clear that while she should be insulted, she's not, but she really wants to be. "If I have to."

Daniel turns into a one-man roller coaster. Traveling on foot will get them caught, apparently, because he's gone off the habit. Instead, outstretched, he soars in graceful arcs. His every movement is gentle and smooth, slicing through the fluid haze rather than crashing into it as it seizes. The motion is utterly silent, even when the arc ends with him clinging to the backside of some bookcase.

Despite what Daniel said, he's definitely doing at least one thing she can't. Her arms are too short to span the bookcase. Daniel grabs both edges of a bookcase at once. His body is in an unreasonably stable inverted iron cross. This, of course, wedges Ellie between his body and the back of a bookcase. Just as obviously, this doesn't occur to Daniel until after he does it.

"Oh, sorry," Daniel murmurs. "I forgot you were there."

"How do you forget someone hanging on to you?"

"It's not like you weigh anything." He sounds extremely defensive.

She bites down her response. Daniel will be Daniel. In the world according to Daniel, he is the typical one. Everyone else is short and small. Nothing about him could possibly be worth pointing out. In any case, like him, she's upside down. The longer they talk, the longer she has to engage her core to avoid flopping over, and it's starting to burn.

Ellie has no idea where they're going. Bookcases revolve around her in way too many degrees of freedom. After every move, they are inevitably on top of, hanging off of, or stretched behind one bookcase or another. Daniel stops to listen. The clicks sound like they're coming from all around Ellie. They don't sound any louder or softer than before.

Someone speaks. Daniel's head snaps in the direction of the voice. Ellie recognizes the language. It's the lingua franca her mom taught her from birth. Unlike Mandarin, she can count the number of times she's used it to speak to someone she didn't know.

"This is ridiculous. You're clearly one of Ahdi's, or I would have tracked you down by now." The voice is low, hollow, and a little breathy. "Show yourself, we'll go to the reference desk, then you can go back to whatever you were researching."

A kind referral is not what Ellie expected. Chris has scared Ellie with stories about isolationists ever since she was a kid. Even if isolationists have been nothing more than convenient scapegoats for Chris, it's not like Ellie has heard anything about them from anyone else.

Ellie peers past the edge of a bookcase in the direction of Daniel's gaze. The librarian looks like a tree trunk merged onto a giant spider and is closer than she expected, only a few bookcases away. A gauzy tunic with sleeves fitted around the segment branches cover the tree-trunk-like torso. An elegant wrap surrounds the giant, spider-like lower body. Segmented legs distribute weight onto eight points against the haze. The librarian clearly has no problems staying stable and upright.

There are an infinite number of cultures. Ellie doesn't recognize the librarian's at all, although she's sure Mom must have at least mentioned it at some point. Daniel looks puzzled. Given that it's Daniel, this doesn't have to mean anything, but he probably doesn't recognize the librarian either. So much for following Daniel's lead as she had with Xu.

Looking at the librarian, Ellie decides she and Daniel are in trouble but not in any actual danger. It's not that the librarian couldn't cause some serious damage if they wanted to. The twig-like fingers radiating off the hand on each of their branches end in points as sharp as the points of their legs. They are, however, curled back, safely out of the way. The librarian's branches cross each other, and one of their legs taps the haze. They look peeved, not ready to attack.

"We're over here." Ellie ignores Daniel's glare and waves smoothly, rippling the haze.

"That close?" Their voice rises. "I should have heard you."

Ellie tugs at Daniel, and he reluctantly comes along. They emerge from one side of the bookcase, Daniel wearing his most irked face. The librarian skitters back a few steps at the sight of him.

"Of course. You." One of their tree-branch limbs points at Daniel, as though that explained everything. "A veritable silent sirocco, sweeping undetected through the archive."

Ellie's eyes dart between the librarian and a very surprised Daniel. His mouth forms a small O but he doesn't say anything.

"We've met once. Daniel is memorable in spite of themself." The librarian's gaze sweeps Daniel up and down, mostly up. "They were a bit occupied at the time so I'm not surprised they don't remember."

The lingua franca doesn't mark pronouns for gender. Sadly, the verb-tense system is ridiculously complicated. In Mandarin, Ellie had any number of conversations with her mom where Mom spent most of it correcting Ellie's measure words. When they spoke in this lingua franca, Mom corrected her verbs.

"How does everybody know you?" After some wandering, Ellie's gaze finally lands on Daniel. "Is there anybody you don't know?"

"I'm sure there's at least one, cuz." Daniel's words are surprisingly well-enunciated under the circumstances.

"Cousin." The librarian extends a branch to Ellie. "You must be Ellie, then. My condolences on your loss."

Part of her wonders how she is supposed to behave when someone built like a robust oak fused onto a giant spider extends one of their branches to you. The rest of her wonders how they know which cousin. At the funeral, Ellie couldn't have flung a floral bouquet without hitting one. A cousin that knows how to come here narrows things down a lot. Still, she's not the only one.

Daniel's eyes bulge, willing her to accept the clasp. Ellie stretches her hand out. They grasp it for a moment, their twig-like fingers gentle against Ellie's skin, then let go. Insult avoided, she hopes.

"How did you know it was me?" Ellie blurts out, in the correct language to her surprise. "Daniel might have brought Chris."

"Oh, no." The librarian brandishes their fingers, and for a moment, Ellie thinks maybe she hasn't avoided insulting them. "Chris is not welcome here. Not that Daniel would ever want to, but they know better than to bring Chris here."

Ellie tries to compose a response. Suddenly, it hits her what language she's speaking. Some things are easy until you realize what you're doing. Then it's like walking by explicitly choosing which muscles to tense, by how much and when. You fall over when if you'd simply let yourself walk, you'd at least take a few steps first.

"Oh, settle down, child." The librarian's tone is kinder than their words. "I've heard this language mangled far worse."

The librarian curls their fingers away. The cast of their bark seems friendly, at least.

"Follow me." They turn and start to leave. "Perhaps it is the reason why you are here, but you two have picked the worst time to show up."

CHAPTER 18

The librarian who found them turns out to be the Head Archivist of the isolationists' archive. This doesn't occur to Ellie until she is ushered into their office. It barely has room for the three of them and is as typical as possible under the circumstances. More than anything else, what impresses her is that they have an office.

They sit on a round stool, their legs dangling around the sides. Neat stacks of papers and folded planes sit on a table that serves as their desk. To the side is a wall of cabinets with drawers. The drawers are deeper than the cabinets but Ellie doesn't gather much more than that at a glance. Behind them, columns of pneumatic tube stretch to the ceiling and then splay out in all directions.

Ellie and Daniel are safely ensconced in comfortable chairs on the other side of the table. The chairs aren't the over-the-top creations in Ahdi's dining room, guaranteed to settle you in a position where you're simultaneously absolutely relaxed and yet still able to feed yourself. They do reconfigure, though. One of them puffs itself up to deal with Daniel's long torso and legs. Daniel forgets that he's still irked at being caught in the stacks and reverts back to being the world's biggest puppy. He eeks and claps as the chair accommodates him.

"Ellie, you're a rare duck among maintainers." The Head Archivist glares at Daniel to settle down before focusing their attention on Ellie again. "I don't know how many of them would have done what you did."

"Not very many, apparently," Ellie says. "You should have seen how many people pretended I didn't exist at my mom's funeral."

"Oh, I did. We livestreamed it." Their upper set of branches spread. "Your mother's will managed to be both quite specific and quite coy about who should set up the stream."

"And Chris let you do it?" Ellie's voice rises with disbelief despite herself. "They wouldn't even tell me when to show up."

"'Let' is putting it a bit strongly." Their smile is a secret and they pause a moment before sharing it with Ellie. "Your mother took precautions to make sure all their friends could attend."

"You knew my mom?"

"I did. We worked together for most of their life." They draw in their branches, weighing their words before they continue. "Your mother spent a lot of time researching here. Most of their work involved removing perversions maintainers installed for their own personal gain."

Ellie's brows pull up in shock. Regardless of what Chris always insists, whoever chased Mom and Ellie whenever they made changes in the skunkworks couldn't have been isolationists. Not if Mom had been here first, working out what needed to be undone. Not if the isolationists let her have access to their archives. Not if Mom insisted they witness her funeral. Chris lied about this, too.

"You shouldn't be surprised." The Head Archivist is sanguine. "There's an appalling amount of drama among the maintainers of your universe."

"Their sister takes hits out on them." Daniel blanches when Ellie glares at him and the Head Archivist twists toward him in surprise. "What? I'm not wrong."

The Head Archivist pivots back to Ellie. Unusually, their trunk seems to untwist inch by inch from bottom to top over the course of days.

"They aren't joking, are they. . . ."

Ellie slowly shakes her head. Dread traps her like a slick of sweat on a muggy day. Isolationists aren't out to kill anyone. That's obvious now. The people who chased after Ellie and her mom when they fixed the skunkworks, the ones Daniel led away while Ellie dismantled the monstrosity that kept her mom stuck between life and death, they couldn't have been isolationists. The room wobbles around her as she realizes whom Daniel must have led away: Neeson's maintainers.

Admitting that, for most of her life, she thought isolationists were stone-cold killers out to prevent changes to the skunkworks at any cost would be humiliating. This seems to be the weekend for humiliating conversations. They've gone surprisingly well so far, but the Head Archivist has to find what Ellie used to think of isolationists insulting. Maybe if she ducks and swerves she can jump off the rails of this conversation.

"Chris has this thing about keeping me on my toes."

"In case you found yourself on the wrong side of some faction of maintainers? Your sister wants to make sure you'd survive?" Their bark crinkles uncannily like a raised brow. "Chris? Even if one agrees with the highly questionable assumption that trying to kill you is the right way to go about that. Chris?"

They had that "I'm joking, but I'm really not" tone in their voice. The joke isn't that maintainers have factions. It's not even that those factions have wrong sides, or that being on the wrong side might be deadly. The joke is that Chris, who is unwelcome in this archive, would prepare Ellie for it. Or maybe the joke is on Ellie for being enough of a fool to believe whatever Chris says. Some small part of Ellie is offended on Chris's behalf anyway.

"Actually, that's a good point." Daniel screws up his face. "Who did Chris say has been out to kill you for years?"

The thing about Daniel is that no matter how much one may be tempted to punch Daniel, one knows better. At Chris's birthday a few years ago, in a volleyball game, Chris's husband hit him by accident trying to bump the ball. The poor man's arm broke against Daniel's body. He was stuck in a cast for months.

Besides, it's not like Daniel knows how insulting the answer to his question is. He doesn't deserve to be punched. Probably.

Ellie takes a deep breath. Since Daniel has caught her swerve and set her back on the rails of this conversation, she might as well get it over with.

"Isolationists." Ellie's tone concedes everything. "They used to scare me into doing what they wanted by saying that they'd sic the isolationists on me."

The Head Archivist's laugh sounds like a little kid overblowing a contrabass recorder. It squawks up and down their range, squeaking at the top and booming at the bottom. They rock back and forth on their stool, several branches clutching their desk for balance.

"What did they think we would do to *you*?" The Head Archivist manages an additional word or two between laughs, sometimes repeating them as they master themself. "Assault with a deadly question? Death by documentation?"

It's a good minute or two before they calm down. Ellie waits, not nearly as embarrassed or humiliated as she thought she'd be. Daniel keeps waving his hand, trying to interrupt, which riles them up again. Honestly, that's at least thirty seconds of their laughter by itself.

Eventually, Ellie plows on, speaking over them. Against all odds, she's going to defend Chris. There were a few years where Ellie thinks maybe Chris meant it when she said she was training her. Certainly, Ellie ended up trained. Also, Chris is her sister. Ellie feels obliged regardless of how little Chris deserves it.

"Maybe they misunderstood what isolationists do. We didn't learn much about you at school."

The Head Archivist sobers up. Their once-rippling bark hardens.

Their trunk steadies on their stool, planting pointed legs solidly on the ground.

"No, when they were younger than you are now, not only did they make unwarranted changes to your skunkworks, but they were part of a group that tried to destroy the archive. I assume they all were trying to eliminate records of the perversions they installed. However, they were quite indiscriminate. It was hardly a surgical removal of specific records." They cross a couple of their branches. "Your mother was quite beside themself."

Ellie didn't know any of this. Maybe Chris is always angry at Ellie because the perfect daughter can never be angry at her mother. Mom disapproved of Chris's work, and Chris couldn't be angry at Mom about that. It is infinitely more acceptable to be angry at Ellie instead. Maybe an angry Chris decided Ellie was Mom's favorite simply because Ellie never did anything that betrayed everything maintainers stand for, things that made Mom stop working with her. Even in Mom's final days, though, when Chris hid food from her and locked her in at night, Mom refused to say anything bad about Chris. Mom spent much of those days defending Chris as a sister, if not as a maintainer, to Ellie.

"Head Archivist?" Daniel is still waving his hand for attention. "We came here for a reason."

"Right." They relax, their fingers now interlaced and resting on the desk. "Ellie, forget your sister's lies. No one would ever deny you permission to study the abomination that trapped your mother into a living death. You didn't need to go skulking among the stacks."

"We weren't." Ellie points a thumb at Daniel. "The silent sirocco here got lost."

"That's a bit harsh." Daniel's smile undercuts his rolling eyes. "I knew where we were. I just didn't know where to go."

"Spoken like a true maintainer." The Head Archivist is utterly deadpan. "All the information we've gathered about that abomination is ready for you in a study room."

"Oh, that's not why we're here." Daniel bounces as he leans in. "Maintainers are making changes in our skunkworks right now and we need to figure out what they're doing."

"So your maintainers are at war with themselves again. That explains why we're so busy."

Ellie says "War?" at the same time Daniel says "Again?" The Head Archivist looks them both over, slowly twisting their trunk back and forth.

"You're both so . . . young." For a moment, their bark seems not only wrinkled but tattered. "You don't have to be involved in the vendettas of your elders."

"But there's a secret cabal." Daniel rumbles more than he speaks. "We need to understand their changes and probably revert them."

"Oh, I daresay there is more than one secret cabal of maintainers." Their bark crinkles in a way that's unmistakably amused. "I mean, *you're* obviously not making any changes right now."

Ellie stops herself from sighing. Maybe the reason no one talks about secret cabals is to keep smart-asses from making the obvious joke. Then again, Daniel's the one who stepped into it this time. Once she realizes that, she has to stop herself from smiling. This is probably bad, but it's not that bad. This sort of snark is wasted on Daniel. Sheer size isn't the only reason the man is a walking mountain.

"I'm a verifier. All I do is manipulate planes of air and tell people that their designs don't work." The walking mountain is predictably matter-of-fact. "I don't make changes to the skunkworks."

"Not yet." They rifle through a stack of papers and pull one out. "You're not a verifier. You're a generalist, or you will be. You're one of Ahdi's and still practically a baby. They like generalists. At the rate you're going, give it a few years."

That catches Daniel up short. He stares at his hands, as if they'll suddenly spark like Ellie's of their own will.

"Literally no one thinks all changes are good." Ellie doesn't roll her eyes but the attitude plays anyway. "And, these, we don't even know what these do yet. Right now, they don't do anything, but it can't possibly stay that way."

"And you, Ellie, do not get to be smug." The crinkle of their bark pivots toward her. "At least Daniel here has made their choice. They know who they're fetching water for."

"There's no mystery." Daniel can't help being chivalrous, no matter how much Ellie wants him to stop. "The Chief Architect asked them to look into this."

"They wanted to know who was behind the side channel," Ellie says simply. "As far as I can tell, we did it to ourselves by accident about a century ago because some of us really wanted quantum mechanics in our universe."

"Again, this is all very 'maintainer.'" The twist the Head Archivist puts on that last word could set it spinning for centuries. "I take it there's no thought of reverting quantum mechanics from your universe."

"I think that ship has sailed." Ellie can be dry, too. "Besides, it's backward compatible with the physics as it was. And the side channels are fixable. Quantum mechanics will still work without them."

Ellie is guessing. But anything Ahdi can do overnight, a crack team of maintainers has to be able to do. In a month or three.

"You don't think this secret cabal is removing those side channels?" the Head Archivist asks.

"Not according to the guy Daniel threw out their apartment window."

"This is forcing me to believe what maintainers across multiple universes say about you, Daniel." They grab a pen and start scribbling on the paper. "What does Ahdi think of you defenestrating someone?"

"I live thirty feet up." Daniel looks as though that excused everything. "The man had plenty of time to get somewhere safe."

"So it left Ahdi speechless."

"Pretty much," Ellie answers for him.

"Back to my point, Ellie." They lay a few of their hands flat on their desk. "You don't have to be part of your elders' machinations. It's not what your mother wanted. Your sister involved themself, and your mother stopped working with them entirely."

"What?" Ellie almost falls off her chair.

Daniel, for his part, remains perfectly calm. Chris would have to do something good to surprise him.

"I thought I was quite clear." They stop scribbling for a moment. "Your sister threw their lot in with Neeson, who has since become your Chief Verifier, whose perversions your mother worked tirelessly to remove. I'm not surprised that, when your mother fell ill, your sister tried to cut them off from their allies."

The first time she saw Mom sneaking out of Chris's house, it was because Amtrak was late and Ellie didn't get there until after midnight. Just as Mom had told Ellie to let Chris have her way, Mom swore Ellie to secrecy. She refused to explain why, but it wasn't like Chris would ever let Mom out unescorted. Ellie kept Mom's secret.

"I helped sneak them out at night." The words fall slowly from her as she tries out all the ways the puzzle pieces can fit together. "In their final months of consciousness, Mom needed more and more help sneaking away. I had to pick the lock to let them out of their room. Maintainers came to pick them up. They wouldn't say what for. I didn't recognize them and they didn't say who they were."

What Ellie doesn't say is that, by then, Chris, who had force-fed

Mom before chemo started, had started to starve her. Ellie secreted away food during the day to feed Mom once she was sure Chris was asleep. In the mornings, whenever Chris asked whether she heard any noises during the night, Ellie smiled sweetly and lied.

Chris took care of Mom the way she had taken care of Ellie as a kid, with an added dollop of "everyone must see how hard I'm working." That was enough to explain why Mom couldn't leave her room whenever she wanted. No schemes involving secret cabals of maintainers necessary. However, "Chris was always going to keep Mom locked up regardless" is not the slam-dunk argument Ellie needs to refute the Head Archivist.

"Your desire to help your mother is commendable." The Head Archivist reaches for and squeezes Ellie's hand. "However, they kept you in the dark. They pointedly did not tell you what they were doing. Getting involved is not something they would have wanted."

"Mom couldn't know things would turn out like this." Ellie's gaze drills through the Head Archivist. "They built some monstrosity to trap Mom in a comatose half death. With that, they exploited apparently already existing side channels in our universe to take advantage of the speculative presents where Mom survived. I didn't make any friends when I dismantled their monstrosity. And now, they're tampering with the machinery of our universe. Does that have something to do with my mom? Having uncovered this, I need to get to the bottom of it."

"Oh, Ellie. Your curiosity and insistence on the truth speaks well of you. You would have made a fine isolationist." They maintain their disappointed gaze. "The cycle could end if everyone stops."

"Look." Ellie digs the tiny cube out of a pocket. "Ahdi said to present you with this."

"I wouldn't say you didn't make *any* friends. Do you understand what it means if I accept this cube from you? Ahdi has their enemies. From now on, they'll be your enemies."

"They tortured my mom. I need to understand why."

They pluck the cube from Ellie's palm. It sparkles and glitters between their fingers. Its internal folds twist and turn and the cube shifts from gray to brown to gray again as it catches the colors of the room. The Head Archivist peers at it closely and looks resigned. They squeeze and the cube disappears.

With a sigh, they take the paper they'd been writing on, fold it into a capsule, and launch it up one of the pneumatic tubes. The capsule swooshes as it flies up and over them.

"Well, that's that then. I hope you've made the right choice, Ellie." The cast of their bark is not unkind. "Change records are streaming in as we speak. You'll have a chance to look at them as we sort and index. But, first, you are going to study the material we've collected on the abomination."

"But we need to understand what they're doing right now." Daniel's voice is an earthquake, more felt than heard.

"They have a point," Ellie follows up, having been beaten to the punch.

"Then you two had better get started. You get access to the change records once you see what you need to see about the abomination. There is a trail outside my office for you to follow." Their branches reach for and gently pat Ellie and Daniel. "Good luck. I hope that I'll see you both again. And under happier circumstances."

With that the meeting is over. Ellie and Daniel exchange glances, then set out on the trail.

CHAPTER 19

The study room is a giant wooden crate. And, apparently, alive. The floor, walls, and ceiling form one seamless rectangular bubble of wood with suspiciously flat sides and rounded corners. The room has no windows or doors. When Ellie concentrates, she feels the respiration in the wood. A slight current scatters oxygen throughout.

The monstrosity floats in the middle of the room. Not the real thing, not even a thing really. Built out of air and light, it's an artifact of the very real waist-high rectangular ring of machinery hunkered on the floor. Levers, dials, keyboards, and displays cover its beveled surface.

Daniel practically hovers over it, his eyes wide and mouth agape. He flits from one set of controls to another, twisting one and pulling at another. One might think sheer momentum would make him overshoot or trip over himself, but one would be wrong. The monstrosity breaks apart into an exploded view. Several internal switches are highlighted. One of the displays fills with text. Daniel stands in front of it and vibrates, his jaw stretched so low that his mouth could hold a hamster or medium-sized songbird.

"I've always wanted to use one of these." Daniel claps. "It's supposed to make sifting through design changes tractable."

Daniel stares intently at a display. His hand nudges a lever. Text scrolls up the display and he nods slowly. He looks dismayed and nudges the lever again.

Ellie slumps. Every second she spent dismantling that monstrosity was agony. It felt as though Mom died with every gate she removed and pipe she sealed. If she never laid eyes on it again, it would still be too soon. Daniel, however, scurries around the ring, oblivious of Ellie. They are clearly not leaving until Daniel has exercised all the bells and whistles.

Daniel's hands fly over a keyboard. The clack of keys blurs into a hum. The sections of the monstrosity fly away, leaving only one hanging in midair. It grows to fill the ring. Its switches and pumps are the sort of precise and pristine that you never see in the real skunkworks. Reservoirs fill in zero time. All the flaps open and close simultaneously and in less than an instant.

"Ellie." Daniel hits one final key and the section rearranges itself and flattens into a schematic. "Why would you build it like this?"

Out of context, what's floating in front of her could be any network of switches and reservoirs. It's also a mess. Thin pipes jogging this way and that around each other become a tangle of crisscrossing lines. Even though all the elements are idealized, the block of equations that would describe the network might take pages. These wouldn't be the most elegant equations, but give her enough time and she could write them out. Then again, so could Daniel.

"I don't know. Are you asking why it can't be coherently decomposed into reasonable-sized chunks?" Ellie's gaze passes over the schematic. "What am I looking at, anyway?"

Daniel looks pensive. He stares down at the ground for a moment. A sliver of ice appears in his hand and flips over and over as it melts.

"I think they tried to contain the changes so that they only affected Aunt Vera." He punishes his now-wet hand with an "I'm a dumbass" glare and rubs it against his jeans. "Not saying that it worked, of course."

Ellie studies the schematic again. Text around the edges annotates the input and output signals. Whoever made the annotations either has a sense of humor or thinks that names like "This almost means 'It happened on Earth'" and "State change is inside a human body or, oddly, various types of swallows" are good signal names.

"Are the annotations accurate?" Ellie walks up to a screen and keyboard. "Do we even squirrel away where things happen?"

The rules of the universe don't change based on location. Or at least they haven't. In theory, anything is possible as long as you can build the machinery for it into the skunkworks.

"Not explicitly. But it's not like stuff happens in the universe at no place in particular." He types something, runs around the ring twisting knobs and adjusting levers as he speaks. "I think this is what they tried to recover the location. Back their way into it, as it were."

The schematic dissolves, replaced by yet another mess of intertwined pipes, pumps, and reservoirs. Ellie eyes the screen next to her and nudges a lever. The mess pitches down, exposing interconnections that other pipes had hidden. It doesn't look any more elegant from this angle. She searches through the help screens and pieces together which commands she needs to type and which knobs she needs to adjust. Multiple versions of the mess now stand side by side. The differences between adjacent versions are outlined with a golden glow.

"Heh." Ellie sighs. "They were just throwing in changes, weren't they. . . ."

"Yeah. I'd like to think they did some verification first, but yeah. The thing I don't get, though." He stares at the controls in front of him, then flits from one section of the ring to another, twisting a knob here, nudging a lever there, tapping keys everywhere as he speaks. "It seems to me like this version might have kind of worked. But then the design starts to get wacky."

Ellie's gaze follows Daniel around the room. A giddy grin is plastered on his face as he races around the ring.

"Can't you control this thing standing in one place?"

"This is faster," he says as he whizzes past her.

This may even be true, if only for him. He may also be enjoying this way too much.

The multiple versions of the mess disappear, replaced by the exploded view of the most complicated version. Pipes and reservoirs disentangled and scattered across the room make the mess look simpler than it is in reality.

Ellie experiments with the levers, nudging them up and down to see what happens to the mess. The exploded view pitches, yaw, and rolls. At the same time, it zooms in and out. A switch grows to fill the room one instant and the whole mess is a sparkling dot in another. It settles down as she masters the controls. Ellie studies the mess from various perspectives, inspecting how the switches are placed and how the pipes entwine around each other.

"I'd have to work through it to be sure, but I'd be shocked if— Hold on, how do you do this?" She taps a few keys, the mess spins, she taps a few more, and the mess is flattened into a schematic with one glowing path. "I'd be shocked if, for example, we could get from this reservoir to that reservoir before its gate closes."

Gates only open for a short time but they do so on a regular cadence. It's as if the skunkworks were a rat maze with gates at the entrance and exit. The builder's goal is to design paths through the maze where a rat can enter the maze when the entrance gate opens and reach the exit by the time that gate opens. If the timing's off and the rat shows up too late, the skunkworks doesn't behave as designed. The more paths that fail timing, the less predictable the behavior.

"Why would anyone go through the trouble of building something that they have to know doesn't make timing?"

"Maybe they were counting on the rules of the universe the

skunkworks lives in changing—" Ellie's gaze falls on a screen. "There's a list of builders who put in these changes."

"Oh, right." Daniel's voice rises. "When they can see who is working on the skunkworks, they annotate that, too."

"One of them is Chris." Ellie feels empty and the words tumble from her lips. "She's responsible for some of what doesn't make sense given the physics of the skunkworks."

"Surprised" is not up to the task of describing how she feels. Even if you've suspected all along but refused to admit it to yourself, being confronted with the fact is still a shock. Part of her still doesn't want to believe Chris would torture her own mother. The rest of her can't deny it anymore.

It's one thing to owe Chris some love because she is kin. It's another thing to ignore the agony that Chris put Mom through, that Chris prolonged. Ellie can't do it. All she can see is Mom struggling to take a step, Mom doubling over in pain, Mom lying comatose on her bed.

None of this changes what Mom wanted for them. She tried so hard to keep the peace between them, but Ellie can't care what Mom wants anymore. Keeping the peace trapped Mom in a living death and exploited her as a source of speculated existences. Chris did that. She can't come back from that.

Daniel's gaze is still focused on a nearby screen. He taps a few keys and a diagram fills the screen.

"Oh. Just so." His syllables are utterly anticlimactic. "Hm. We probably should have thought to look this up before."

Ellie stares at Daniel, tears streaming. Daniel gasps when he notices. Immediately, he wraps Ellie in a hug. For a few moments, the only sound in the room is the faint whir of respiration, exchanging the air in the room.

"I'm so sorry, cuz." He slowly strokes Ellie's back. "I know you wanted to patch things up with Chris, but she's content with who she is. She's never going to admit she's wrong, she's never going to apologize, and she's never going to change."

"You're not surprised?" Ellie gently pushes him away, and wipes away her tears.

"I didn't say that." Daniel shrugs. "It's just Chris always made sure everyone knew she was doing everything possible to save Aunt Vera's life. That apparently included trying to rewrite the rules of the universe, not to mention the universe surrounding ours, if necessary. If she's involved in all of this, there's nothing like morals or norms stopping Neeson's cabal from doing whatever they want to the universe."

A piece of paper drifts down from the ceiling. Daniel's gaze follows it down as it teeters toward Ellie. She grabs it as it bobbles overhead. It's from the Head Archivist. Now that they have seen what they needed to see about Chris, Ellie and Daniel get to leave now. The Head Archivist has laid a trail to the incoming change records.

"I would have believed it if you'd just told me instead," Ellie shouts at the ceiling, but really at the Head Archivist, shaking the paper at them. "I mean, why would you lie?"

"Believe what?"

She hands Daniel the note. He mumbles to himself as he reads, then smirks.

"Didn't this knock the wind out of you like thirty seconds ago? Life moves fast." He folds the paper and stuffs it in a pocket. "Anyway, anything else about this monstrosity you wanted to study before we head off to look at change records?"

"I didn't want to study it in the first place."

She shoots him a look. He shrugs as they both dissolve.

CHAPTER 20

Pneumatic tubes fill the space above Ellie. They are an organized chaos, making the ceiling a cascade of frozen, rumpled waves. Overlapping high-pitched whines fade in and out. Whenever Ellie's attention wanders, the transfer station nestled among the tubes insinuates its way into Ellie's mind. Canisters rush in and are switched from one tube to another. One tube goes down into a station against the far wall. A couple of canisters wait in the queue.

A grid of desks fills the floor. An unlatched canister or two litter every desk. Each canister holds a change record, a tiny crystal that sparkles against each desk's slate-gray surface. Archivists sit or stand at each desk. Some of them are bipedal. A few might even commute from Ellie's universe. Assuming where anyone comes from is a bad idea. Each one pores over a change record, fills out a catalog entry, and places the change record back into the canister with the paperwork. Perversely, from here, each change record goes into an archive and a copy is immediately bounced back for Ellie and Daniel to study.

Daniel paces in a ring around the grid. As he does, he pointedly gives the archivists a wide berth. One archivist or another is always walking or rolling to the station. He never changes direction and his gait is so smooth, he might as well be gliding. Whenever an archivist approaches the station, though, Daniel always manages to be somewhere else.

Reverse-engineering a model of the cabal's revised physics

from schematics is really Daniel's bailiwick. Unfortunately, they don't have schematics. What they have is a pile of change records Ellie can compile into schematics. Parsing schematic change records is not something verifiers generally do. If she's going to do that, she might as well go straight to a model they can both analyze. So, Daniel gets to do what Daniel loves the least: nothing.

Ellie sits at a table tinkering with a folded plane of air and scribbling on a pad of paper instead of rolling her eyes at Daniel, not that she doesn't want to. Daniel on the prowl is Daniel dying to understand exactly what the archivists are doing, and it's taking every bit of restraint he can muster not to charge into the grid of desks and interrogate each and every one of them. The only way it could be more obvious is if fireworks lit "I'M DYING TO UNDERSTAND WHAT YOU DO" in bright, bold letters in the air.

A canister lands in the station against the far wall. An archivist rolls over. Daniel lengthens his stride so fluidly it doesn't look like he's sped up at all. Daniel is on the opposite side of the room by the time the archivist intersects the ring Daniel is wearing into the floor.

The archivist looks at the label on the canister and brings it to Ellie. She thanks him as she takes it. He nods with a shrug before he rolls away.

A shimmer ripples across her model as Ellie applies the change record. Her model crinkles in a way that's both subtle and disconcerting. She started her folded plane of air as an accurate enough model of the skunkworks as she knows it. After changes the cabal have made, it's fallen into the uncanny valley. Nothing lines up quite the way she expects. None of the angles are true. The way it refracts light, it unscrambles the test patterns into lines that are almost but not quite parallel. It generates almost but not quite the correct physics. The differences are so tiny that the vast majority of the time, no one would notice.

None of this is a surprise. Ahdi said as much in Daniel's apartment.

Ellie needs to work out how Neeson's cabal plan to alter the universe the skunkworks lives in. That's the only way to build a model of the skunkworks accurate enough to see what effect the changes will have on her universe. Ideally, she figures all this out before the physics that the skunkworks operates under changes. Once she understands what the cabal is doing, its changes may be easy enough to remove for now. Making changes to a skunkworks without thoroughly understanding the physics of the universe it lives in, though, is too dangerous to consider. Ellie tamps down her rising sense of panic. If she can't derive the physics that makes the cabal's changes take effect before both universes change, it may be too late for even Ahdi to do anything for either universe.

Scratched-out equations fill dozens of pages of her pad. She turns it over to a fresh sheet and starts scribbling again. She flips back a few pages, rereads what she wrote, flips ahead, and continues her scribbling. The physics the cabal's builders expect for the skunkworks' universe can't be too different from what it is now. The parameters for a universe that can sustain life as we know it are pretty narrow. Ellie hopes they aren't trying to kill all life, including themselves.

Ellie stares at the dense block of equations she's written, checking it over for anything stupid. It's probably her imagination, but she can still smell the acrid heat of attempt number five. A sign error made the physics she applied to the model unstable. Shattered fragments covered the table. Daniel pointedly continued his prowl around the librarians as though nothing happened. Her embarrassment cut deeper than if he'd made a fuss instead. At least the archivists only turned their heads for a second before returning to their work.

She applies the physics she's scribbled out to her model. Some folds straighten while new ones form. It teeters and totters and it writhes and twists. Folds that rested against the table migrate deep into the structure as new folds take their place. The model squeals. Its high-pitched whines are simultaneously faint and immediately present. Ellie stares oddly at the ever-shifting plane of air. Not that she's had a lot of experience with this, but she's never had a model behave like this before.

The room is suddenly silent. The model looks both radically changed, with sharp spikes striking out in all directions, and as though it had never moved in the first place. If the physics she came up with isn't the physics they're targeting, it must be close enough. The cabal's changes to the skunkworks have taken effect. She tries out the test patterns and all refract into unerringly parallel lines. At first glance, the physics they want is compatible with the physics they have.

Daniel sprints toward Ellie. An archivist heading toward the pneumatic-tube station is between the two. She's large, crystalline, and moves in slow, liquid steps. An unstoppable force is about to slam into an immovable object, and Ellie is dead curious about how it comes out. She starts to warn him and immediately feels stupid. It's not as if Daniel can't see the archivist in the way.

The roundoff back handspring takes Ellie by surprise. In retrospect, maybe she should have seen it coming. At first, it looks like maybe Daniel tripped, but no one trips that precisely, not even Daniel. That sets him up for the half twist and layout over the archivist. She's remarkably calm, all things considered. As Daniel sprints through his landing, she continues toward the station. Daniel's stunt blurred by so quickly, she didn't even break her cadence.

"Was that really necessary?" Ellie side-eyes Daniel as he stops at her table.

"We're in a hurry." Daniel is not out of breath. "Ahdi needs to know what they're up to."

Daniel gestures at the now-spiky plane of air, and Ellie takes a closer look. She was so relieved to find a plausible physics for the universe the skunkworks lives in that she never noticed which physics the model of the skunkworks generates. Large chunks of the machinery could have been ripped from the monstrosity Ellie dismantled. Not only did they trap Mom between life and death to exploit various side channels, they were also using her to try out the machinery they planned for the universe as a whole.

Ellie pushes all that away. There will have to be time for that later.

The new physics would work differently for different people. Her model isn't detailed enough to work out all the ramifications, but what Ellie sees is disturbing. Only certain people would get to be maintainers. It's not clear from her model who those certain people are. It would be a very tidy way for Neeson to disarm his enemies, though.

What maintainers do would only work for some people and not others no matter how hard they strove for it or how much they practiced. It'd be as though a light turned on when one person flipped the switch but never when another person flipped the same switch. Some people—no, some maintainers—would always get that favorable bounce or dodge that bullet. The universe would simply work better for them. The realization is a punch in the gut and Ellie has to catch her breath.

"This is all wrong. The systems within our universe are already unfair. We should be fixing them. Corrupting the universe makes just systems impossible. Why would you do that?"

"World domination." Daniel is utterly sober. "Bending the world to your will has to be easier if the universe itself is on your side."

"Wait, what?"

"This is overkill if your master plan is just to disrupt shoelaces as well as aglets. There are easier ways."

"They want to install themselves as a permanent overclass."

"There's more. We're going to screw over the universe our universe generates. Its skunkworks wasn't designed to function under the new physics. That's going to affect not only that universe but also the skunkworks within it and the universe it generates and so on." Daniel holds up a hand. "Changes still being filed away allow causality violations, breaking the speed of light—"

"How do you know all this?"

"Oh, I read the changes as the archivists were processing them."

Ellie stares at Daniel oddly. Daniel stares right back.

"You know how to parse schematic change records?" Ellie is annoyed Daniel never mentioned that. "I thought you were pacing in circles to stop yourself from browbeating the archivists into explaining every aspect of their work to you."

"Well, yeah. That, too." Daniel looks a little hurt. "I can multitask."

Daniel has this way of explaining things without actually explaining anything. Like how he managed to read a change record from a few dozen feet away or how he kept them all straight. Ellie doesn't bother asking. The answer is going to be some exercise Ahdi put him through.

"But you need to know the physics to understand how the machinery functions—"

"There are only so many physics families their new physics could belong to. I just tracked all the possible behaviors. Then when you figured out which physics—"

"Which you recognized from the other side of the room."

"The room's not that big. I've seen—for that matter, you've seen—Ahdi sense things from farther away. Anyway, since you figured out the physics, I knew what their changes do. Enough talk. We have to get going."

Daniel shrinks Ellie's model and stuffs it in a pocket. He then dissolves into nothingness. Ellie follows quickly in his wake. Daniel, of course, never said where they were going.

CHAPTER 21

On first glance, Daniel's living room is pretty much as they left it. The shades are open. The coffee table is now ever so slightly askew. Ahdi is gone, but now that she knows what Ahdi did to the walls, it blares in Ellie's head. At least for now.

Daniel rushes to the sofa. Belt is lying face up, his eyes glazed. Daniel kneels by his side and gently taps his face.

"Hey, Belt." Daniel's voice is a soft rumble. "How ya doing, sailor?"

Belt blinks. He shakes his head and props himself up against a sofa arm with a push.

"Well, that was a trip." Belt rolls his shoulders. "Not literally. I clearly am not going to understand this apartment well enough to get here except by Metro."

What Ahdi did was subtle and tricky. All Belt needs is someone to explain it to him.

"Belt." Daniel's face grows somber. "Who did this to you?"

"Did what to me?" Belt looks oddly at Daniel. "I'm fine."

"Tell me, slowly, what you can remember of what happened." Daniel wraps his hands around Belt's waist.

"Daniel, you're doing that thing again where you're incredibly sweet and yet somehow also incredibly annoying. We've talked about this." Belt places his hands on Daniel's shoulders. "I came to study the apartment like you texted and how Ahdi reconstructed the walls is clearly a little beyond me. You'll have to explain to me what he did."

"Daniel, he's fine." Ellie puts her hands on her waist. "It's the same sort of woozy you get after a particularly stressful oral exam."

"Really." Daniel's head turns toward Ellie, followed by the rest of his body. "How are you so sure?"

Daniel's arms are still wrapped around Belt's waist. As Daniel stands, he lifts Belt up with him. Surprisingly, Belt is unsurprised. Secure in Daniel's grasp, he quickly wraps his legs around Daniel.

"The human body is a kind of machine." Ellie's voice catches. "When I look, it's not like I can't figure out whether something's wrong. Too bad I don't know how to fix a human body."

Daniel and Belt both look at her sympathetically. Their collective gaze creates the space for Ellie to go on but only if she wants. It's the opposite of pressure. Ellie, however, shakes her head. This is not the time to talk about her mom. Even if it were, she's not sure it would be with them. She'd hoped it would be with Chris, but that ship has clearly sunk.

"So you're fine?" Daniel, dubious, turns back to Belt.

"Yes." Belt doesn't even try to hide the exasperation in his voice. "I literally got lost in my thoughts. That's all."

Daniel's gaze shifts between Belt and Ellie. He flattens his lips into a thin line before he outright frowns. Daniel's body stiffens, and he heaves several deep breaths. For a moment, he is some supernatural being bound by the chains of the laws that allow his existence. In other words, he's miffed at being wrong.

"OK." Daniel's voice is downright audible. "I'm sorry, Belt. I saw you dazed on the couch and catastrophized."

"Don't worry about it." Belt sighs. "But you can set me down at any time."

Daniel's eyebrows leap up. It has finally occurred to him that he's carrying his boyfriend.

"Oh, sorry." Daniel sets Belt upright on the floor the way one might a soap bubble. "It's not like you weigh anything."

Daniel doesn't need an excuse for himself, but it sounds like he's making one. Ellie and Belt share a look of mutual recognition. Daniel will endure any number of jabs from, say, the Chief Architect, but a casual comment from Ellie or Belt gets his back up.

"Daniel, it's fine." Belt is the epitome of warmth and calm. "You're just being your inexplicably lovable self."

"Belt." Ellie notices a note on the coffee table. "Was anyone here when you got here?"

"No." Belt keeps glaring warily at a spot next to the TV. "I assume Ahdi was here at some point, but he was gone by the time I showed up."

Daniel walks across the room to where Belt is staring. He places a palm on the wall next to the TV.

Ellie picks up the note. It's from Ahdi. His handwriting is exactly what she expected: precise, elegant, and like nothing she'd ever seen before. The form is so breathtaking that it feels like continents have drifted, reunited, and drifted again before she acclimates and can even see the text as words.

"Oh." Daniel smites his forehead. "Ahdi left a trail."

"Are you sure it's Ahdi?" Ellie is still staring at the note.

"Yup." Daniel gestures at the wall. "Study it for yourself."

"Here, read this." Ellie hands him the note.

"Seriously?" Daniel is beside himself. "Why would he set up a trail for us to follow and leave us a note telling us not to look for him?"

The trail presents itself to Ellie right away. Daniel is right, of course. It's too neat and precise to be laid by anyone else. Wherever it ends, the trail seems to start in the middle of a wall stud. It curves immediately through some other universe, and Ellie would have to follow to know where. On first glance, it could be a feature of the wall. That it can send someone who doesn't quite have the hang of it yet spiraling into a mental fugue isn't all that surprising. As usual, Ellie admires the precision. It has to be this precise or it'd be useless.

"At least he won't be hard to find."

Daniel purses his lips. He looks down at the note.

"Maybe we should send him a text and wait for him to get back to us?"

"Daniel." Ellie folds her arms across her chest. "You're the one who's in a hurry to find him."

"I know but he said . . ." Daniel shrugs and points at the note.

Ellie's phone buzzes. It's a text from Chris. Ellie's not reading it now, maybe not ever.

"Would someone like to clue me in?" Belt waves at them as though the other side of the room were an ocean away.

"Oh, sorry." Ellie lets her arms fall. "Some secret cabal of maintainers—"

"You mean, like you and Daniel?" Belt at least tries to hide the smirk.

"Some *other* secret cabal of maintainers." In her mind, Ellie is shooting useless virtual daggers at Belt. "Is making dangerous changes to the skunkworks—"

"Different laws of physics depending on who you are. Causality violations," Daniel interjects.

"—and we're not absolutely certain who's behind it but it's probably not Ahdi." Ellie sighs. "If it were, we probably wouldn't have detected signs of it in the first place. Not to mention, if it were Ahdi, he'd probably be done by now and the new physics would be in effect."

For a few seconds, the room is silent. The three just stand there, staring at each other.

"So why are you still here?" Belt opens his palms.

"Yes, Daniel, why are we still here?" Ellie turns to him.

"Ahdi has to have a good reason to keep us away."

"Fine." Ellie turns her focus back to the wall. "You stay. I'll go."

"No." Daniel is practically inaudible, but the room vibrates in sympathy.

Belt's mouth forms a small O and he takes an involuntary step back. Ellie rolls her eyes.

Ellie's phone buzzes again. This time, the notification on its screen stops Ellie cold. The text is from Chris and starts with "I'm sorry." Ellie's heart pounds and races. She's in uncharted territory. Chris has never apologized to her before. Not for anything, not even in jest or as a prank.

She unlocks her phone and reads the text. It's a paragraph long and everything Ellie has been afraid to hope for. Chris admits to trying to kill her, to torturing and gaslighting both her and Mom, especially the past couple of years, to nurturing her resentment because she wanted to show Mom and Dad that she was a better daughter than Ellie. Chris says outright she was wrong and apologizes for making Ellie's life horrible. Mom is gone, and Ellie is the only one left. Chris doesn't want to lose Ellie. She wants Ellie to come over right now so that she can make amends.

"I can't believe this." Ellie hands her phone to Daniel. "She did it. She finally admitted she was wrong and apologized."

Relief floods Ellie's body. It feels like she's soaring through the air. Cool, clean wind washes across her and every bit of tension and stress drains from her. Chris has been relentless for decades and, now, not only has Ellie been right about all of it, but it's over. Or at least it can be, she decides when her brain kicks back in. Chris's apology is just the first step toward the door Ellie has left open for her all these years. Perhaps, eventually, Chris will finally walk through, and they can have some approximation of a normal relationship between two sisters and what Mom always demanded will be satisfied in a way that Ellie can bear.

"You realize it's a trap." Daniel's tone is friendly but flat. "This is the person who laughed at my suicide attempt when I was a kid. She was a cruel teenager, she became a cruel adult, and she'll be cruel until the day she dies."

Ellie is caught dumb for a moment. Daniel has never mentioned this before. Even Belt looks stunned.

"Your . . . suicide attempt?" Ellie treads carefully.

"You try living as a gay boy with my parents sometime. Sure, it wasn't a very good attempt, but I didn't deserve to be mocked. She was sarcastic and disdainful, laughing as she taunted me to try again. I'll never forget it." Daniel is completely casual about all of this. "After I met Ahdi, I told him about her, who told Aunt Vera, who couldn't believe him, just like she couldn't believe you."

Belt tries to hug Daniel, but he steps out of the way and waves Belt off. He doesn't want to be hugged at the moment.

"I'm so sorry, Daniel." Ellie struggles for words that are at least adequate. "I had no idea."

"Of course not." Daniel is warm and kind. He hands her phone back. "You were like six. No one should have told you."

"It's like I said, though. Mom's dead, and she no longer feels the pressure to be the best daughter."

"Who texts their sincere, heartfelt apology?" Daniel puts his arm around Belt's waist. "At least make the phone call."

"He has a point." Belt stretches his arm across Daniel's back. "And if she really is sorry, there's no reason to tell you to come over right now."

Daniel looks oddly at Belt for a moment. His eyes widen and his jaw drops. He disentangles himself from Belt, sits down, and studies the note.

"Ahdi always explains himself. Sometimes to a fault. So I can decide for myself." Daniel stands, folds the note into quarters, then slides it into a pocket. "I don't think he wrote this. I mean, it's his handwriting but it's not his writing. I don't think he's the one who doesn't want us to go to him."

Ellie can't not hold on to the hope that Chris is finally ready to be her sister. Still, Belt is right. The Chris who has changed will wait.

"Then why *are* we still here?"

Daniel waves goodbye to his boyfriend, then throws himself at the wall. Rather than bouncing off or, more likely, crashing through the wall, he melts into it.

"OK, that's a lot." Belt whistles. "I am never doing that."

"The last time he left here, he threw himself out the window." Ellie shrugs. "See you later, Belt."

Ellie does not aim for the wall. She dissolves into the air, like a normal person.

CHAPTER 22

As Ellie falls to the floor of Neeson's office, a few thoughts blur through her mind. Who would end a trail twelve feet off the ground? Actually, she knows who. How does someone end a trail twelve feet off the ground? It's one thing if you haven't gotten it completely together and you have problems with reentry. It's another if you're Ahdi, who has it several orders of magnitude more together than most maintainers if not all of them. That leaves Ellie's last thought in less than six feet of falling. Why would someone end a trail twelve feet off the ground?

Daniel is right below her. He crashes into Neeson from above. This has the effect that one might expect when a mountain materializes in midair and gravity does its thing. The victim crumples like a beer can.

"Daniel, keep him down!" Ahdi shouts from the other side of the room. "I'll explain in a moment."

Ellie rolls off of Daniel and lands crouched on all fours next to him. Neeson struggles in vain beneath Daniel, who is way more diligent than he needs to be. His hold on Neeson is never going to break, but Daniel screws up his face and keeps his body taut as though if only he can maintain control until the end of the period, he can beat the world champion in Greco-Roman wrestling on points. From his dedication, one might think it's a challenge to keep Neeson under control. One would be wrong. His casual easy breaths are a dead giveaway.

"Ellie, I have to make some changes to the structures of this office." Ahdi points at the door. "Meanwhile, I need you to stop anyone from coming in. If you can do that without killing them, that would be preferable."

Ellie's not sure whether that last sentence says more about Ahdi, what Ahdi thinks of her, or what she has gotten herself into. Nevertheless, now's not the time to figure that out. The commotion of two maintainers falling to the ground has alerted whoever is on the other side of the door. Footfalls pound. Loud words fall over each other. Some sort of high-pitched whine floats above all that.

A nickel coating makes the door and the jamb promising enough to look into. Just as Ellie hoped, every once in a while Neeson also needs the door barricaded for his own reasons. Underneath the nickel coating, two layers of rare earth alloy lie in concentric rectangles, one surrounding the door, the other surrounding the jamb. It'd only take a nudge to turn the alloy into a magnetic one. Neeson had a door installed here that one of his minions can stick shut.

Ellie lurches past Daniel. Her hands slap the door. That's close enough for her to give the alloy the push it needs to become magnetic. The door binds to the jamb. The footfalls stop. The door rattles or at least it tries to. It also muffles the swearing from the other side. Someone pounds on the door but the sound is more of a dull thud than the splinter of wood. There's every possibility that the door will hold for a bit. Hopefully, whichever builder Neeson normally keeps around to bind and unbind the door is busy in the skunkworks wrecking physics. Either way, they'll still have to track that builder down and that might take a minute or three.

"OK, I figure we have a few minutes." Ellie leans against the door. "Ahdi, what is going on?"

Ahdi leans against a desk on the other side of the room. His thick, meaty arms are folded against his chest. He smiles pleasantly, waiting. The silent countdown running in his head becomes obvious when it reaches zero and he nods.

The changes to the structure of the office explode in Ellie's mind. She slumps to a sit, still pressing against the door. Ahdi has manipulated the curled-up dimensions beyond the third but only within the walls. Ellie makes a mental note to ask him what he's done and how at some appropriate time, which is not now. Daniel still has Neeson crushed under him. The former still looks determined and utterly unaffected. The latter spasms for a moment, for all the good it does him.

"Everyone OK?" Ahdi smiles when Ellie and Daniel both nod. "Excellent. You two have helped me win a bet I made with the honorable Mr. Neeson here."

The honorable Mr. Neeson grunts. Daniel shifts his weight and pulls a note out of his pocket.

"Did you write this?" Daniel shows Ahdi the note with one hand, while he keeps Neeson down with the other. "It's your handwriting."

"Some alternate version of me did." Ahdi stares at Neeson. "One of the side channels lets you fish out artifacts that might have existed. The honorable Mr. Neeson fished it out. I bet you two would show up anyway."

Daniel turns Neeson's head around. Neeson, wary, stares at Daniel.

"Can you retrieve anything?" Daniel's face is bright with anticipation. "Like, say, a complete original-cast recording of *Follies* or *The Golden Apple*, the latter with the correct ending, of course. Or, even better, *Shuffle Along, or, the Making of the Musical Sensation of 1921 and All That Followed*."

"Daniel!" Ahdi and Ellie both shout at the same time.

"They would be historically invaluable." Daniel's gaze both doubles down and pleads with the both of them. "It's not like I would actually accept it."

"Your sister's apology is not counterfactual," Neeson chokes out. "Meeting with her now was my idea. She will wait until you're willing."

"We could have shown up in the other order," Ellie says to Ahdi, ignoring both Daniel and Neeson.

"Then you'd be keeping the honorable Mr. Neeson occupied and Daniel would be keeping people from coming in." Ahdi rubs his hands. "Now, either we can take this office apart or the honorable Mr. Neeson can honor the terms of the bet and tell us where the images are."

The honorable Mr. Neeson grunts again. One of his arms flails at a spot on a wall. A hidden hinge becomes obvious once Neeson points it out. Taking in the room, Ellie realizes the office is a maze of secret compartments within secret compartments and portals to container universes. The smug smile on Neeson's face dares Ahdi to try to find the images.

What Ahdi does next reminds Ellie of a not-a-trick she saw a master at sleight of hand do once, goofing around. The magician covered a ball with a cup, pointed at the cup, then removed the cup, revealing the ball. It looked like she hadn't done any sleight of hand at all. She repeated the not-a-trick, more obviously, breaking down the steps. The ball was never under the cup. She palmed it as she set the cup down. As she picked up the cup, she set the ball on the table. It was a lot of sleight of hand for something that looked like no sleight of hand at all.

Ahdi goes to the wall, opens the secret compartment, and takes out a bunch of crystals. He drops them into his shirt pocket. It looks like all he did was pull open a drawer, but what he did was a nontrivial amount of understated pyrotechnics. The difference between this and the cup-and-ball not-a-trick is that the understated pyrotechnics was necessary. Without it, there would be no drawer to open in the first place.

Neeson grimaces and makes another attempt to lurch free that never stood a chance. Daniel looks both diligent and bored. Whatever he does to stop Neeson is barely a shift in weight or the slight tensing of a muscle.

"Do you have documentation of the changes his associates made to the skunkworks?" Ahdi asks.

Daniel fishes the tiny crystal he made of Ellie's work at the archive from yet another pocket. He holds it out and Ellie hands it to Ahdi, who nods slowly as he studies it.

"Excellent." Ahdi pointedly catches Ellie's gaze. "Good job, both of you."

"Now can you tell us what's going on?" Ellie asks.

"The honorable Mr. Neeson here is blackmailing the good folks who maintain the physics of the universe our skunkworks lives in." Ahdi gestures to the crystals in his shirt pocket. "Or rather was. If he doesn't have his builders revert their changes to our skunkworks, I'll make it known who's responsible for them."

Ahdi shows Neeson the evidence in his hand. It lingers for a bit in front of Neeson's face so Neeson can sense what Ahdi has. Ahdi flashes a quick smile before he puts the crystal in a pant pocket.

"Blackmail. Not exactly respectable, is it?" Neeson ekes out the hypocrisy.

"Oh, please. You all slayed me with the respectability silver bullet years ago. If nothing comes to light, everyone will think I was behind these shenanigans in the skunkworks instead." Ahdi turns his attention back to Ellie and Daniel. "My advice to you two is leave this office as soon as possible. The folks who can unwedge that door will arrive sooner or later. The honorable Mr. Neeson won't lay a hand on either of you. Others may not be so restrained. Now, if you'll excuse me, I have some evidence to return."

Ahdi nods to Ellie then to Daniel. There's a twinkle in his eyes Ellie thinks may be metaphorical. It's the last bit of him that disappears, though, when he dissolves.

"Well, that's that, I guess." Daniel lifts his head toward Ellie.

"Say, are you hungry? We haven't eaten all day. How do you feel about Ethiopian?"

"Sure." Ellie shrugs. "I should go see Chris, though. Get that apology that's been decades in the making in person."

Daniel starts to speak, but stops. He looks down at Neeson.

"Excuse me." Daniel renews his grip on Neeson. "You don't get to listen to this conversation."

A blindfold materializes around Neeson's head, blocking his eyes. Clear putty blocks his ears. That Daniel has this move at the ready makes Ellie wonder exactly how Ahdi has been training him. He examines his work and pronounces the blindfold and earplugs good before he starts speaking again.

"I told you, Ellie. It's a trap. She doesn't mean any of it." It should sound rude but, coming from Daniel, it doesn't.

"I told her that the next time she wanted to talk to me, she should text me like a normal person. Not only did she do that, but she apologized. Before I write her off for good, I have to check."

"One shouldn't enter a trap on an empty stomach. At least eat first. I'll come with."

"Yeah. Let's do that."

A sense of contentment settles on Ellie. It would have never occurred to her to ask. He offered, though. Having him along to deal with Chris feels right.

The blindfold and earplugs disappear. Daniel, however, doesn't move.

"About time." Neeson manages to sound entitled even while squashed. "Have a good chat?"

Daniel doesn't react. He merely maintains his effortless, unbreakable hold on Neeson. Ellie doesn't answer either. Neeson shouldn't have the chance to warn Chris that Daniel is coming with her, just in case. Neeson summons up an impressive amount of imperiousness as he continues on.

"True, he didn't say it explicitly, but I believe your boss implied that you could let me go."

"If you don't mind"—Daniel's voice is its usual soft but unusually polite—"I'd feel better if I hang on to you until we leave."

The door starts to splinter. The folks on the other side have apparently given up on finding someone to undo the magnetic lock.

Ellie and Daniel exchange glances. Daniel lets go of Neeson and dissolves. Ellie follows. She nudges the rare earth alloys in the door and jamb back to their original nonmagnetic forms first, though. No sense in leaving the door locked.

CHAPTER 23

Ellie unlocks Chris's front door. As she steps through, the emptiness and chill slams into her again as if it were the first time. That same sense that something has been ripped away and can never be replaced still screams in her mind. Maybe the house will warm again over time, maybe she'll get used to the insatiable void, or maybe this is how Chris's house will always be for her now.

Chris's hug is an ambush, one that Ellie notices in the nick of time and chooses not to avoid. Ellie meets Chris's open arms with open arms of her own. They hug and, in the end, the hug is only a hug. There isn't a secret shiv that Chris slices into Ellie's back or a takedown that leaves Ellie flat on her back with Chris in full control of her body. Ellie was prepared for both possibilities and a dozen more. Old habits die hard.

"You're here. I can't believe you came." Chris gives Ellie one last squeeze before letting go. "I'm so sorry for everything. It was all my fault. Let's forget the past and start over from scratch."

Daniel follows Ellie in. Chris registers his existence. Something unreadable flickers across her face before she ambushes him, too, for a hug. Daniel avoids it, dodging Chris's grasp with a stumble too precise to be convincing. She doesn't try again.

"I'm sorry to you, too." Chris offers a hand, which is not accepted. "I've been awful to you over the years, and you didn't deserve any of it. If you can't put any of that behind you yet, I understand."

Daniel remains silent. A vague, genial smile rests easily on his face. He looks completely relaxed, but Ellie is certain that one aggressive move from Chris, and she'll be unconscious and slumped to the floor before Ellie can blink.

"Come on, you two." Chris walks toward her office door. "There's something I want you to see. I've been working on it for weeks."

The door handle glints the instant before Chris twists it. It glints again as she pushes the door open. Chris never carries a key. She always extrudes the correct one from the air when she needs it and then makes it go away when she's done. As a reflex, Ellie feels her pockets for the keys to her apartment and lab at school. She doesn't even need them right now.

Chris's office is as cold as a morgue and nothing like what it was the last time Ellie was here. Back then, it looked like an office, if not a usable one. A desk was pushed to one wall, a row of file cabinets to the opposite wall. The bookcases were always against the third wall. The shades were drawn on the window that lined the fourth because who needed anything as useless as light. A computer, a small trash can, piles of papers, and piles of books cluttered the desk. All this was to make room for the daybed that Mom lay on for most of her coma. There was just enough room around the bed for two people to stand on either side and reposition Mom every couple of hours.

All of that is gone. The room shimmers. The desk, the daybed, and everything else in the room have all been broken down into their raw materials and transformed. The contraption that now occupies the office is an empty box that stretches from ceiling to floor, hugs the walls, and blots the windows. A coffin stands open in the middle of the room. It has its own fair share of almost invisibly small gadgetry. Tendrils connect it to the machinery in the walls on all sides. They trap it taut like a fly in a spiderweb. The near-microscopic machinery is dazzling and Ellie has no idea what any of it does. It involves structures she has never seen before. Some of the machinery seems designed to function in a physics nearly but not exactly the same as the physics Ellie derived from the isolationists' change records. The irrefutable confirmation makes Ellie's stomach sink. The only people who knew ahead of time what the new physics would be were Neeson's cabal of maintainers.

The door shuts behind them and disappears. The rest of the world is gone. It feels like this room is the entire universe. Nothing exists on the other side of the walls.

Chris folds her arms. The disapproving frown reappears on her face. The gash it reopens in Ellie's heart never really closed in the first place. That for a minute, Ellie saw the Chris she hoped for is now a retractor that tears and keeps the wound open. Her frown is never a sharp frown. If it were, it might slice right through. The blood would seep but the wound would be clean and she might not even feel it until it was too late. Instead, Chris's frown is always dulled. The lips are set just so. The brows are furrowed but not too furrowed. The arms are taut but not tense. The gaze is always focused a little past Ellie. It's aimed at Ellie but refuses to admit she exists. The dulled frown rips and tears as it hacks through Ellie. It always has and always will.

"It would have been easier if you'd shown up next week like I told you to, Ellie. You made me work nonstop to get this done in time. I've spent all day today making the final adjustments." Chris gestures at Ellie to go into the coffin. "I've sacrificed myself for Mom and, Ellie, it is, at long last, finally time for you to do the same."

Chris closes in. She reaches for Ellie.

"What are you talking about?" Ellie shakes off Chris's grasp and backs away from both Chris and the coffin.

"The rules of this universe have changed. I can violate causality." Chris's gaze shifts for a moment to the ring on her hand. "This holds everything I need to re-create the Mom I know and love, except the body of one of her direct descendants."

The diamond ring glints against the room's shimmer. Ellie studies the diamond. Its facets and internal structure are folded and twisted like the planes of air Daniel constructs. Mom really did give Chris the ring. It's just some alternate version of Mom from a universe that might have existed but didn't. That's who Chris wants. If Ellie makes it out of this house alive, she's never coming back.

"No, we got Neeson to revert the changes and stop blackmailing the maintainers one universe out." Ellie dodges Chris's lunge for her. "The physics of this universe has not changed and is not going to change."

"Chris." Daniel waves his hand to get her attention. "Aunt Vera's dead. You can't bring her back. Let her go."

Filaments dart out. They wrap themselves around Daniel and bind him to the wall. Daniel strains against them. His body puffs up but the more he pushes against them, the thicker they grow and the tighter they bind. The filaments, now thick cords, fray a little as they squeeze his chest, but they don't break. A restraint Daniel doesn't break out of with an easy shrug must be a new experience for him.

Ellie gapes. Only Chris's words sawing through her brings her back.

"You're lying." Chris points to Daniel. "If you don't get into the coffin, I'll let the wall crush Daniel."

"If I'm in the coffin, how am I supposed to know whether you've freed him?"

"You don't trust your own sister?" Chris sounds righteously aggrieved. "And don't count on Ahdi to help you. Even if he's still a maintainer, the machinery in the wall is constantly reconfiguring the room. He's not showing up without killing Daniel first. No one, not even Ahdi, gets in or out of this room."

Ahdi hadn't occurred to Ellie at all until now. Maybe he would show up to help. It says something that Chris figured this out before Ellie. The Head Archivist implied that Ellie had made at least one friend. The realization that the Head Archivist was right is useless at the moment but still heartening. She'll keep it in mind for the future if she makes it out alive.

Ellie's gaze shifts between Daniel and the coffin. He's stopped struggling for the moment. His face twists with a nuclear rage and anger she's never seen in him. In that instant, she understands why almost everyone else is afraid of him. Heaven help Chris if he ever breaks free. Or maybe Ellie herself if she goes into the coffin. She can't tell which. Maybe both.

Ellie is so tired of someone being angry at her for no reason that she just doesn't care anymore. What pops into her mind is something her driver's ed instructor told her. When faced with more than one danger, try to separate them and deal with them one at a time. Daniel's rage can wait.

Even with Daniel, motionless, strapped against the wall, the cords continue to tighten. Chris is going to let the wall slowly crush Daniel until he suffocates. Nothing says she has to stay in the coffin.

"Fine." She goes into the coffin.

"No!" Daniel shouts, if a choked rumble counts as shouting.

Chris slams the coffin shut. Ellie straightens. A dizzying array of machinery smothers her. The sheer density forces the tiny spinning gears and flapping gates into her consciousness. A few seconds pass before she realizes that she's trapped in a dark, cramped space with no airflow. Chris needs the body of a direct descendant, but it doesn't have to be a live body. In fact, dead may be better. Chris may have meant to keep Ellie on her toes at first, but she changed her mind long before Mom got sick. All the times Ellie escaped death must have been frustrating as hell for her murderous sister. Of course, Ellie is now slowly suffocating in a coffin in Chris's office, so who's really gotten the last laugh? She throws that unhelpful thought away and focuses on the task at hand, freeing herself.

Ellie pushes against the coffin lid. Locked, of course. She probes the machinery. In theory, she can find the mechanism trapping her and reengineer it to pop the lid. In practice, she'll run out of air before she even finds the lock. There's a better way to spend her remaining time alive. If nothing else, at least she'll finally get some things off her chest.

"All my life, Chris." Ellie struggles for breath. "Your standards for me have always been way higher than your standards for yourself."

"That's not true. I was the one who took care of Mom while you loafed around in Boston. You could have quit grad school."

"I made all the arrangements to transfer to George Mason and do research at night and weekends. I was all set to throw years of work away and start over before you decided that wasn't enough for you." Ellie pants and struggles to push out a few more words. "What did you do?"

Chris has a tech job. With the right infrastructure, she could have done it from the moon. While Mom was still alive, she worked nights and weekends, exactly what Ellie proposed for herself. She saw this with her own eyes every weekend and every school break. Not that she expects Chris to admit now that what she didn't think was enough sacrifice for Ellie was plenty enough for herself.

"I'm going to save Mom. You killed her."

"Do you seriously think that perverting the physics of this universe is something Mom wants?" The air is thick and Ellie wheezes. "Chris, Mom's dead. You have to let her go. Are you doing this for her or for you?"

"How dare you even think that?" Chris's condescension is even thicker than the air. "I've never done anything for myself. It's all been for Mom. This is the literal only thing I have ever asked you to do for her, and you have the nerve to complain."

"Please, I saw you at the reception. The praise and adulation was off the charts. You've spent years making sure that everyone knows you're the 'good daughter.' You didn't let me help, didn't let Daniel help, because if we helped, you'd lose out on chances to show how fucking dutiful you are."

Ellie gasps for oxygen that is barely there. The coffin starts to sway and spin as suffocation starts to set in. She spends three seconds thinking about cutting her way out. Unfortunately, sparks from her hands would excite the air. Oxygen atoms would split off and combine with each other. The by-product, unfortunately, would be carbon monoxide.

"I *am* the good daughter. Mom realized that I have been doing my filial duty all along, eventually, and gave me her ring." Chris's voice drills through the coffin. "Everything I'm doing, I'm doing for Mom, because I love her. You would go quietly, if you loved her, too."

Ellie is really sick of hearing Chris talk about how much she loves Mom and how much Ellie doesn't. That the Mom she loves isn't even the Mom that existed is galling. The diamond ring isn't supposed to exist. Just like the note Ahdi didn't write. Just as Mom never led Tom to Daniel's apartment. At least she won't have to deal with Chris for much longer.

"No, you don't love Mom. You don't want Mom back." Ellie has very little air left. She might as well go out in a blaze of glory. "You want the Mom-shaped monster who thinks perverting physics is a good thing, the one who likes the ways you're corrupting the skunkworks, the one who kept working with you when you tried to destroy the isolationists' archive."

"Don't be ridiculous!" Chris sounds so angry that Ellie is positive that she's right. "Mom stopped working with me because of you."

Ellie hears a high hiss from outside the coffin. A miniature beam of focused light makes tiny incisions in the coffin. The machinery changes around Ellie. The coffin creaks and groans as gears morph into gates and vice versa. They swirl around her and settle into a new configuration. Whatever this machine was meant to do, it's now going to do something similar but different.

The coffin clicks. The lid flips open. Ellie doubles over and takes a deep breath. When she straightens up, a stone-faced Chris glares at her.

"You don't deserve to sacrifice yourself for Mom." Chris pulls Ellie out of the coffin and substitutes herself inside. "I'll show you who really loves Mom. There's nothing *I* wouldn't do to save her life."

Chris slams the lid shut. Ellie feels the coffin for seams. There must have been at least one but now the surface is perfectly smooth. She can just make out the remnants of the reactions that bonded the lid to the rest of the coffin.

"Don't worry. Mom will be back just as you remember her," Chris shouts through the coffin. "She will have to live with the fact that I was the one who fulfilled the filial obligations we owe her. She will hate being back, and it will all be your fault. She will know you shirked your duty and hate you like she hates me."

Ellie has no idea whether Chris has even one redeeming quality, but Ellie doesn't want to be responsible for anyone's death, even Chris's. If Ellie were vindictive, she'd also say that Chris doesn't get to escape. Chris has to live with the mess she's creating.

"No. Chris, let yourself out." Ellie pounds on the coffin. "Physics hasn't changed. You can't bring her back. All you can do is accept that she's gone."

Ellie takes a step back. The coffin is still a confusing maze of machinery. She's not sure what it's doing but it's doing something. Probably not to Chris, except suffocating her. But that's what happens when you lock yourself into a box with no vents.

Something cracks behind her. It sounds like someone making popcorn down the hall in the kitchen.

"Ellie." How Daniel looms behind Ellie is palpable. "Anything I can help with?"

Ellie looks back at Daniel, who is pleasantly, if incongruously, calm and attentive. His T-shirt is ripped. Scratches run across his arms and chest. He either hasn't noticed or doesn't care.

"Yes, you'll do." Ellie points up at the coffin. "Can you lift me to the top of the coffin?"

Daniel looks at her as though the answer should be obvious. He puts his hands on her waist. An instant later, she is looking down at the coffin.

A thin tendril of fire darts from her index finger. One by one, she drills thin tunnels into the coffin. To reach the empty space inside, they have to twist and bend around the active machinery. She still has no clue what any of it does or what might happen if she nicked any of it.

A dense matrix of tunnels now covers the top of the coffin. It's still going to be too hot and stuffy, but Chris will have oxygen. Ideally, something should actively exchange the air. Designing anything, though, has never been her strong suit. She's always been much better at taking other people's designs and making them buildable.

"OK, I'm done. Thanks." Ellie studies Daniel after he sets her down. "How are you even here? Did Chris actually free you?"

Daniel's jaw drops. Astonished, for a moment, he stares dumbly at Ellie.

"Have you *met* your sister?" Daniel places a hand on her shoulder. "Ellie, I'm a verifier. Finding failure modes is what I do. I freed myself."

Chris is listening to all of this. The realization hits Ellie, and she expects to feel awful, but she doesn't. Let Chris hear. Let her know how her horrifying plan has gone wrong.

"So what did Chris do wrong?"

"It's a pretty shallow bug, really." Daniel's face brightens at the idea of having to explain something. "Whatever force I used against the cords, they responded with a multiple. So, when I rested up a bit and exerted hard enough, they attempted a response that exceeded the tensile strength of the materials they're made of and the cords shattered."

Ellie eyes him skeptically. Daniel is either bragging or being humble to a fault. She can't tell which.

"So, what you're saying is that the cords weren't strong enough to hold you."

"That's such a limited way of looking at it." Daniel laughs. "Besides, I didn't break the cords. They broke themselves."

"That is, at best, a technicality."

"Ellie." Daniel's face grows serious. "I need you to repeat these words: 'His life means nothing to me.' When someone tells you to do something or else I'll be crushed or whatever, the right response is always 'His life means nothing to me.' OK?"

Ahdi appears behind Daniel. As usual, he should have displaced air and made a noise but didn't. Despite whatever Chris did to stop him, whether he's supposed to be able to show up here at all is apparently a mere technicality. Maybe he's just that good, or Daniel broke the machinery reconfiguring the room when he broke free, or that machinery would have worked correctly only if physics had changed, or maybe Chris flat-out lied. Honestly, it could be any, some, or all of those things, and even if Ellie exhaustively examined the machinery, she doubts she'd ever truly know which.

"You've saved yourselves. Excellent." Ahdi beams with approval. "When I realized what some of the side effects of the changes to the skunkworks were going to be, I figured I should at least try to find my way in."

"We're OK. Chris, on the other hand . . ." Ellie points to the coffin. "I don't think I can get her out."

Ahdi's gaze shifts to the coffin. He walks around it, weaving over and under the cables that link it to the walls.

"Impressive." Ahdi nods with satisfaction. "Had the rules of the universe changed, this might have brought Vera back."

Chris's sobs fill the room. They are raw, harsh waves that overwhelm Ellie, threatening to pull her under. Finally accepting that your mother is dead is awful. Ellie ought to know.

Mom always loved Chris, but she never showed it in a way Chris could recognize. For Chris, maybe the desperation to see that love distorted the filial piety anyone would expect from their children into something monstrous. Chris had almost got a Mom who would show her love in a way that Chris could see. Now, she never will.

Trading Ellie's own life for Mom's has an elegant simplicity that Ellie can't help but find appealing. Mom would be alive again. Chris might, for once, be happy with Ellie. True, Ellie herself would be dead, but frankly that might be the only way Chris can be happy with Ellie. Not exactly the way the relationship between sisters should go, but perhaps the only way this one can.

It hurts that Mom is dead, but Ellie's not sorry that Mom's not back. Mom spent her life stopping maintainers from perverting the universe. Doing exactly that to bring her back is, at best, ironic, at worst, corrupt. The Mom Ellie knew would not want to be alive again and her rage at being yanked back would brand fear on everyone responsible. Or, worse, Chris might have brought back some Mom-shaped monster. She'd work to pervert the universe more rather than work to stop it.

From the depths, Ellie rises until she only skims the waves of Chris's grief. When Chris makes it to shore—if Chris makes it to shore—maybe she can take some comfort, solace, or whatever she needs to deal from the fact that she was willing to sacrifice her life for Mom and Ellie was not. In any case, Ellie's done trying and failing to navigate these waters.

"Get out," Chris manages between sobs. "Go hide in Boston, Ellie, and don't ever come back."

The three exchange glances. Ahdi makes the lid seam reappear on the coffin. Chris, however, remains in the coffin and continues to cry. Ahdi restores the door into the room. It's an infinity before anyone manages a word.

"When do you leave, Ellie?" Ahdi's tone is kind and gentle. "I'll see you off."

"The Amtrak back to Boston leaves around nine PM."

"OK." Ahdi nods. "I need to check to make sure everyone has kept their word. And you two should update the Chief Architect. I'm sure she'll want to hear it in person. I'll see you at the station."

Ahdi disappears. Ellie raises her eyebrows and shrugs at Daniel. There really aren't any words that are right. Slowly, the two see themselves out.

CHAPTER 24

Ellie rings the Chief Architect's doorbell. A tallish, solid man opens the door. This one has brown rather than blond hair. He meets Daniel's gaze and instantly adopts the demeanor of an ice wall. His face grows serious and his body becomes taut but not stiff.

"What do you want, Daniel?" The man's voice is harsh and his gaze never leaves Daniel.

Ellie is half tempted to jab him in the stomach to find out what happens if the attack he's braced for comes from her rather than Daniel. Instead, she waves to get his attention. He shifts ever so slightly, and Ellie decides he might have blocked her attack or at least would have seen it as it came.

"Have we met?" Daniel, for his part, is his usual somewhat befuddled.

Maybe it's because the stakes at the moment are so low, but Ellie is amused that half the people who see Daniel assume Daniel must be out to kill them. If Daniel were trying to kill someone, Ellie suspects they'd never see it coming. Part of her wants to say nothing and see how long the ice wall can maintain his vigil. However, all of her has a train to catch.

"Hi, I'm Ellie." Ellie waves again. "We're here to see Mary. I called ahead."

At the sound of her name, a relieved expression relaxes onto his face. The ice wall melts back into a man.

"Oh, right. She's expecting you. I'm her son, Ray." He shakes Ellie's hand. "Come in."

He leads them through the family room and gestures at the stairs. Daniel gets a wide berth as he passes by. Ellie follows him down into the basement.

Only as many folded planes of air as will fit ring the room. There aren't any at all beneath the tables. The room looks even more composed, a carefully cultivated microcosm where everything has a place and every place has a thing. The Chief Architect sits at a table in front of a folded plane of air. Daniel's annotations are attached to it at odd angles. Her hands are deep in one of them, opening its folds and crevices. She turns to Ellie and Daniel as they reach the foot of the stairs.

"Hello, Ellie." She refolds the annotation she was inspecting. "Daniel."

The Chief Architect swivels her chair around to face them. Daniel stays by the stairs, trying not to loom and failing. Ellie steps forward to deliver the news.

"We can show that the side channel you demonstrated is a long-standing bug. However—"

"Good." The Chief Architect nods. "Jerry told me that his team is putting in a fix for it as we speak."

Daniel growls softly. Ellie doesn't hear it. She feels it just as she can feel his body grow taut, ready to punch Neeson into next Tuesday. That Neeson isn't here is beside the point. The Chief Architect doesn't notice.

"He did?" Ellie's eyebrows rise. "As we speak?"

If the Chief Architect wondered about all the activity in the skunkworks, Neeson has presented her with a reason why. It's a lie, but it serves the purpose. She, however, probably wasn't wondering. Not that many maintainers ever notice changes as they are made. Neither she nor Ellie is one of them.

Giving the Chief Architect a reason makes Ellie's job harder.

In her mind, she shoots rays of hate at Neeson, not that they are a thing. Maybe they would have been if Neeson and his crew had succeeded in changing the rules of the universe. For a moment, she feels a tiny bit sad that the rules haven't changed. Then it hits her that a universe where Neeson made rays of hate a thing is also one where the only people who get to shoot them are Neeson's chosen few, and she feels a bit guilty.

"That surprised me, too." The Chief Architect nods. "Jerry is usually a stickler for process. But we don't have a Chief Builder right now and everyone who has to do the work is already working with him on the audit anyway. The fix is apparently quite involved."

The reason there isn't a Chief Builder right now is because Mom is dead. Ellie hasn't even thought about that rat's nest until now. Dread pools in her gut. Who ends up coordinating the builders is not her fight, she hopes. The power struggle is yet another way to corrupt the system that Neeson has already corrupted so much that he nearly rewrote the physics of the universe to suit his whims. Nothing within the system stopped him.

"It's not only the one bug." Daniel stands next to Ellie. "There are whole families of bugs of the same sort."

"Daniel, you know the process." The Chief Architect seems puzzled that she needs to say this. "Write up and file the bug reports with Jerry Neeson."

All is well, apparently, between the Chief Architect and Chief Verifier. Neeson covered his tracks well enough with her. She doesn't suspect a thing, It doesn't take a genius to predict what Daniel would say the next time he saw the Chief Architect. Neeson made sure she'll never believe it.

Daniel either doesn't notice or doesn't care, because he is about to burst. Ellie holds a hand up to forestall the oncoming torrent where he explains in too much detail everything that has happened. He spots her hand and growls softly again. Ellie would explode too if she could get away with it. Neeson is about as likely to deal with bug reports about side channels as he is to resign from his hyper-innovative disruptive tech company and devote the rest of his life to the fervent worship of fermented soybean products. The Chief Architect would hear Ellie's growl, though.

"Daniel has to take me to the train station, so we have to go."

Ellie waves to the Chief Architect, then hustles Daniel up the stairs. Daniel, for his part, doesn't resist. He merely stares oddly at her over his shoulder as she hurries him up the stairs. After a few steps, he faces forward and takes the stairs several steps at a time. Ellie hurries after him out of the house.

Daniel leans against his car, his arms folded across his chest when Ellie catches up to him. He still has a puzzled look on his face.

"Ellie, why didn't you tell her about Neeson?" He lets his arms drop. "She needs to know."

"One, I'm not sure she'd believe us. Two, the skunkworks still has all that extra machinery that needs to be cleared out."

Realization is a grimace that creeps across Daniel's face. His brow furrows and his mouth twists.

"Oh, I see." His arms go back across his chest. "If Neeson is going to try this again, we want him to start from scratch and the only thing getting him to remove his work is the fact that no one else knows except us."

"Pretty much." Ellie shrugs.

"You know, the Chief Architect could believe us." He spreads his arms out. "The idea isn't that outlandish."

"Are you prepared for the chaos that would unleash? Who knows how many of the maintainers on the planet work for Neeson one way or another right now." Ellie jabs him in the chest. "If you want war, you should be ready for it first. For now, all we can do is keep to our half of the blackmail."

"It's annoying." He goes to the driver's side of the car and unlocks it. "I don't have to like it."

"Honestly, I don't think you're supposed to."

He gets in and unlocks the passenger side. Ellie gets in.

"So that's done then." He starts up the car. "Let's get you to the train station."

The traffic is surprisingly reasonable. Even with a detour to Daniel's apartment to pick up her luggage, they'll get to Union Station with time to spare. They are, however, not done. Daniel knows it too, probably. Ellie slouches in the seat and, for a moment, lets herself doubt whether the universe they saved is better than the universe they prevented.

CHAPTER 25

The waiting room at the train station has both a glorious coffered ceiling and rows of really crappy plastic chairs. Travelers crisscross the room, dragging their roller bags behind them. Their voices, the click of footsteps against the shiny floor, and the low-key rumble of wheels echo in this vast space. Every once in a while, boarding announcements blare over the PA system.

Ellie sits in a crappy plastic chair, her roller bag parked by her feet. Daniel sits next to her, his fingers tapping against an arm of his crappy plastic chair. They're both watching the people walk by. Ahdi will probably appear when they least expect it, but that's no reason not to watch for him.

"Why do you always take the train down?" Daniel asks.

"It's cheaper than flying."

"That's not what I mean. You know Chris's house well enough."

"For one, I have to lug this with me." Ellie taps her roller bag.

"You don't have to carry it all with you." Daniel clearly doesn't understand that his idea of traveling light is way lighter than hers can ever be. "You can just go back to Boston whenever you need something."

"That's not any less exhausting." Ellie rolls her eyes. "And, honestly, if I ever did that, she would have found the time to change something to stop me from doing it again. I mean, she never even let me on the house Wi-Fi. Not that it matters anymore."

Daniel peers at her roller bag. He crouches down, puts a palm beneath it, then tests its weight. His hand moves as if the roller bag weren't there.

"I could deal with this, maybe. You know my apartment now. Next time, if I study your apartment, I could take this back and forth for you." Daniel sets the bag down and sits back in the chair. "There will be a next time, right?"

The sound of a throat clearing behind them interrupts whatever Ellie is about to say. She turns around to see it's Ahdi and wonders how long he's been standing there.

"Will there be a next time, Ellie?" Ahdi walks around and sits on the other side of Ellie. "You look like you have questions. Ask away."

Ahdi's smile is gentle and patient. Ellie sifts through the past two days. She expected to go to a funeral, spend the next day or so arguing with Chris over inconsequential things because that's what they always did, then she'd go back to Boston. And that's what happened. Sort of.

"Mom didn't want me involved in, as the Head Archivist of the isolationists called it, the vendettas of my elders?"

"In her defense, Vera couldn't have predicted how the latest outburst would start." He shows her his palms. "And 'vendetta' is not the word I would use."

"What word would you use?"

"It's complicated." Ahdi leans in to hold her gaze. "At heart, it's a philosophical dispute or, less pretentiously, a disagreement over a norm that holds until it doesn't. Nothing prevents maintainers from refashioning a universe in their own image except other maintainers. We need the norm, though, because we can't be trusted, and the thin end of the wedge is so easy to argue."

"Really?" Ellie chews on this for a moment. "Either you're reworking the skunkworks to give yourself an edge or you aren't, right?"

"Oh, Ellie." Ahdi's voice drips with exaggerated sincerity. "These changes aren't for you. They aren't for me. They're for your mother. Isn't she worth changing the universe to save? These changes will be limited, tiny—"

"OK, OK." Ellie throws her hands up in defeat. "I get it. If you're fine with that, the next thing is just a tiny step further."

"Exactly. I should have realized what was really happening and looked into that abomination when they started building it." Ahdi's expression grows somber. "I'm sorry, Ellie. I could have kept you out of it. You didn't need to be exposed to any of this."

"I don't see how I could have avoided it." Ellie shrugs. "I mean, Neeson tried to recruit me yesterday. He might have done that even if I hadn't gone to him first. I was going to end up on one side of this or the other."

"So which side are you on?"

"Seriously?" Her eyes want to pop out of her skull.

"Seriously." He nods earnestly.

"Self-serving changes to the physics of a universe can't possibly go well. At best, it makes the universe unfair at such a fundamental level, we can't possibly create and maintain a fair and just society. We impose guardrails on ourselves for a reason."

Ahdi holds up his hand for a high five and Ellie obliges. She wishes she could take the approval as the consolation he undoubtedly means it to be. Some part of her will always wonder about the world where her mom is here and she is not.

He stares at his hand for a moment. It's not quite the same "you dumbass" glare that she's seen Daniel deploy. It's more of a disappointment. Apparently, he's decided going for the high five was a mistake.

"That puts you and your sister on opposite sides." Ahdi mindlessly rubs his hand against his pants. "Is this something you want to talk about?"

"No, not yet." She shakes her head. "Besides, what is she going to do? Stop trying to kill me?"

Ellie laughs at her own bitter joke. It's been a rough weekend. Ahdi looks profoundly uncomfortable, unsure what anyone can say in response. Who knows when she'll be ready for that conversation. Whenever she gets to the point where she can talk about it, though, it will probably be with Ahdi and Daniel. They've earned at least that much, and she can't imagine who else she could talk to about this. For now, she lets him stew for thirty seconds too long before speaking again.

"Have we really accomplished anything? The Chief Architect believes the various side channels are bugs. This, technically speaking, is true in that maintainers a century ago probably didn't intend them. To the extent that anyone noticed any recent funny business in the skunkworks, they probably think it's just Neeson's audit or believe Neeson's story about putting in a fix for a side channel. Anyone who recognizes that it's really something else probably thinks you're behind it. That's assuming anyone even cares." Ellie can't side-eye anyone looking at her so gently. "Neeson is the Chief Verifier. His job is literally to make sure no one builds harmful changes into the skunkworks. He tried to do exactly that and there will be no repercussions because he's the guy who metes them out, and he's all for it. What's to stop any group of maintainers, much less Neeson's group of maintainers, from rewriting the rules of the universe whenever they want?"

"Well, that we are riddled with side channels will become common knowledge, at least among maintainers. All the excess hardware Neeson's maintainers put in is being taken out. But that's not what you're really asking." Weariness takes over Ahdi's face for a moment before he fights it back with a smile. "My first instinct is always to go in and fix things myself. This time, what's broken is the system that maintains the universe. The entire system is broken. I can't fix that by myself."

"So will there be a next time, Ellie?" Daniel literally sticks his head into the conversation.

Ellie involuntarily jerks her face away from him. He's been so quiet that she forgot he was there.

"Daniel." Ellie eases herself upright. "Can you please take a walk around the concourse or something?"

Daniel looks confused and a little hurt. His gaze shifts to Ahdi, who nods ever so slightly. He shrugs and leaves. Ellie will apologize later.

"You want to know why he has been so . . . prepared for this weekend." Ahdi's gaze follows Daniel across the waiting room. "The man has a reputation. He finds that distressing. You sent him away so he doesn't hear you bring it up."

"Basically, yeah."

"Nothing changes in the skunkworks without the change being verified first. No one wants to cause a cascade of failures that destroy all the universes one after another in turn. Verification is Daniel's clear strong suit, and he's always been too guileless for his own good." Ahdi's gaze shifts back to Ellie. "He had to become someone who could refuse changes, make that decision stick, and survive the repercussions. I may have gone overboard in preparing him."

"That's it?" Ellie is openly skeptical.

"No. You know what he's like when he's excited about something." Ahdi nods. "He's not doing anything he wouldn't have tried anyway. All I did was teach him how to do it well."

"It's not fair." Ellie slumps. "If everybody just did what they're supposed to, limited ourselves to finding bugs, fixing bugs, and replacing failing parts, we wouldn't even be having this conversation."

"No, it's not fair. And what I'm asking of you is extremely unfair. If you dropped out completely, if you avoided even the occasional bit of maintenance, no one, not Daniel, not me, would blame you. A universe is at the whim of whoever can change its skunkworks, though. We could use the help." He reaches for Ellie's hand but waits until she nods before he gives it a gentle squeeze. "It's a thankless job. When we succeed, no one will ever notice. But when we fail—or worse, no one even tries—the effects ripple through all the universes because each universe generates the next until the last generates the first in an unending loop—"

Ahdi turns around. Ellie wonders why until she finally spots Daniel being the silent sirocco. He has this way of looking like he's just strolling casually while hurtling toward you at the equivalent of a dead sprint. Long legs help.

"So." Daniel, looking and sounding impossibly earnest as usual, stops in front of Ellie. "Will there be a next time, Ellie?"

"Daniel." Ahdi is openly reproving. "She doesn't have to plan out her life right now and certainly not for your comfort."

Fuzzy words squawk over the PA system. Her train is starting to board. Not that she needs an excuse to leave.

"I should get going. Until we meet again, you guys." Ellie stands and drags her bag out of the way. "Ahdi, we need to find some time to cook together."

"Oh!" Daniel claps his hands with joy. "Can I come with?"

"Yes, Daniel." Ellie wonders what she has to teach a professional chef, but it'll be fun having him around. "Of course."

Ahdi shakes her hand. Daniel gives her a hug that could easily have become deadly with a few minor adjustments. They wave as she walks away, roller bag in tow.

She sleeps through the trip back to South Station. The T takes her back to Alewife. The recorded voice announces the arriving train. It's still out of sync.

ACKNOWLEDGMENTS

Writing and publishing a novel takes time. This novel has its genesis in a short story I published in 2015. The world has changed since then in ways one might not have expected. For example, we now have a different definition of the kilogram. Back in 2015, it was still a hunk of platinum-iridium alloy called the International Prototype of the Kilogram with effectively identical copies all over the world. In 2019, scientists created a new definition of the kilogram based on Planck's constant. Also, Alberto Fujimori died during one of the final revision passes. This novel doesn't take place in this universe anyway. Or does it?

Writing and publishing a novel also takes a village, and everyone in that village deserves my thanks. Eric Showers, my agent, and Jennifer Gunnels, my editor, with assistance from Julianna Kim, were crucial for getting this novel into its best form. They asked the right questions at the right times and spurred me to write what are now some of my favorite parts of this book. Ann VanderMeer acquired and edited "Hold-Time Violations," the aforementioned short story that started it all. This novel simply would not exist without her unwavering support and guidance. Thank you to everyone who read one version of this book or another. They include Fran Wilde, Marissa Lingen, Margaret Ronald, John Murphy, and Max Gladstone. All of them, especially Max, saved me from myself more times than I can count. Simon Neely, at one point, sang "Shut up and write!" at me to the tune of the song by Walk the Moon. Honestly, that was probably exactly what I needed at that moment.

Thank you to everyone at Tor who has had a hand in publishing this novel. This includes copyeditor Terry McGarry, proofreader Ingrid Powell, cold reader Katherine Kirk, jacket designer Katie Klimowicz, managing editor Rafal Gibek, production editor Dakota Griffin, and production manager Jim Kapp. Emily Honer and Lauren Abesames were in charge of marketing and publicity, respectively. Claire Eddy, Will Hinton, Lucille Rettino, and Devi Pillai oversee the whole show. Lastly, thank you to Weston Wei for the spectacular cover art. I've shown it to everyone who's given me even half an opportunity.

Finally, thank you, dear reader. The world does not maintain itself, and while the arc of the moral universe bends toward justice, it doesn't do it all by itself. When I started working on the short story that became this novel, I could not have imagined the world I'd find myself in as I write this acknowledgment. The arc of the moral universe, however, is long. Let us all bend it toward justice together.

ABOUT THE AUTHOR

Tim Seiger

John Chu has published short stories in *Boston Review*, *Reactor*, *Clarkesworld*, and *Uncanny*, to name a few, and many have been reprinted in multiple Year's Best anthologies. His short story "The Water That Falls on You from Nowhere" won the 2014 Hugo Award for Best Short Story, and his novelette "If You Find Yourself Speaking to God, Address God with the Informal You" won the 2022 Nebula Award for Best Novelette and was a finalist for the 2023 Hugo Award for Best Novelette.